HMSM HOLLAND II

Brenda Murray

Published by

MELROSE BOOKS

An Imprint of Melrose Press Limited
St Thomas Place, Ely
Cambridgeshire
CB7 4GG, UK
www.melrosebooks.co.uk

FIRST EDITION

Copyright © Brenda Murray 2014

The Author asserts her moral right to
be identified as the author of this work

ISBN 978-1-909757-20-2

Printed and bound in Great Britain by:
Grosvenor Group (Print Services) Ltd
London

MIX
Paper from
responsible sources
FSC® C041357

Chapter 1

As usual, the weather on the way to the Clyde Submarine Base was rather murky, a typical March day. Kit was driving towards the base coming from the direction of Helensburgh, and there was a fine drizzle, not enough to have the wipers going all the time, but annoying when she had to use them as they squeaked when she did.

She was nervous enough as it was, for she was joining her first command of an all-female crew on HMSM *Holland 2*, and the squeaking of the windscreen wipers only seemed to exacerbate and add to her nervousness. As the *Holland* was the first submarine to be driven by an all-female crew she had to get to know the crew and whip them into shape and prove that females were just as capable as their male counterparts, so she had her work cut out. Fortunately she had a good Executive Officer that she had asked for, plus a few of her other officers, and the powers that complied with her request.

The first thing she must do was get this long journey over and report to the Flag Officer Scotland, Northern England and Northern Ireland/Flag Officer Reserves, Admiral Richard Guy Ambrose RN. What a mouthful, she grinned.

She had only driven from Dumbarton today, but her journey had started in London two days before. She had left her flat in Chelsea, not far from Sloane Square, and had stopped off in Preston on the way and stayed with friends. Kit used to share the flat with her husband, Clive, who had been killed on this same journey. Apparently, as he rounded a bend he was hit head on by an articulated truck that was driving on the wrong side of the road. He didn't stand a chance. He was killed outright. That was six years ago, on his way to his first command, also in Faslane. Kit sighed and tried to forget him and concentrate on the road ahead, but Clive was always there, at the back of her mind.

Her full name was Christine Georgina Carson, Commander RN. She was nicknamed 'Kit', after the legendry cowboy, Kit Carson. She had joined the Royal Navy in 2005 with a degree in engineering. She was a Direct Entry at the rank of Sub/Lt and she volunteered for submarine service in 2015. She was a Lieutenant Commander and she had served on four boats – as submarines were called – in the past. The last, a now obsolete Trident class boat called *Vindictive*, after which she went on the Command course at HMS *Neptune* in the Clyde Submarine Base, where she was going today, and the 'Perisher Course' also at HMS *Neptune*. All the boats she had served in had been based at Faslane, so she was very familiar with the journey from London. Soon after the course in HMS *Neptune*, she became a Commander.

She arrived at the main gate and used her swipe card to gain access to the base. She went straight to her in board cabin and showered and changed from civvies to her best Number One uniform before reporting to Admiral Ambrose's office at 1100 hours. The Admiral's First Lieutenant stood up as she entered and smiled at her. 'The Admiral will only be a minute, Commander Carson, so if you would care to sit down he will buzz when he is free.'

'Thank you, but I would rather stand.' She smiled back at him and walked over to the window and stood there with her hands clasped behind her back.

The Admiral's First Lt looked at her back which was ram-rod straight and motionless. She was, at a guess, five foot ten inches tall, very slim and smart, and the creases in her trousers were so sharp that it looked as though you could cut a loaf in half with them. He smiled to himself.

Kit was thinking that even though she was nervous about this interview that was about to take place, she was really looking forward to her first command. She noticed that it had stopped raining and the sun was shining. She could see across to the other side of the Gareloch. She smiled as she thought of what the locals said – "If you can see across the Gareloch it was about to rain, and if you couldn't see it, it was already raining!" At that moment the buzzer went.

'You may go in, Commander.'

Kit nodded and smiled her thanks and went over and knocked on the Admiral's door. At his, 'Come in,' Kit entered the inner sanctum.

Admiral Ambrose stood up and shook hands with Kit. 'Sit down Commander,' he said then sat down himself.

'Thank you, Sir,' Kit said.

He looked down at some notes on his desk then looked over to her and smiled, saying, 'What does it feel like to be selected as the first Commander of an all-female crew of submariners?'

'Very proud, Sir. I just hope that the choice in me being the first will lead to even more all-female crews.'

'I see from your file that your great, great, great grandfather, John Philip Holland, built the first modern day submarine in the early 1900s.'

'Yes, Sir. My Grandfather often tells me about him, from tales that were told to him by his father, so it makes me doubly proud to be the first, especially on a boat named after him. I just hope I can live up to my Grandfather's expectations as well, Sir.'

'I am sure you will, Commander Carson.' He looked down at his notes again and continued, 'your first duties for the first month will be working the boat up to an efficient standard, obviously, and teaching your crew all the new systems too.'

'Yes, of course sir,' Kit said, although it was a rather obvious statement for the Admiral to have made.

'Anyway, you know yourself what is expected of you, and with your past experiences you should come out with flying colours.' He stood up, ending the interview, but as a passing shot he said, 'A lot rests on your shoulders, Kit.'

Kit said, 'Yes, Sir. Thank you, Sir.' With that she stood up and shook his proffered hand, gave him a final smile and about turned and walked proudly out of his office.

CHAPTER 2

On leaving the Admiral's office she looked at her watch and saw that it was time for lunch, so she made her way to the Wardroom. She hadn't had time to book in for it earlier so went and asked the Chief Steward if it wasn't too late to book in now for lunch? The Chief had a soft spot for Commander Kit Carson so he told her that it was okay as they always did an extra amount in case there were any latecomers. She smiled her thanks to the chief and walked into the wardroom.

When she entered the first person she saw was Shelagh Bennett, who was to be her XO (Executive Officer) in the *Holland*. 'Hi Wiggy. How's it going?'

Shelagh looked up and saw who had spoken to her and when she did she stood up and said, 'Not too foul, thank you Ma'am.'

'Do sit down and tell me about the boat,' Kit said laughing, and sat herself down opposite Shelagh.

Shelagh Bennett was a dark haired, short but determined Lt/Cdr, and she wouldn't take any nonsense from anyone. But everyone who was her subordinate would do anything for her, and they knew her bark was worse than her bite. She had been XO on her last boat and her captain had been very pleased with her and given her an excellent write up.

Kit asked her what the new boat was like. Shelagh said it was typical of a new boat, the smell of fresh paint, the bright shiny new fixtures and fittings. What she thought was fantastic was that both the Commander and she had a big single cabin each with an en suite shower especially for them, and as she was used to sharing a shower with all the other officers in the boat, this was positively luxurious.

Kit said that she would like a tour of the boat after lunch, and to meet whatever crew had arrived already.

'Of course, Ma'am. I've had all the girls scrubbing out, not that there is much to do at the moment, being brand new that is, Ma'am.' She smiled at Kit who smiled back and said, 'When we are on our own you can call me, Kit. And I'll call you Wiggy or Shelagh, whatever you prefer.'

'Wiggy will be fine Ma'am, I mean, Kit.'

'Good.' She smiled at Wiggy then she heard the Chief Steward saying that lunch was ready. 'Shall we go in?' Kit said to Wiggy.

They found a quiet corner where they could talk about the boat and the team, as they called the crew, but Kit kept getting congratulated by fellow officers on her achievement in becoming the first Commander of an all-female crew.

Both Kit and Wiggy were glad to make their escape. Kit said to Wiggy that she would be down on the boat at 1400, so that would give Wiggy a while to do any last minute checks and brief the crew that the 'Captain' would be coming down at 1400.

'Aye, aye Ma'am,' Wiggy said. Kit raised her eyebrows and they both laughed.

'See you at 1400 then.'

Kit went back to her cabin and changed from her No.1s to working rig. It was identical to No.1s except that she didn't wear her medals, just the ribbons, and of course her Dolphins that were worn above the medal ribbons on her left breast.

At 1400 she was entering HMSM *Holland 2* via the conning tower, or fin as it was called. She heard the whistle of a bosun's pipe, piping her aboard. When she got to the foot of the ladder and turned around, although she didn't show it, she was surprised to see some of the ship's company standing to attention. Wiggy, wearing her hat, smartly saluted and said, 'Welcome aboard, Ma'am.'

Kit returned the salute equally as smartly and said, 'Thank you, Lieutenant Commander Bennett.' She turned to the crew and smiled at them and said, 'I will be seeing you all later, so carry on.' As one they turned smartly to the right and then dispersed to their various positions on the boat.

There were a few officers still standing to attention in the passage way and she said to them, 'At ease, and carry on.' She turned to Wiggy and was about to say, 'Shall we get on with it,' when Wiggy forestalled her by saying, 'The steward has made a fresh pot of coffee for us, so if you would like to come to the Wardroom for a cup, then you can meet those officers that are already on board.'

'Thank you Commander, I will be honoured. Lead the way.' Although Kit had studied the layout of the boat and knew exactly where the Wardroom was, and everything else, she didn't want to detract from Wiggy's little ceremony. She was taking in all the bright work gleaming, and sniffed at the smell of fresh paint and the polish on the glittering decks, and as they got near the galley she could smell fresh bread baking. 'The crew will have to make the most of the fresh bread in harbour as they won't get any when we are doing work ups,' Kit said.

They arrived in the wardroom and Wiggy asked Kit to sit down. 'Thank you.' Kit sat where she was shown and had a look round at the pictures on the bulkheads. She was most surprised to see the same picture of *Holland 1*, that her grandfather gave to her to hang on her cabin wall.

'Coffee, Ma'am?' a Leading Steward said from behind her. She turned and said, 'Please.' As she looked up at the steward she recognised her from her last boat. 'Jeffries, it is nice to see you again, and with your hook too. Congratulations.'

'Thank you, Ma'am.' She carried on pouring coffee for

the rest of the officers then went back to the steward's pantry. Elaine Jeffries was very pleased that Commander Carson recognised her. She was instrumental in recommending her for her Leading rate.

Kit was introduced to the other officers. Some she recognised from previous boats and some she didn't. The first one was the Weapons Engineer Officer, the WEO Lt/Cdr Valerie Kennedy. Kit had met her on *Truculent*. 'It's nice to serve with you again, Val.'

'Thank you, Commander. It is nice to be with you again too.' She smiled at her new boss. The next one to be introduced to her was the Marine Engineering Officer, MEO Lt/ Cdr Joan Shakespeare (Willy). 'It's very nice to meet you, Joan.'

'Willy, Ma'am,' Joan said with a smile. Kit chuckled.

There were only a handful of officers on board, and Kit met all that were there with exception of the Doctor, Lt. Surgeon Penelope Soames, who was testing the air throughout the boat. The Supply Officer, Lt Susan Osgood, she hadn't met before, but had heard of her. She told Kit that she had put the order in for the food and stores that would be required.

'That's good, Sue. For the first four weeks we will be running daily on work ups so there won't be as much food to take with us, but naturally we will really need to be topped up for when we do go to sea.'

'I've already got that in hand, Ma'am. At the moment I am working on a six months' supply of stores and food of course,' she said, hoping that it wouldn't be much longer as she was getting married in early October.

Kit didn't contradict her as she didn't know herself how long the first patrol would be yet. 'Thank you.'

Wiggy got up and said to Kit, 'Would you like to see your cabin now, Commander?'

'Yes please. Thank you for the coffee. Ladies…' Kit got up

and followed Wiggy to her cabin. She heard a mumble behind her when she left the WR. She smiled to herself.

When she saw the cabin she said, 'Good God! It's huge.' Wiggy laughed and said she'd said exactly the same thing when she'd seen her own cabin. 'The people who designed it must have known that the great, how many greats are there Kit?'

'Three.'

'They must have known that a great by three, granddaughter would be the first one to drive this boat, so decided to go all out on luxury for her and her XO too.'

'You just can't compare the two, can you Wiggy?'

'No Kit. What do you think of the officers you've met so far?'

'They seem a good bunch, but we'll soon see in the first few weeks. Tell me something, how did you know about my three times great grandfather?'

'Oh, someone mentioned it in the WR the other night.'

'Oh. I see,' Kit said then added, 'I'll just take a wander through the boat and I'll move on board at 0800 tomorrow. Perhaps you'll have a list of the crew still to join and when they will be joining so that we can get this show on the road so to speak, Wiggy.'

'Very well, Kit. Do you want me to come round the boat with you?' Wiggy asked.

'No thanks, I can find my way around alright. I'll see you tomorrow morning.' Kit smiled, moving off towards the galley.

CHAPTER 3

Kit finished the visit to HMSM *Holland 2* at 1600. She decided to go back inboard to her cabin in the WR and have a lay down before dinner. Back in her cabin she stripped off and hung her uniform up and lay down on the bed. Surprisingly, she fell asleep almost straight away.

A loud knocking woke her up at 1815. 'Wait one,' she said as she struggled into her dressing gown. 'Who is it?'

'Wiggy, Kit.'

'Right. Come in,' she said, opening the door, still tying her dressing gown. Wiggy was there wearing civvies.

'Oh. I am sorry. I didn't realise you were having a sleep. Sorry,' she said once again, looking chagrined.

'That's okay. I am glad you came as I would have slept through dinner otherwise. What can I do for you?'

'A couple of us officers wanted to know if you'd care to join us for a drink before dinner,' Wiggy suggested to Kit.

'That would be nice. But I'll have to take a quick shower though.'

'That's okay. We'll see you as soon as you can make it, Kit.'

Kit had a quick shower and got dressed in a skirt and blouse with a cardigan and high heeled shoes. It felt nice being in female clothes again as all day she had been wearing trousers, first with civvies on her journey here then with uniform. She studied her reflection in the full length mirror, fluffed out her hair and checked her make up and then proceeded down to the Wardroom bar.

She saw the women as soon as she entered the bar. When she approached they all stood up in deference to her rank and the fact that she was their boss. 'Do sit down ladies. Good evening.'

They all sat back down saying, 'Good evening, Ma'am.'

A steward came over to take her order and she asked if any of the others would like one, but they already had nearly full glasses. 'Just a horse's neck for me, please. No ice, thank you.' She smiled at the male steward.

'Thank you, Ma'am.'

Wiggy asked her how her look around the boat went. Kit told them that it all went smoothly. She told them that in the junior rates dining room they were queuing for tea. There were two apples left, a large one and a smaller one, and two people left in the queue. The first one, a rather big killick, took the large one leaving the smaller one on the tray. The last girl in the queue said, 'If I were you, I would have taken the smaller one.' The big girl looked at the smaller one and said, 'Well you've got it, aint you? So shad up and stop complaining.' They all laughed and one of them told Kit, 'That sounded like Tug the Thug, LMEN Wilson, the boat's resident comedienne.'

'She definitely sounded like a right character.'

'There's a few characters on board like her,' Willy said.

'No doubt I'll meet all of them soon enough,' Kit said.

'Have you met the Chief of the boat yet, Denise Danvers?' Penny said.

'You will tomorrow,' one of them said.

At that moment the steward came and told them that dinner was about to be served. They all ambled into the dining room and sat at a comparatively empty table and the officers regaled Kit with little anecdotes about some of the crew members.

'I look forward to meeting them all eventually.'

Dinner over and coffee and liqueurs to hand, they sat in companionable silence, each having her own thoughts until Kit

got up and said, 'It has been a very pleasant evening, but you'll
have to excuse me. With the drive here and the first visit to the
boat, it's been a rather tiring day. So I'll say goodnight to you
all. See you some time tomorrow.' She made her way back to
her cabin, set her alarm for 0630, creamed her face and washed
it, then cleaned her teeth, got undressed and fell into bed.

She slept right through until the alarm woke her at 0630. She
yawned and stretched and got up and showered. She arrived for
breakfast at 0700 and went and poured herself a cup of tea. Kit
sat down near the window and noticed that the weather was
just as murky as it was yesterday and it was also raining and
dark. She was thinking that she ought to buy an apartment or a
small house locally and sell her flat in Chelsea. She should get
a good price for her flat in Chelsea, more than enough to buy a
small house near the base. It would be a better idea than travel-
ling back and forth to London every leave she got as it looked
like she would be here for a few more years yet. Although her
parents were still alive and living in Westminster, not far from
her flat, she could always stay with them when she wanted to
go down to London.

A steward came to her and asked what she would like for
breakfast. Kit carried on thinking about the idea of a small
house or flat. The more she thought of it the more she liked the
idea. *Yes*, she thought to herself, *I'll have a look in the local
rag later on today*.

Her breakfast came, two poached eggs on toast, so she
concentrated on her eggs and toast and pushed the idea of
moving to the back of her mind.

After breakfast she went back to her cabin and finished her
packing. At 0750 there was a discreet knock on Kit's door and
she told whoever it was to come in. It was Leading Steward
Jeffries from her boat. 'Good morning, Jeffries.'

'Good morning, Ma'am. The First Lt was wondering if you

would like a hand with your bags.'

'How thoughtful of her, yes please, that suitcase over there and the grip please. I can manage the rest, thank you.' She smiled at Jeffries as the steward picked up the luggage that Kit had indicated and went ahead of her.

When she got downstairs she went to see the Duty Hall Porter and told him that she was moving onboard *Holland* so wouldn't be needing her cabin for a few months.

'Very well, Commander. I will have any of your gear packed up and stored for you until you tell us differently. The best of luck with your new Command, Commander.' Kit smiled her thanks to the Hall Porter and followed Jeffries out and down to the boat.

It was just as well Kit had worn her Burberry, as it was hosing down with rain. 'What typical Scottish weather,' she muttered to herself.

When she got on board, Wiggy met her at the bottom of the ladder and said 'Good morning, Ma'am. I'll have some tea sent along to your cabin. There are some files on your desk, but nothing urgent that needs any action today.'

'Good morning, XO. Have you looked outside lately? It is not a very good morning at all,' Kit laughed, 'but thanks for the tea though.'

Kit made her way to her cabin and when she opened the door she was struck by the aroma of freesias, her favourite flowers. Someone must have done their homework. There were only three freesias in a small bud vase, but she was rather touched by the gesture.

She poured herself a cup of tea and glanced at the top few files. Like Wiggy had said, there wasn't anything urgent that needed doing today.

As she was doing some unpacking, Wiggy came in to discuss what routine Kit wanted to adopt. 'I'll address the crew at 1000, telling them what I expect of them in the meantime. But I'll draw up a set of orders that must be adhered to at all times. Other than that I'll leave your department to issue daily orders, Wiggy, as you see fit.'

'Of course, Kit. I'll have tomorrow's daily orders on your desk by 1530 this afternoon for your signature. Okay?'

'That'll be fine, Wiggy. Carry on with whatever you were doing,' she said dismissively and turned and got on with her unpacking.

All she could think of was what she was going to say to the ship's company. She had a good idea but she was going to wing most of it even though she had a few notes.

At 1000 she switched on her microphone and addressed the ship's company. 'Good morning to you all. This is Commander Christine Carson, your commanding officer, just in case you didn't know who I was.' She heard a few chuckles from outside, but continued. 'As you are all well aware, this is the first "all female" crew to ever take a submarine to sea. A lot will be riding on all our shoulders, and I mean ALL of our shoulders, including mine, especially mine, so I hope you won't let me down. We will make mistakes at first, we are bound to, but that is what these next four weeks are all about. After that, when I say we are ready for sea, I mean one hundred per cent, so I won't want any excuses. Everyone on board is dependent on the other doing her job efficiently and I won't take any excuses from anyone, and I mean anyone.

'Now, a few do's and don'ts. There will be no smoking in any part of the boat at any time except in the messes at stand-easy time and when you are in the mess off duty. Other than those times and places, there is definitely No Smoking anywhere else on the boat. God forbid that any one of you get caught smoking outside those designated times and places.' (There were a few groans that Kit heard from the outside.)

'Secure will be at 1630 daily except on Fridays when it will be 1530 for those who are not on duty, until Monday morning 0730 for Junior rates, and 0800 for Senior rates. This, of course, is when we are in harbour.

'There will be a list of orders which will become standard for this boat and will be promulgated as part of the *Holland's* standing orders.

'That is all I have to say at the moment and if there is any change, of course you will be the first to know. Thank you ladies, I wish us all the luck that is going.'

She switched off her microphone and went along to the control room where she thought she may find Wiggy. She was on her own, looking at some charts. When Wiggy looked up and saw Kit she smiled at her and asked her what was the penalty if anyone got caught smoking.

Kit said, 'They will be instantly disrated.'

'That's a bit harsh, isn't it?'

'Yes.' And she walked back to her cabin, leaving Wiggy staring after her. *So that is the way of things*, thought Wiggy.

When Kit got back to her cabin she played back what she'd spoken into the recorder and just added the bit about being disrated if getting caught smoking. She pressed the print button for twenty copies. That done, she took them out of the printer and put them into an envelope and addressed it to the XO, and put it in her out tray.

Kit looked across at the framed photograph of Clive, taken the day he was promoted to Commander, on his way to take up his first Command that he didn't make. Kit took his death rather badly and it took a couple of weeks of crying, too. Fortunately, she was given two weeks' compassionate leave so afterward when she rejoined her boat she was over the worst of it. A tear came to her eye even now as she thought of him and spoke as if he were alive, 'I wonder how they will get on with the smoking rule?' She looked in the mirror and noticed her eyes were bright so rinsed her face just as there was a knock on her cabin door. She said, 'Come in.' It was Ldg. Steward Jeffries to tell Kit that lunch would be served in the WR in thirty minutes' time. 'Thank you, Jeffries.'

Kit went to the WR and found a nice white crisp linen napkin in her space in the napkin box and sat down where she was directed to by Wiggy.

Lunch was a very informal affair with everyone chatting and laughing. There was a lot of banter between the SO and the WEO, the WEO finally asking Sue if there was plenty of fresh spinach on board? Sue said that there was a bit but it would have to be eaten soon. But she had ordered a large box of frozen spinach. The rest of the officers groaned at this and threw their napkins at Sue. Sue laughed and said it was all good healthy stuff and full of iron. Sue added that her father used to say that it put lead in your pencil, 'not that I ever knew what he meant.'

Kit looked up at Sue and realised that she was serious, and burst out laughing with the others. Sue looked rather bewildered and looked at the others, all innocent.

Kit said, 'Someone explain it to her please,' and laughed again. The Doc explained it quietly to Sue, who said, 'Oh, oh,' and laughed and blushed at the same time, starting the others off again.

After everyone had calmed down the WR got back to the sedate place it should be and they all enjoyed their lunch that included spinach. Despite the groans of earlier when spinach was first mentioned, Kit noticed that they took some when it was offered.

Kit excused herself, saying that she had work to do. 'I'll see you all later.' She went back to her cabin and worked her way through the files and initialled them and passed them on for the next person on the distribution list. She noticed that the orders she'd printed off had been collected.

At 1415 Wiggy came in with the list of Officers and ratings that were arriving the next day. 'That is our full complement now with this next batch, Kit.'

'Good, then we will able to start these work ups on Thursday. When you do daily orders for Thursday will you tell the team that all shore leave will end at 0700 Thursday and Friday please.'

'Of course Kit. Will there be anything else today?'

'I can't think of anything else at the moment, Wiggy. I'm just going topside to have a look around the securing lines then I'll come back and have another walk about the boat. Would you care to come with me?'

Although said as a request, Wiggy thought it sounded a bit like an order.

'Yes, I'll just get my hat and Burberry. Won't be a tick.' Kit was already shrugging into hers.

When Wiggy came back, Kit was waiting for her. They both went up the ladder to the outer casing. They were surprised to find that it had stopped raining, but there was a chilly wind coming up the Gareloch. It was just as well they had their Burberrys on as they counteracted the wind. The Trot Sentry saluted them and held her gun at the correct position, and Kit returned the salute. She had a quick word with her and she was saluted again as she walked off the casing to the jetty to join Wiggy.

'What do you honestly think of the crew we've been given, Wiggy?'

Wiggy was a bit hesitant and thought for a minute before answering. When she did she said, 'On the whole we've been given a good team, but naturally there are a few weak links in the chain, nothing I'm sure that can't be ironed out within the next few weeks on this work up.'

'Good. I'm relying on your judgement on this, Wiggy, but should you have problems or are unsure of anyone, please don't hesitate to tell me.'

'Yes Ma'am. With the final lot that are joining tomorrow there is just one Officer and two Ratings that the *Holland* will be their first boat.'

'Right. Perhaps when they have settled in you will send them to me so that I can give them a pep talk.'

'Yes, of course, Kit. The officers are all watch keepers and there are six including the one that hasn't been to sea before. The ratings are mostly seamen with the exception of a leading hand and rating who are both Logistics.'

CHAPTER 4

They sailed from the Gareloch at 0900 hours on Thursday morning. Kit conned it on the surface along the course the navigator had plotted on the chart until they were at their designated place for diving just halfway from Gareloch and Rathlin Island, which was the usual place to dive the boat when they were going on patrol. The order was passed for all hands to secure the boat for diving and to clear the upper deck. When all sections had said they were closed up and ready for sea, Kit gave the order to take the boat down to periscope depth.

There was none of the noises of loud claxons and the shouting of 'Dive, Dive, Dive,' as depicted in all submarine movies. Rather, it was done by the Captain saying over the tannoy system, 'Diving the boat to periscope depth.'

'Periscope depth, Ma'am,' said the Duty Watch Officer after she had read the gauges on her consul.

Kit asked for the search periscope to be raised. When it was raised she adjusted to the focus of her eyes – and that was where it was to remain at all times. She did a quick 360° sweep around the boat and lowered the periscope. There was nothing in sight and nothing on the sonar screen.

'Remain on this course until further orders, but take the boat down to 400 metres.'

'Aye aye, Ma'am.

'Watch the trim, Cox'n,' Kit said.

'Yes, Ma'am.'

Kit was looking at all the gauges that were displayed on her consul so she knew what was going on throughout the boat and around it. Everything so far was going as planned.

'When you've reached the 400 metres depth line, let me know,' Kit ordered.

Everything and everyone was quiet; there was just the slight sounds of the creaking and groaning of the pressure hull. It seemed like everyone was holding their breath. The silence was broken by the navigating officer saying, 'Clearance below of 1,000 metres plus, Captain.'

'Very well. Take the boat down another 150 metres.'

The boat was taken down to 550 metres and when it was at the correct depth Kit said to keep it that depth and to steer the plotted course until further notice or unless the depth changes. She was going for a walk around the boat. 'You've got the con, XO.'

'Aye, aye Ma'am,' answered Wiggy.

Kit knew she had left the boat in very capable hands whilst she herself was going from one end of the boat to the other, checking on the results of the dive to see if there were any leaks, not that she was expecting any. And, of course, there weren't.

After her look around the boat, she then went around the personnel, checking on them and having a quiet word with the new members who were on their first submarine. Although during training they had gone to sea in a submarine for one day, this was to be their home for the next year or two and a lot depended on whether or not they could handle themselves in any given situation.

She spoke to most of the crew that she encountered and had a friendly word or two with them. They were all rather surprised and pleased when Kit remembered their names. That was one thing she was good at because she had a photographic memory and she could remember how all the systems worked too, so she didn't (or wouldn't) take any bullshit from any members of the crew, or any officer for that matter. That was probably why she was where she was at this moment.

She went to the galley last before she went to the control room to see how things were there. The duty chef was Leading Cook Kimble, and she was stirring some soup up in a big pot when Kit spoke to her. 'What flavour is that soup, Kimble, as it smells delicious?'

'Tomato and basil, Ma'am. Do you want a cupful?'

'I'd love some, but I have to get back to the control room, and I can't very well go there with a mug full of soup. But I'll look forward to some when we have our late lunch, thank you.'

Kimble chuckled. 'Yes, Ma'am.'

Kit made her way back to the control room and stood at her consul after having ascertained that everything was running smoothly.

'Would you pipe to the off watch members of the crew that lunch will be served in fifteen minutes' time and for duty men it will be when they have finished their watch at 1400, XO,' Kit instructed Wiggy.

CHAPTER 5

The rest of their first dive went off very well with no incident. They got back to Faslane at about 1645. Kit addressed the ship's company when they arrived alongside. 'Thank you ladies, everything seemed to go fairly well for the first day. Tomorrow, however, we will be sailing at 0830 so I will want you back on board and closed up ready for leaving harbour at 0745. Thank you.'

Those that were going home or ashore left the boat leaving just the duty watch and a few others on board that didn't have a home to go to or didn't want to go ashore. Kit and Wiggy were two of them, also the WEO, Val Kennedy. Although Val was married, her husband, a Lt Cmdr who too was a WEO, was serving on another boat at sea at present and as they hadn't been married very long hadn't bothered to get a MQ, (Married Quarter) and definitely had no time to look for a house in the locale. Her husband, Ron, whose boat would be in the following Friday, would at least have time to go ashore and maybe, just maybe, Val would have the weekend off and they would be able to get a room at the Ardencaple Hotel at Rhu, if not the Cairndhu or Commodore hotels between Rhu and Helensburgh for a night or for the weekend. There was quite a lot of choice, so if one was booked up there were still the others to try.

Val was sitting in the wardroom when Kit walked in. Val was nursing a gin and tonic. Val stood up as Kit walked in, but Kit told her to sit down. She, Val, asked Kit if she would like a drink too? Kit asked for a horse's neck, no ice.

Just as Val was ordering, Wiggy walked in. 'Would you

like a drink, Wiggy?'

'Yes please, Val. A G and T, thanks. Good evening, Kit. Not going ashore then?'

'I was thinking of going after dinner actually. Would you both like to come with me?'

Wiggy looked at Val, who nodded, and Wiggy said that they'd both like to join her. As an after-thought Wiggy asked Kit where she was planning to go.

'I hadn't thought that far ahead yet, but how about the Ardencaple? I haven't been there for years.' Both Wiggy and Val said that was alright with them. So it was decided.

The three women spent a pleasant hour and a half over dinner and Kit asked the duty steward to ring for a taxi for them and to ask the trot sentry to ring down when it arrived.

All three had cars but none of them wanted to drink and drive so a taxi suited all three of them.

When they got to the Ardencaple Hotel, they went into the lounge bar. There were a few sailors with their wives there who must be from the nearby estate where the ratings' and senior rates' MQs were. There was no one other than themselves from the *Holland*, so they could relax and enjoy their drinks that Kit had bought. Kit used this interlude to get to know the two others better. She knew that Val was married and after a couple more G and Ts, Val felt really relaxed and opened up and she told them that her husband would be in on Friday so she must book a room for them here before she left this evening. She blushed as she said it, and both Kit and Wiggy smiled.

'How long have you been married, Val?' asked Kit.

'Five months, Kit. We haven't had time to put in for a MQ or look for a house in this area,' she said. Then she looked at Kit's third finger on her left hand and noticed she too was wearing an engagement and wedding ring and was halfway through asking the same thing when she suddenly remembered that Kit was a widow. 'Oh. I am so sorry Ma'am. I'd forgotten that you were a…'

Although Kit's eyes had clouded slightly, she put the younger woman at her ease by saying, 'That's okay, Val. I don't expect everyone to know my marital situation. I suppose I should take these off, but not yet, as it hasn't been that long.' She smiled at Val, putting her at her ease again.

Val said lamely, 'I'm sorry, Kit.'

To change the subject, Wiggy asked Kit what her ancestor would have made of his great (however many) granddaughter being put in command of the first all-women crew of a submarine named after him.

Val smiled her thanks across to Wiggy. Kit looked thoughtful for a moment then said, 'He would probably be aghast at it.' She smiled at the two others. 'But I'd expect he'd also be pleased, secretly, that one of his ancestors was in charge. Although he was an American of Irish descent, his son sailed to England in the late 1890s and met his wife here and my great, great grandfather came here from the States, who was John Philip Holland's grandson – all very complicated – and settled here. What it boils down to is, all my ancestors since John Philip have been in the submarine service in one way or the other, at least that's what I've been told by my grandfather. I've never bothered to get it authenticated. I just assumed that it was so. So there you are.' Kit smiled and shrugged.

Wiggy said that she couldn't see any reason why it shouldn't be true.

'I can't see what difference it makes in any case,' Val added.

'That's true,' said Kit. 'Anyway, enough of me. What about you, Wiggy?'

Wiggy thought for a minute then said, 'There's not much to tell really. As you know I'm not married or engaged, but I nearly was married once, but I chickened out.' She gave a rueful laugh as she thought of it.

'Why did you chicken out, Wiggy?' asked Val.

Kit was wondering that too but didn't have the nerve to ask her, so Val had saved her the trouble.

Both Val and Kit looked at Wiggy expectantly. Wiggy stared into the bottom of her drink and took a deep breath and looked up at the two women who were expecting an answer. When she looked at them they could see the pain in her eyes and Kit said, 'You don't have to tell us if it hurts too much, Wiggy.'

'Thanks, Kit, but I may as well tell you. It was a couple of years ago now, but it still hurts when I think of it. I was on a 'T' boat and we had come in a few days' early, so I went straight to our flat that we were setting up ready for when we got married.' She paused a while then continued, 'I could see lights on so assumed *he* was already there.' She didn't mention his name. 'He was alright, but in what was to be our bed, with another woman. I just stood there, rooted to the spot. I couldn't move or speak at first, then, I just took off. I ran all the way back to the base and went straight to my cabin inboard. I cried my eyes out for a few hours, and since then I haven't let myself get close to any man again.' When Wiggy finished telling Kit and Val her story she looked up at the two women with tears at the back of her eyes. Kit leaned across and squeezed her hand. At that, Wiggy excused herself and went out to the ladies.

What made matters worse was that her so-called fiancé didn't seem too bothered that Wiggy had caught him 'at it'. That is what really hurt. How many times before had this happened, and was it with the same girl?

Kit and Val looked at each other but didn't speak at first, just drank their drinks. Then Kit turned to Val and said, 'What a big shit he turned out to be. It was just as well she found out before they were married and not after.' Kit went to the bar and got them all doubles and she was just putting them on their table when Wiggy returned. She looked at the drinks and said that it was her round, but Kit told her she could get the next one.

It was obvious that she had been crying, although she had repaired her makeup pretty well; however the two others were too polite to say anything.

Wiggy downed the drink that she'd left on the table then took a sip of the new one. She winced and said, 'Good God. That's a bit strong.' She laughed and said, 'Thanks Kit. I needed that.' 'I thought we all did,' Kit added. To change the subject completely, Kit asked the other two how they thought the first day at sea had gone.

Val said, 'I thought it went surprisingly well considering it was the first time that the crew had ever sailed together, Kit.'

Kit then looked across at Wiggy, who smiled weakly back at her and spoke honestly too. 'Like Val, I thought for the first time of the crew being all together, it went quite well. But there are still a lot of areas that need ironing out of course.'

'Like what?' Kit asked, curious.

'Well, little things that, if we let them go, the crew will think are the norm, and they will always do it and I think they will get quite sloppy in the long run. As I said, little things, and this is just one of them, like securing the lines.'

'Hmm. I think I know what you mean, Wiggy. I noticed a few things myself too. Like that, tying up alongside and the way things were secured generally around the boat. Perhaps you will make a broadcast tomorrow when we are underway?' Kit looked at Wiggy and smiled. 'I have a few other tricks up my sleeve for tomorrow too.' Both Wiggy and Val laughed, imagining what it would be, but guessing correctly what the tricks were.

'Last orders, Ladies and Gentlemen please,' the landlord told the customers.

Wiggy looked up and asked the other two if they'd like one for the road, but both said no and Kit said they could have one back on board.

'Okay, then I'll phone for a cab.' She did so, on her mobile.

Back onboard they went straight to the Wardroom where the duty steward was about to shut the bar. On seeing the Captain, the XO and the WEO, she smiled and said, 'What can I get for you Ladies?'

Wiggy asked the others if they would like the same again? To which they both nodded so she signed for the drinks and handed the bar chit to Ldg Steward Jeffries, and went and sat down with the other two.

Jeffries brought the drinks over with a small bowl of peanuts. They all thanked her and Wiggy said that she could go off watch now as they would see to themselves and secure the bar when they were ready. 'Goodnight Jeffries.'

'Goodnight and thank you, Ma'am.' Jeffries nodded to the two others and both said, 'Goodnight.'

The three women sat there for another hour just talking quietly amongst themselves and drinking their drinks then they all went to their cabins. Wiggy secured the wardroom bar and went to hers.

Chapter 6

Kit took the boat out to exactly the same spot that they dived at the day before. When she came down from the fin she was frozen as there was a very stiff wind up there today. Although it had been cold yesterday it wasn't half as bad as it was this morning.

She wouldn't normally have been up on the fin yesterday and this morning, but for the first time at sea she felt that she ought to be there. She definitely wouldn't be conning the boat from up there the next time, but leave it to the Officer of the day (OOD).

Kit gave the order to prepare the boat for diving. The OOD made sure all the casing party were down below, and the ensign stowed properly and reported to the Officer of the Watch (OOW) that everything up top was secured. When the rest of the sections said they were also closed up and ready for sea, Kit gave the order to dive to periscope depth. When at periscope depth she had a quick 360° sweep around and saw that everything was clear then told the OOW to take the boat down to 550 feet, remaining on the same course as was marked on the plot as yesterday

'Aye, aye, Ma'am,' she said, and soon after, 'Depth at 550 feet. All clear to 1,000 feet.'

Kit went over to Wiggy and had a quiet word with her. What Kit had said to her was to make a pipe saying that there was a fire in the forward torpedo compartment but make sure that the ship's company knew it was an exercise. First Wiggy went forward to the torpedo section and let a couple of smoke

28

bombs off. Then the pipe was duly made.

'For exercise, for exercise, for exercise. Fire in the forward Torpedo section. Duty watch muster at the scene.'

Kit turned her TV screen on that covered all the work sections of the boat. The smoke bombs that Wiggy had set off before coming back to make the pipe were going very well.

The duty watch was all down at the forward torpedo section. Wiggy was over with Kit and they were both watching the screens on Kit's consul. 'They are looking a bit bewildered by it all,' said Wiggy.

'Yes they are. Give it a couple of minutes to see if anyone comes forward and shows some initiative,' Kit added.

A killick had come onto the scene and told half of them to get breathing apparatus and when they had got theirs to bring spare sets for the rest of them.

A couple of the team seemed to know something about what they were doing. Eventually they put the 'fire' out, but it took them three-quarters an hour to do so.

'That wasn't good enough,' Kit announced over the tannoy. 'You have all done fire-fighting during your training and although this was an exercise it must be treated as though it were real. It took far too long to find the seat of the fire and when you had, too long to put it out. Next time, and there will be a next time, I can assure you, I will expect the fire to be out a hell of a lot quicker than that. The rest of the ship's company are relying on you to deal with it. This is the Captain, so mark my words and remember them. Leading Stoker Hills to report to my cabin in five minutes. Thank you.'

Kit looked over to Wiggy and winked. Wiggy nearly burst out laughing, but managed to control it. 'I'll be back in about ten minutes so I'll leave you with the con, XO,' Kit said to her.

'Yes Ma'am.' She was still smiling.

Kit went along to her cabin where Ldg Stoker Hills was

waiting for her.

Kit told Hills to come and sit down. Hills looked very nervous, waiting for Kit to speak. Eventually she did after making a couple of notes on a file. She swung her chair around to face Hills and put her arms on the arms of her chair, made steeples of her fingers and looked at Hills shrewdly. It was making Hills nervous, waiting for her Captain to speak. Eventually she did, and when she did it made Hills look surprised. 'Well done, Hills. I was waiting for someone to show initiative.'

'Thank you, Ma'am.' Hills looked very relieved.

Kit said to her, 'You look as though you were expecting a bollocking just before I spoke.'

'I was, Ma'am.'

'Oh and why?'

'It was a shambles. No one knowing what to do so I thought someone ought to do something. So I did.' She looked down at her shoes.

'That will go on your report. Now I want to speak to the rest of the duty watch who was on that exercise. So thank you again, Hills. When I ask for the rest of the party to muster in the junior rates' dining room I'll want you along too.'

'Yes, Ma'am.

Kit said, 'Thank you,' dismissing Hills.

When Kit got back to the control room, Wiggy asked her how it went and Kit told her okay, but she was going to speak to the rest of the duty watch that were on the fire-fighting debacle. Wiggy just smiled at her. Kit carried on and made the pipe. When she'd done that she invited Wiggy along as well. Wiggy left the control room in the hands of the OOW.

When they both got to the junior rates' dining room they could hear a lot of muttering from within that promptly ceased when the Captain and the XO arrived. The Petty Officer called them all to attention. They seemed very surly when they eventually were all at attention.

Kit looked all around at the faces of the duty watch in the mess deck. She spoke, 'That exercise…' When she did the duty watch seemed to stand at ease and this made Kit angry. 'Who told you to stand at ease?' They all came smartly to attention again. 'That's better. Why I called you all in here was to tell you that I wasn't at all impressed with your fire-fighting efforts. They were disgusting, until someone showed some initiative and took charge.' She looked at one of the junior rates and the girl lowered her eyes. 'What do you think would have happened, Davidson, if it had been a real fire?' Davidson was the girl the Captain had just looked at, and she raised her eyes to Kit and said, 'I don't know.'

'I don't know what, Davidson?' Kit said angrily.

'I don't know what would have happened, Ma'am.' Davidson looked at her feet in embarrassment. 'That's better.' Kit was about to berate her again but switched her venom over the rest of the team and asked, 'Does anyone know what would have happened?' Her eyes roved around the room again. They all lowered their eyes. Kit carried on looking around at them. She was definitely angry by this time, so she said, 'You mean to tell me that none of you can tell me if that had been a real fire that got out of hand, what would have happened…? Don't be shy. There must be one of you that must have some idea?'

One of the juniors put her hand up tentatively. It was one of new members who had joined the boat on Wednesday and was in her first submarine. Kit looked at her and smiled. 'Yes, Andrews?' She was a slight girl with very blonde hair looking no more than twelve at this moment with a smudgy face and her hair all over the place. 'Go ahead, Andrews.'

'The fire could have got out of hand and caused everyone who wasn't wearing breathing apparatus to asphyxiate, Ma'am.'

'Very good, Andrews.' Kit smiled at her.

Kit looked around the rest of those mustered and said, 'It took someone who has never been to sea in a submarine before to tell us all what could and will happen. As for the rest of you, I am very disappointed in you all. You all have been on boats before and possibly have had to fight real fires at sea as well, so there must have been a lot more of you that knew this as well.'

Kit looked all round at the girls present and added, 'The boat could have sunk if the fire got out of hand. There will be other fire exercises soon. You are all dismissed.' They started shuffling back to their usual place of duty.

When Kit and Wiggy were out of earshot of junior rates, Kit turned to Wiggy and said, 'How was that, Wiggy?' Wiggy laughed. 'Very good, Kit.' And chuckled again.

When they got to the control room Kit asked Wiggy to pipe hands to lunch. 'Very well Ma'am.' She did as was asked.

They went to lunch themselves and Kit asked Wiggy to start smoke bombs off in the Missile compartment after lunch and have another fire exercise carried out. Wiggy said to Kit that it would be a different watch on this time. Kit said, 'I do realise that but a buzz must be going round the junior rates' dining room about the fact that the last watch got a right bollocking because I wasn't very pleased with their efforts.'

'Yes. I suppose you're right.'

'Damn sure I am.' Kit laughed at Wiggy.

They enjoyed their lunch and the rapport between the officers. Naturally most of the talk was about the fire exercise that had taken place earlier and other banter as well.

Wiggy duly announced for exercise that there was a fire in the Missile compartment and duty watch to muster at the scene. Both Kit and Wiggy watched on Kit's consul again. They said that things seemed to be going better than they had earlier, especially when someone had the initiative to get the Thermal

Imaging apparatus to the fire so they could find the source of the fire quicker, through all the smoke. At least all the team had on breathing apparatus this time.

When they had put the fire out, Kit announced over the tannoy, 'Well done everyone. That took about half an hour. That was a lot better than the last efforts so you must have learnt something from this morning's debacle. But next time I expect it to be done quicker. Thank you.'

Kit looked at Wiggy and shrugged. Wiggy smiled at her but didn't say anything.

'Will you take the boat up to periscope depth please, XO?'

'Aye, aye, Ma'am.' Wiggy gave the appropriate directions then turned to Kit and said, 'Periscope depth Ma'am.'

'Thank you.' Kit did her usual 360° sweep before lowering the periscope. 'OOW, turn the boat around and go back to Faslane please.'

'Aye, aye, Ma'am,' replied the OOW, which today happened to be one of the new Lieutenants. Kit didn't know her well yet, but she seemed to be doing okay. Knowing Wiggy, she would keep her eagle eye on her.

'I'm going to my cabin to write up the report. If you have any problems, XO, just let me know please. You have the con, XO.'

'Aye, aye, Ma'am.'

Kit went to her cabin and buzzed through to the wardroom. When the Duty Steward answered, Kit asked her for a pot of tea. 'Yes, Ma'am, right away, Ma'am.' The voice on the other end of the line sounded like Steward Jones, a good kid and becoming a good steward.

It didn't take long for the tea to come, and on the tray was a plate of McVities half-covered chocolate biscuits, plain chocolate that Kit preferred. 'Thank you Jones,' she smiled at the young steward. Jones must have had lessons from Ldg Steward

Jeffries, Kit smiled to herself.

She got on with writing her report and drank some tea and ate a couple of the biscuits then stretched out on her bunk for half an hour. She nearly dropped off to sleep but Wiggy spoke to her over the intercom. 'We are on the surface in the exact spot we dived at, Ma'am.'

'Thank you, XO. Continue conning the boat until we get to the Gareloch please then let me know. Carry on.'

'Yes, Ma'am,' Wiggy said.

Kit got on with writing her report. Time seemed to fly by and she was surprised when Wiggy told her that they were in the Gareloch.

Back in the control room, Kit spoke to the ship's company over the tannoy. 'I am very pleased with the first two days at sea. I know we have had hiccups, but that is only to be expected with a new crew who haven't worked as a team before. Anyway, when we get back to base, those of you that are off watch can stay ashore until Monday am 0700…'

She heard cheers in the background and smiled, then continued, 'Then we will be going to sea for five days to see how everything goes. Have a good weekend, and thank you.'

CHAPTER 7

When they got back to Faslane, those going ashore left the boat and left the duty watch on board plus a few of those who had no homes to go to.

Kit and the XO and a couple of the other officers who weren't going for the weekend made their way to the wardroom where the steward had left a big pot of coffee and some sandwiches.

As it was 1700, Kit thought it too late in the day to get in touch with estate agents. She had the rest of the weekend and many other weekends to look around the area for accommodation. She thought she'd drive in to Helensburgh on Saturday morning. She would just relax this evening, have a meal and a few drinks and an early night.

She had a cup of coffee and ate a few sandwiches then went back to her cabin. She finished up the report of the first few days at sea.

After she had finished the report, she locked it in her safe and went and showered and got dressed into some civvies. She was sitting at her desk, staring into space, when Wiggy knocked on her door. It shook Kit out of her reverie and she said to enter. Wiggy was smiling as she came in to Kit's cabin. 'Are you coming to dinner, Kit?'

Kit looked at her watch and said, 'Is that the time? I was miles away. Thumb up bum and brain in neutral.'

Wiggy laughed and said, 'Dinner will be ready in about half an hour, and I was wondering if you would like a drink before then?'

'That sounds a good idea. Lead on McDuff.' She laughed as she followed Wiggy to the wardroom.

There were a couple of others there already and as Kit entered with Wiggy, they stood up but Kit told them to relax and sit back down. She said good evening to them all and went to the bar. She ordered a horse's neck for herself and asked what Wiggy would like. 'A G & T please, Kit.' Kit wrote the drinks onto a bar chit and added her mess number and signed it. They sat down in a couple of vacant armchairs with the others. Kit took a large swallow of her drink and visibly relaxed as she unwound. 'Boy, I needed that,' she said to the mess in general.

They smiled at her and a few of them murmured, 'I know what you mean'.

'I think we all deserve a drink after the first few days we've all been through,' said Kit. Kit downed her drink pretty quickly. She was about to get up and get herself another when Wiggy forestalled her. 'Same again, Kit?'

'Please, Wiggy.' Wiggy asked if any of the others would care for another drink. A couple of the others took her up on her offer. She went to the bar and ordered them. The steward took the order and said she would bring them over.

Wiggy sat back down and noticed that Kit had a vacant look on her face again. She said, 'A penny for them.' Kit smiled at her and said she was sorry, and went on to tell her that she was thinking of getting in touch with an estate agent with the view to buying an apartment or a small house.

Wiggy thought about what Kit had said for a few moments then suggested a couple of estate agents to her. Kit took a note of the addresses and thanked Wiggy for them and sat back and enjoyed her drink and chatted with the rest of those present about the pros and cons of an apartment over a house. 'I don't know what I want yet, but I'll know when I see it. I'll have to sell my apartment in Chelsea, but I can't foresee any problems over that as apartments are always in great demand in that area of London.'

'Yes, I think they would be in that area. Whereabouts in Chelsea is it?' asked Penny Soames.

Kit looked at her and smiled at her interest, and answered her, 'Just around from Sloane Square.'

'Wow!' uttered Penny. 'It should make a mint in that area.'

Kit laughed at Penny's enthusiasm. 'It sounds as though you know that part of London, Penny.'

'Oh, I do as I used to live in Vauxhall Bridge Road as a kid. I was there until I was eighteen, then I started my medical training at St Mary's. Then I joined the Royal Navy.'

'Do your family still live in Westminster?' asked Kit.

'No, not now, they've gone back to Coventry where they came from originally.'

The rest of the women were listening to the exchange between the Captain and the Doctor and during their silence Wiggy asked where everyone had come from – their roots to be exact.

Sue Osgood said she was from Edinburgh, Joan Shakespeare was from Portsmouth. One of them said she was from Gloucestershire and another from New Zealand. This caused a bit of a stir in the wardroom, so much so that Kit asked her, 'What brought you to the UK then, Jean?'

'Well, my parents are both Brits and although I joined the RNZN, they didn't have a submarine service. As my parents decided to come back to the UK I thought that was a good chance for me to transfer to the RN. So here I am.' She smiled.

'Don't you miss New Zealand, Jean?' asked Wiggy.

Jean thought about the question then answered, 'Sometimes, but when I see the surrounding area around here, it is very reminiscent of parts of NZ in the South Island. The Royal Navy is far stricter than the New Zealand Navy. The people of NZ seem to be very laid back, in fact they seem practically horizontal at times!' The rest of the wardroom burst out laughing at Jean's comment.

Just then the steward came and told them dinner was ready. They all trooped in and sat down. The table looked very nice. Someone had even put some fresh flowers on the table that everyone thought was a nice touch. The talk returned again to the pros and cons of an apartment over a house. The majority suggested a house and a few, an apartment. Looking around the faces Kit still didn't know what to go for.

She got on with her dinner and let the talk flow over her head, just answering when a direct question was put to her.

* * *

The next morning Kit drove into Helensburgh and went to the first estate agent on the list Wiggy had given her. She wasn't too impressed with their selection, so she said no thanks and went on to the next one on the list. Here she had better luck. The agent, who was a woman, had come across people like Kit before, not really knowing what they want, but when she sees it she knew that was the one she wanted. Therefore she showed her what she liked herself and that usually worked. The agent, Jean MacAlister, noticed that Kit was wearing a wedding ring and asked her, with raised eyebrows, 'Will your husband want an input into this?'

Kit laughed and apologised to Jean, telling her that she was a widow and that she should have told her straight up front, but never gave it a thought.

Kit then went on to tell Jean the general area in which she was looking, so that gave Jean something to work on. She also told her that she would like at least two bedrooms.

So started a marathon of looking at flats, houses and

apartments.

Kit saw about nine in all and got a bit confused with those she had seen and needed to sit down to look at the brochures Jean had given her. She suggested coffee, which Jean agreed to. Kit had asked if Jean would mind going to the Ardencaple Hotel. Jean had no objection to Kit's suggestion so they found a nice quiet table in the lounge.

Kit sat and ummed and aahed over the various layouts of the places she'd seen, but couldn't make her mind up. Jean quite understood Kit's dilemma and sat in silence so Kit could peruse the brochures.

'How much of a hurry are you in, Kit?' asked Jean.

'Not much really as I only thought of it earlier this week. I've still to sell my apartment in Chelsea but I can't see any problem with that.'

'No, neither can I. If you like we can call it a day for now, and I can look up some more places in our records now I know what you need, more or less. Are you free tomorrow?'

'As it happens I am.'

'Perhaps you would like to try again tomorrow?' Jean asked Kit.

'Yes, I'd like that if it's not too much trouble for you.'

'Of course not, it's my job. If you could meet me at the office at ten o'clock if that is not too early for you, Kit.'

'No, that will be fine.' Kit stood up and shook hands with Jean and thanked her, saying she would see her tomorrow. Jean departed and Kit paid for the coffees then went to her car and drove back to the base.

CHAPTER 8

When Kit got back on board, she was just in time for tea. Wiggy was just walking in to the Wardroom as Kit was walking to her cabin. She asked Kit how she had got on and Kit told her she'd tell her in a minute.

She went to her cabin and put her coat and handbag on the bed and then went to the mess for a cup of tea. There was only Wiggy there so Kit asked where everyone was. Wiggy said that some of them went to the hockey match and the rest of them were probably having a kip or had gone into Helensburgh. Then Wiggy asked if she had found anything. With that, Kit produced all the brochures she was given by Jean and they both browsed over them. Wiggy said she liked a couple of the properties but Kit said there wasn't much about any of them that she liked, although they looked alright in the brochures. She said that she was meeting Jean the next day at ten to start the process all over again.

Kit was starving as she hadn't had any lunch so she ate a good few of the sandwiches the steward had prepared and drank three cups of tea. She told Wiggy that she got very confused and all the places seemed to run into one, if she knew what she meant.

When she was full she turned to Wiggy and said, 'Thanks for that list of estate agents. I only saw two of them this morning. The first one was useless. He didn't seem the least bit interested. He seemed more interested in picking horses for some race or other today. The second one was okay though. That's who I'm meeting again tomorrow morning.'

'I hope you have some luck with that one,' Wiggy said.

'Anyway, I'll go back to my cabin. Will you be at dinner tonight?' Kit asked Wiggy. Wiggy answered in the affirmative so Kit said she'd see her then.

Kit went back to her cabin and put her gear away, then stretched out on her bunk and had a doze until six pm. At six she had a shower and got ready to go to the wardroom. But first she decided to ring her mother and father to tell them that she had decided to sell her apartment in Chelsea. When her mother answered the phone, Kit noticed that she was as immaculate as ever. She said, 'Christine, how lovely to hear from you. You are looking a bit tired darling.'

'You are always saying that, Mother. And you look as lovely as ever.'

'I presume you are phoning from your cabin and I must say it looks very pokey.'

'This is sheer luxury compared to what I'm used to.' Her mother had no concept of what it was like on a submarine.

'Anyway, Mother, I was wondering if you and Dad would do me a huge favour please.'

'Of course, dear.'

When Kit told her what it was her mother nearly had a fit. Kit explained to her mother why she was selling and why she was unable to get down to London to do it herself. She seemed to have placated her a bit and said she would speak to Dad tomorrow evening as he wasn't there just at that moment. She would ring at six o'clock.

Before her mother could say anymore Kit said, 'Goodbye Mum.'

'Goodbye darling. I am sure you are making a mistake.'

'Goodbye Mother dear. I love you. Love to Dad. I'll ring tomorrow.'

She hung up and heaved a sigh of relief. As much as she

loved her mother she could be a bit much at times. It would be easier speaking to her father tomorrow.

Kit went to the wardroom and found no one there so she read the local newspaper. There was a bit about property in it but Kit had had enough for one day and just skimped through it then picked up a copy of the *Times*. Its format hadn't changed in years. It had been the same for as long as she could remember. Although she could have read it online she and Clive had always liked reading an actual paper on a Sunday, and even though Clive was gone now, Kit still kept up the practice.

Wiggy came into the wardroom and Kit got up and went to the bar. 'Usual, Wiggy?'

'Please, Kit.'

Kit had her usual horse's neck and brought the drinks over to where Wiggy was sitting. She said to Wiggy, 'I have just rung my mother.' She raised her eyebrows and sighed. 'It was hard going.'

'I know what you mean. Mine hasn't a clue. I'm sure she thinks it's all a big game. I don't try to disillusion her, I leave her to her thoughts about how wonderful everything is.'

Kit laughed at what she had said. 'That sounds just like my mother. You'd think with Dad being an ex-submariner she'd have some idea. The latest was that she thought my cabin was pokey,' laughed Kit. 'Little does she know. When I asked her if she could sell my apartment in Chelsea, she nearly had a fit.' Wiggy laughed at that and Kit said, 'I'm going to ring Dad tomorrow evening and have a word with him about it all.'

'A good idea.'

At that moment the girls who had been to the hockey match came into the mess. Wiggy took one look at their attire and said, 'You know the rules at weekends after six o'clock in the mess. You should be tidy and no overcoats on, or boots.'

'Sorry, Ma'am. We'll go and change straightaway.'

'Good. But before you do, did Neptune win?' Wiggy asked to soften the reprimand.

'Yes, Ma'am,' they said as one before they went off to change.

When they'd gone Kit laughed, but Wiggy said that they knew the rules, standards are standards. 'Anyway, they should have known better, especially with you here, although that shouldn't make any difference.'

'Quite so,' said Kit, with a smile on her face.

Wiggy laughed too as she could see the funny side of it.

Kit started to tell Wiggy about her grandmother who was in the WRNS before they became the RN way back in the nineties. She said that her grandmother used to play hockey and in goal in the sixties. None of this extra padding that the goalies wear these days.

'Excuse me, Ma'am, for butting in but I couldn't help overhearing what you were saying about your grandmother…'

'That's alright, Penny. I was just telling the XO that she said she didn't wear all the padding that the goalies seem to affect these days. All she wore was a pair of Kickers, something that looked like cricket pads, and a pair of specially padded gloves. And that was it.'

'Wow. She must have been a very brave lady. A goalie these days wouldn't even contemplate going to face the ball without a gum shield,' said Penny.

'No she wasn't brave, not a bit. Back in the "good old days" as she called them, things were so much simpler then.' Kit chuckled and added, 'She also said – my grandmother – that they are all wimps these days.' Kit suddenly burst out laughing. 'I can just picture her face when we were watching a hockey match at the last Olympics. When the teams came on to the pitch, when she saw the goalkeeper she said in her rather high pitched voice, "Good Lord." She says, "She looks just like a

Michelin X Man. You can't even tell whether it's a man or woman under that lot." I didn't like to show my ignorance and ask her what a Michelin X Man looked like, and duly laughed. I've looked it up on the net since,' said Kit, still smiling.

'What is a Michelin X Man?' asked Penny.

Wiggy roared with laughter and said to Kit, 'You asked for that, Kit.'

'Yes, I suppose I did.' She was still smiling when she went on to explain to Penny, 'Michelin X Man was a large inflated silvery very rotund man used for advertising tyres. He was like a person whose rolls of fat went on forever, from his neck right down to his ankles. That is the best I can do.' And Kit shrugged.

'Thank you, Ma'am.' Penny was still looking confused.

Kit laughed and told her to look it up on the net.

At that moment the steward announced dinner was served, and they all trooped in for the evening meal.

CHAPTER 9

On Monday they sailed at 0800 and the Officer of the Watch was on the fin following the route set by the Navigator. It was one of the new officers that had joined the boat last Wednesday. It was also her first time conning the boat, any boat.

Kit was keeping an eagle eye on her from the warmth of the control room. As usual, in the Gareloch it was a bit blustery. Fortunately it wasn't raining, yet.

Val Kennedy asked permission to go up to the Fin for a few minutes. Kit knew why she wanted to go, so smilingly she gave her consent, warning her to wrap up warm.

After Val had gone up top, Wiggy looked across at Kit and smiled knowingly. Kit smiled back, and looked at her consul. She was just in time to see Val struggle up to the Fin and greet the OOW, then look across to Rhu at a chap who was waving a big Union Jack. It was obviously Val's husband and she waved a white silk scarf back to him, very enthusiastically. She continued waving as did he, until they were out of sight to each other.

Val Kennedy came back down and thanked Kit. Kit said, 'I presume that was your husband waving the Union Jack at Rhu Narrows?'

Val blushed and said, 'Yes, Ma'am.'

'Carry on with your duties, WEO.' Kit was smiling at Val who blushed again, and nodded without saying anything before going to her part of the boat.

For the first day, Kit just carried on with the patrol and there were no nasty surprises for the crew that day. All was quiet.

During the afternoon, Kit left the control room in Wiggy's capable hands, and as she left said, 'You have the Con, XO. I'm going to my cabin to write up some reports then going for a walk around the boat.'

'Aye, aye, Ma'am.'

Kit went to her cabin and sat at her desk. She heaved a great sigh of relief and buzzed the wardroom galley. 'This is Commander Carson. When someone is free I'd like a pot of tea please. Thank you.'

It was the Chief Steward who had picked up the phone and relayed her message to the duty killick who happened to be Jeffries. 'The Skipper wants a pot of Rosie Lee so will you do the honours, 'ookey?'

'Yes Chief.' Jeffries detailed Steward Jones to make it and take it. She watched Jones as she prepared the tray and put some of the Skipper's favourite biscuits on it.

The tea wasn't long in coming and Kit stretched herself and her eyes fell on the colour picture of Clive. *Oh how I miss you my love, especially those long languorous nights we had when we were both on leave or weekend. Many were the nights spent in one of the rooms of the Ardencaple Hotel*, she thought to herself.

At that moment when she was about to take her first sip of tea, the phone went on her desk. She picked it up halfway through the first ring. 'Yes?' It was Wiggy. One of the junior rates was having a fit and trying to get out of the boat.

'I'll be right there. Whereabouts is this happening?'

'In the engine room, Ma'am.'

'Right I'll meet you there.' Kit walked very quickly to the engine room. The Doctor was there already, as was Wiggy.

'What is the situation, Doc?' asked Kit.

'I've given her a sedative and she is quite calm now, but I'd like her in sick bay so I can keep an eye on her.' The doctor looked up at Kit and Wiggy's expectant faces.

'Of course, Doctor. Who is it, by the way?'

'One of the new girls, Seaman Graham, Captain.'

'Right Doctor. Get two of the other seamen to give you a hand getting Graham to sick bay.'

'Yes, Ma'am,' said Penny Soames.

The Captain asked the Chief when she had someone to take over from her to come to her cabin. 'And you too, please XO.'

When Kit got back to her cabin her cup of tea was cold, so she poured it down the sink and poured another. That wasn't much better but it was wet and warm.

There was soon a knock on her door and Wiggy and the Chief came in. 'Now tell us what happened, Chief Hawkins.'

'Well Ma'am, Graham suddenly went berserk and tried to get out of the after hatch. I tackled her down and told one of the other artificers to call the Doc. Doctor, Ma'am.' Jenny Hawkins blushed at her gaff.

'You did well, Chief Hawkins. It could have caused a nasty incident. How was she behaving prior to going berserk, Chief?'

The Chief thought for a moment then she said, 'Very quietly. That's what made me keep an eye on her as she has been quite garrulous since she has been on board. She hadn't opened her mouth for a few hours, Ma'am,' said Chief Hawkins. She looked dolefully up at Kit and over to Wiggy.

Wiggy smiled at her and the Captain did also. 'As I said before, you did well. Don't worry yourself about her, although that's easy to say coming from me who has no children, whereas you as far as I recall have twin daughters about Graham's age.'

Chief Hawkins raised her eyebrows as much to say, 'How the hell do you know that?' but she didn't say it.

Kit saw the raised eyebrows and answered the Chief's query. 'I've read everyone's documents and all that sort of thing is in there, even the fact that your husband Thomas is a serving Officer on HMS *Invincible* as a Lieutenant. As far as I can recall, your mother looks after the children when you are both at sea.' She smiled at the Chief who was looking absolutely awestruck. 'Well done and carry on.' The Chief was still looking shocked after Kit went back to her cup of tea. She left, closely followed by Wiggy. The XO touched the Chief's arm to get her attention and said, 'You are still wondering how the Captain can remember details like that.'

'Yes, Ma'am.'

'Well, she has a photographic memory. It is sometimes hard to keep up with her. She always has everybody's welfare at heart, so don't hold that against her.'

'Oh,' said the Chief, and again, 'Oh.' This time she smiled and went back to the after ends of the boat, still smiling.

By this time the tea was cold but as time was getting on she decided against ringing for a fresh pot and sat thinking about Graham. What to do about her? She picked up her phone and spoke to Wiggy. 'Can you pop along to my cabin when you have a free moment please?'

'Yes, Ma'am.' Wiggy guessed correctly that it was about Graham. She went and collected Graham's file from her Divisional Officer then went to Kit's cabin. She knocked and went in.

'Ah, you must be psychic, Wiggy, as I was going to ask you to get that. What do you suggest we do about the poor kid?'

Wiggy thought for a minute or two and shrugged her shoulders saying, 'Normally, she would be chucked off the boat when we got back to Faslane, but I'm not sure if this is the right answer for her, Kit.'

'No, I know what you mean. She always seems so cheerful and she has always got VG on her History Sheet, and good write ups from her previous ships.' It was Kit's turn to think a bit. 'I think maybe I'll go and see her tomorrow and have a quiet word with her. What do you think?' She looked across at Wiggy, expecting her to say something. It was obvious she wanted to but was in two minds whether to or not.

Kit forestalled her and said, 'I know that it should be her DO's job, but in this case Graham may feel intimidated when she sees me by her bed, but enough to open up with me. What do you reckon, Wiggy?'

'That is a good suggestion, but not the done thing for you to interrogate the poor kid, her Captain!' Wiggy raised her eyebrows. 'Would you like me to go instead?'

Kit frowned. 'No, I'll go tomorrow morning. Yes, I'll do that, Wiggy.'

'Right you are, Kit, it's your call. Naturally I'll be curious to know how you get on.'

'Yes, it is,' she said dismissively, smiling at Wiggy.

'Yes, Ma'am.' And she walked out of Kit's cabin.

* * *

At dinner time that evening everyone appeared to be on a high and everyone seemed to be chatting away about the way things had gone on, on their first day at sea, the first of many.

CHAPTER 10

The next morning, Tuesday, after breakfast Kit made her way to the Sick Bay. It wasn't very big, about half the size of Kit's cabin. Before each patrol all the submariners have a thorough medical check-up so they should all be fit, physically and mentally, so there is not a big area put aside for a Sick Bay.

When Kit arrived there the doctor was just checking on Graham. Penelope Soames saw Kit arrive and gave her a smile. They went to Penny's office and Kit asked her quietly, 'How is young Carol Graham doing, Penny?'

'She seems perfectly normal at the moment, although I have just given her another jab, a sedative, just to calm her down.'

'Good. Will it be alright to go and have a chat with her?'

'Of course, Ma'am,' Penny said.

'Thank you.' Kit went along to Carol Graham's bedside and drew out a chair and waited for Graham to open her eyes. When she did and she looked at who it was, she panicked. Kit put a hand on her arm and gently told her, 'It is okay, Carol. I am not going to shout at you, so calm down. I've just come to see how you are and ask you why you threw a wobbly yesterday?'

At this, Carol laughed and Kit said, 'That's more like it. Do you realise we could've all had a free swim yesterday if you had succeeded in getting out of the boat? As you know, all us roughy, toughy submariners can swim, but we at least like a bit of warning so that we can get into our bikinis.'

Carol laughed again and said she was sorry and it wouldn't

happen again.

Kit asked her what her last ship was like, Graham answered, telling her that it was very good and went on to tell Kit all the foreign places the ship went to. Kit let her talk on, occasionally asking about one of the ports of call they'd visited and chatted about that, the pros and cons of it. When Carol told Kit that she went to Hawaii, Kit told Carol that she had fond memories of Oahu, in Honolulu. 'That's where we were, Ma'am,' said Carol, her eyes glowing.

'Well I never. Clive, my late husband and I, spent our honeymoon there and we had a great time. That was a place I'd always wanted to go, and I wasn't disappointed either.'

Carol smiled and said, 'I bet you weren't.' Then she realised who she was talking to. 'Oh, I am sorry, Ma'am.' And she blushed.

Kit laughed and told her not to worry about it. She had realised that Carol had forgotten who she was talking to, but Kit carried on talking to her and asking what other ships she had been on and Carol proceeded to tell her.

Eventually Kit knew she had the girl's trust. Then she asked her why she had volunteered for the submarine service. Carol thought for a minute and told Kit that she heard about a submarine being built in Barrow-in-Furness and that it was going to have an all-female crew. 'I wanted to be part of that and I felt that I would like to help. Now look where I am.' Tears were starting to well in her eyes.Kit was still talking to her gently like a mother and asked Carol, 'Why did it happen to you yesterday, Carol?' And she squeezed her hand.

The girl thought for a minute through the tears, trying to pull herself together, and put the words together to tell her Captain. 'I got to thinking about all that water above us,' she shrugged.

'The water was above us all last week. Why was it different

yesterday, Carol?'

'I've been laying here trying to think why to myself, Ma'am. I just don't know. Are you going to chuck me off the boat? Please don't do that, Ma'am. I love being on here, and Chief Hawkins is a very nice person and I realise that I have let a lot of people down, especially the Chief. Please let me stay, Ma'am.' She begged Kit through her tears.

Kit said to the girl, 'Wipe your tears away, Carol, or anyone will think I've been beating you for being a naughty girl or something like that.' She laughed and could see that Carol was laughing too through her tears. 'There, that's better. Don't worry, I'm not going to "chuck" you off, although you should be.' Gently, Kit continued, 'But I have decided to give you another chance…' Before she could finish her sentence Carol reached out and hugged Kit saying, 'Thank you, thank you. Oh thank you, Ma'am.'

Kit was blushing at the girl's show of thanks. In fact she was quite embarrassed.

Carol suddenly realised what she'd done and apologised profusely. She herself was embarrassed.

'As I was saying, I am letting you stay on the boat, and if you can prove to me that you are quite over this…' Kit was stuck for a word, 'well you know what I mean, until the end of this week and the following weeks I'll let you stay. Until now you've always had a faultless record, so don't let me down.' She smiled at Carol, who smiled back, saying thank you once again, looking down at her hands shyly.

'Now, stay here until tomorrow then report back to Chief Hawkins after breakfast and apologise to her.'

'Yes, Ma'am.'

'Have you got everything you need, Seaman Graham?'

'Yes thank you, Ma'am.'

Kit stood up and nodded and walked from the Sick Bay.

She went back to her cabin and rang the doctor, telling her to dispense with the injections assuming that Penny thought it was okay to do so, and also told her that Graham was to report back for duties tomorrow.

* * *

Kit picked up her phone and buzzed the XO. It was answered on the first ring. 'XO,' was all she said and listened.

Kit asked her if she would spare a few minutes and Wiggy said she'd be right along.

There was a knock on Kit's door and she said, 'Come in Wiggy, sit down.'

Wiggy looked at Kit expectantly and didn't have to wait too long. Kit said, 'Well, I've seen Graham and had a word with her. She is very apologetic and during the talk she seemed okay and told me why she suddenly went berserk.'

'Oh, and why was that?'

'She said, and I quote, "I got to thinking about all that water above us." Unquote.'

'But what about last week?' Wiggy asked.

Kit laughed and said, 'That was exactly what I said. Anyway, we chatted for quite a bit. At one stage when I said we wouldn't be chucking her off the boat it was quite embarrassing. She flung herself at me and hugged me. It makes me blush just to think of it.'

Wiggy laughed, but said, 'Do you think that wise, Kit?'

Kit steepled her fingers and looked over the top of them before she answered. 'Yes, I think so. I've thought long and hard about it and come to the conclusion that it was just a one-off aberration. That's the word I was trying to think of when I was with Graham, aberration.' She looked up and smiled at Wiggy.

'Well if you are sure, Kit.'

'Yes I am, Wiggy. I have written her papers up just in case she does it again, so no one else will get the blame.'

'That's very fair, Kit.' She got up and said, 'Will that be all, Kit?'

'Yes thanks, Wiggy.' She had already turned and pulled Graham's file toward her.

CHAPTER 11

The next day, after breakfast, Seaman Graham reported to Chief Hawkins. Carol was very nervous about this and she felt her knees starting to tremble as she waited to see her. Eventually the Chief was free and she looked up to see Graham standing at attention, waiting. Chief Hawkins looked at her and saw that she looked perfectly normal apart from looking slightly nervous with a tinge of embarrassment as well.

Before the Chief could speak, Graham launched in with her apology. 'I am terribly sorry about my behaviour, trying to get out of the boat and all that, Chief Hawkins. The Captain said she isn't going to throw me off the boat after all.'

Chief Hawkins said, 'At ease. I know that, but you don't deserve a second chance, putting all of our lives at risk, like that. Captain Carson came and told me that she'd visited you in Sick Bay and she said that she had given you a second chance. You don't deserve it. Anyway, go and get back into working rig and report back to me as soon as you've done that, Graham,' she said with a small wry smile.

Carol Graham came smartly back to attention again and said, 'Thank you, Chief Hawkins. It will not happen again.' With that, she did a smart about turn and marched away, leaving the Chief looking bemused.

* * *

For the rest of the week everything ran smoothly and HMSM *Holland 2* returned to Faslane with no further surprises on Friday.

Kit addressed the crew just as they were going through Rhu Narrows. 'This is the Captain speaking. Thank you all for making this trip fairly smooth. You have all done well and I am proud of you. When we get back to Faslane, those of you who are off watch can go ashore and return Monday at 0800 for junior rates and 0830 for senior rates. There will be Captain's Rounds on Monday morning at 1100 and everyone will wear their number one uniform for them. Thank you.' Kit could hear groans from around the boat and she just smiled.

She looked across at Wiggy who was smiling too. Kit gesticulated with her head to follow her and she went to her cabin. Once there Kit turned to Wiggy and asked, 'Will you promulgate about rounds on tomorrow's Daily Orders please Wiggy, as the first item on them for Monday please?'

'Of course, Kit.'

'I'm sorry it is such short notice, but it just came to me on the spur of the moment.'

'That's okay,' Wiggy laughed, 'it will be the first rounds they've had since coming on board. It will do them good. We'll soon see what they are made of.'

'Right then. You had better get back to the Control room to keep an eye on things. Who is the OOW?'

'Chambers, Kit.'

'Oh. One of the new ones. I'll wander along to see how she gets on.'

'Right ho. See you then.'

With that Wiggy made her way back to the control room and found everything to be running smoothly.

The new OOW seemed to have everything under control but as her job as XO in the Captain's absence was to see to the safety of the boat she went over to her console and watched with her beady eye, so to speak, what the new one was doing. She had everything running smoothly.

Unbeknown to the people in the control room, except Wiggy, Kit was also watching on her smaller console in her cabin and she noticed that that new officer, Lieutenant Vera Chambers, had it all under control too. Kit had to smile when she thought of the nickname that Chambers had. 'Potty' was what everyone called her and she seemed to take it in her stride, just as she was conning the boat in now, as though she had been doing it for years. Kit smiled again and decided it was time to take her place in the control room.

She made her way to the control just as Wiggy said, 'Watch your speed. We are not at Brands Hatch.'

'Aye, aye, Ma'am,' said Chambers without taking her eyes from the screen.

At that moment, Kit walked into the control room wearing her Burberry, gloves and carrying her hat. Wiggy looked across at her and noticed that she was ready to go up to the bridge. 'Everything is under control, Ma'am.'

'Very good, XO. I'm going to the bridge for a bit of fresh air and once there I'll let you know when I will take over. Carry on, XO.'

Kit took over control of the boat and conned it very smoothly alongside into the berth. 'Casing party, secure the boat fore and aft.' She watched as the casing party sorted the ropes out and secured them. Kit rang down to the engine room, telling the Chief to stop engines. When the boat was secure to Kit's satisfaction she rang down to the engine room, telling the Chief that she was finished with the engines, leaving the casing party to put the gangplank into position and secure it.

Kit was glad to get down to the warmth of the control room. She gave an involuntary shudder. 'It's colder up there than I expected,' she said out loud.

Wiggy looked across to her and smiled, saying, 'As they say up North, "You look nithered to death."' Kit laughed and asked Wiggy to make the usual pipes over the tannoy, and told her that she was just going to her cabin.

On her way to her cabin she could hear Wiggy making the pipes that she was asked to do. When she got to her cabin she hung her Burberry on the back of her cabin door as it was too damp to put in her wardrobe, and lay her hat and gloves on her desk. She went to her bathroom and noticed her hair was rather damp so she towelled it dry then combed it. She had one final look at her reflection in the mirror and she said to herself that would have to do. That done, she went back to the control room.

The OOW was just writing in the log and when she had finished her entry Kit said to her, 'Well done, Lt Chambers.'

'Thank you, Ma'am.'

Wiggy looked across at them and smiled to herself and said, 'I'll secure here, Ma'am, if you want to go to the wardroom for a coffee.'

'That is the best idea I've heard all day. Yes I'll do that.' Smiling to herself she made her way to the wardroom.

* * *

Kit heaved a great sigh of relief as she sat down in one of the armchairs and thought about the second week of the *Holland*'s patrol; well, the prelude to the actual patrol which would probably be in six weeks' time or thereabouts.

She poured herself a cup of coffee and thought about what had gone on in the previous two weeks. She smiled to herself as she thought of the first couple of fire exercises. It was no laughing matter, but she could see the funny side of the debacle of the first one. At least with subsequent ones the crew had got their act together and got the timing down to a fine art. Then there was the incident with young Seaman Graham trying to get out of the boat and nearly giving them all swimming lessons. She thought about her leniency in letting Graham off with just a warning. What would her father have done? Kit thought about it long and hard and came to the conclusion that her father would have been as lenient as Kit had been. On the other hand, if the girl had nearly succeeded in getting the door open she would have been chucked off the boat as soon as they got back to Faslane. If any of them had survived. Thanks to Chief Hawkins' observations of the girl, she had managed to avert the situation. Good for her.

Apart from those incidents, their first two weeks had gone off very well. There were no more repeat performances with Graham trying to get off the boat. In fact, she had returned to her duties and carried them out very well. So Kit's allowance of letting her stay onboard was well founded.

Kit poured her second cup of coffee just as the wardroom was beginning to fill up.

'Thank you, ladies, for all your help these past two weeks. I think they went off quite well. What do you all think?' Kit asked.

With this, they all started to speak at once. Kit held up her hands and told them, one at a time.

They stopped talking and Kit said, 'One at a time please,' and laughed. 'How about going round in order? You first, Wiggy.'

They each had an opinion slightly different to each other but more or less the same as each other just with slight variations, but what they said was just as Kit had thought, that after all their trials and tribulations, they were of the same opinion as Kit.

Kit looked all around at the assembled officers and smiled, saying, 'Thank you Ladies for your thoughts and suggestions. I will think about them this weekend. Now, some of you have homes to go to or things to do. Have a good weekend, enjoy yourselves and I'll see you all on Monday at 0900.'

There was a joint, 'Thank you, Ma'am,' and they all trooped out, leaving Kit, Wiggy, the Doc and MEO in the wardroom.

'What are your plans for this weekend, Ma'am?' asked Wiggy.

'More house hunting I suppose,' said Kit.

At this, Penny, the Doc, piped up, 'Is there anything particular you had in mind, Ma'am?'

'No, not really, I have an open mind.'

'Have you? That's good,' said Penny.

Kit looked at her quizzically and Penny blushed, saying, 'What I meant was that I was talking to the Doc off *Poseidon*. He is leaving, and going back to General Service. Well, he is married and lives in a two bedroomed cottage with his wife and child and he wants to sell the cottage.'

Kit looked over at Penny and asked, 'Where is this cottage, Penny?'

'Gareloch Head, Ma'am.'

'Do you know when it will be available from?' Kit asked keenly.

'No, I'm not sure, but I can give him a ring and find out…'

'That will be fine, Penny. If he asks if I want to see it, could you arrange it for some time on Sunday, to suit them please.'

'Yes, Ma'am. I'll go and do it now.'

'Thanks.'

Penny left the wardroom to go and make the phone call. Kit looked across to Wiggy and grinned saying, 'This could be just what I'm looking for.'

'Yes. You never know your luck.' Wiggy sounded quite pleased for Kit and she was smiling too.

All this time, Joan, the MEO hadn't said a word, although she looked interested in what was being said and spoke up, 'If it is the cottage I am thinking of, it is a very nice roomy place, but cozy, if you know what I mean, Ma'am.'

'Yes. I know exactly what you mean, Joan. It sounds just like my cup of tea.' Kit laughed.

Penny came back with a huge grin on her face and Kit looked up expectantly. 'It's all fixed, Ma'am. 1430 on Sunday if that's okay.'

'That is very okay. Thanks, Penny,' Kit laughed. 'After dinner, if you haven't anything else to do, how do you all feel about having a few drinks at the Ardencaple?' She looked round at them and they all nodded their consent. 'Right then, ladies, I am going for a shower, so I'll see you at dinner.' With that she got up and left the mess.

The others soon followed.

CHAPTER 12

They all went to the Ardencaple as arranged before they'd had dinner. A mini bus picked them all up and Kit paid for it. The others all tried to pay for it but Kit said that it had been her idea. She gave the driver a good tip and asked him to pick them up at closing time. With that arranged she followed the others into the Hotel.

Good, there weren't too many people in there, so they were able to get a table quite near the bar. Wiggy had already placed the order and the waitress said she'd bring them over.

'I presume a horse's neck with no ice is still your tipple, Kit?'

'What else is there?'

Wiggy started to answer, but Kit said, 'I was only kidding, Wiggy.' And they all laughed.

The waitress brought their drinks over to them. 'That's a new thing since Clive and I used to come here.'

'What's that?' asked Penny.

'The waitress. I didn't notice that the place has been redecorated too when we came here a couple of weeks ago. I must have had something else on my mind.'

The others just laughed and Wiggy looked a bit sheepish but Kit never said anything about that incident. Instead she looked across to Penny and asked her if she would go with her on Sunday to the cottage. Penny agreed to Kit's request and they arranged a time to leave on Sunday. That all arranged, Wiggy asked Kit if she would still meet up with the estate agent tomorrow as planned.

Kit said she may as well as she had nothing else to do also it was nice to see what else was available on the market and to get some idea of how much a two-bedroomed cottage would go for.

'I don't know what John and Chris are expecting to get for their cottage as it isn't on the market yet, Kit.'

Kit smiled at young Penny and said, 'That is okay, Penny, by seeing the estate agent tomorrow that will give me some idea how to negotiate if I like the cottage.'

'I suppose it will,' laughed Penny.

That all sorted out, the four women talked about things in general and had a good laugh too. The time seemed to have got away from them and it didn't seem like they had been long there when the landlord was calling time.

Joan asked if any of them would like another drink but they were all of the same mind; they would have one or two back on board. The minibus was waiting for them in the car park, for which Kit was very grateful. Kit thought the rest of them were rather pleased too.

The driver said, 'Back to the boat, ladies?'

As one they all said, 'Yes please.'

After no time at all, the driver was dropping them at the *Holland*'s gang plank and Kit paid him and asked if he had a card for future reference. He gave her one and she said, 'Goodnight and thank you.'

When she got to the mess Joan had ordered the same drinks as they were drinking in the Ardencaple and the steward brought them over a bowl of cashew nuts.

'Thanks,' they all said, followed by Wiggy saying she would secure the bar when they had all finished.

* * *

The next morning Kit met the estate agent in Helensburgh, slightly hungover. She was taken to a couple of places but nothing seemed to suit her. Kit invited Jean to lunch in the Ardencaple and while they were drinking a glass of wine and waiting for their lunch Kit asked Jean how much a two-bedroomed cottage would go for. Jean said in town they would expect £600K but out of town about £300–£350K.

'When you say out of town, where exactly do you mean, Jean?'

'Anywhere from here going North like Gareloch Head and around the loch as far as Arrocher. After that I don't know.'

'Thanks, Jean,' Kit said thoughtfully.

Jean took Kit to see a couple more places after lunch but there still wasn't anything worth buying, although Kit didn't say as much to Jean. All she said to her was, 'I've got enough brochures here to keep me going for the rest of the week. Thank you Jean, I'll be touch with you the next time I'm in. At the moment, I'm not sure when that will be, but I'll get back to you when I do.' She smiled at Jean and said thanks again as Jean drove off back to Helensburgh.

Kit heaved a sigh of relief as she drove off in the opposite direction, back to the boat.

CHAPTER 13

On Sunday afternoon Kit and Penny left in Kit's sports car for Garelochead, with Penny showing Kit the way to her friend's cottage. It didn't take long to get there so, as they were a bit early, Kit drove around the surrounding area. Then they drove back to the cottage, arriving dead on 1430 as arranged between Penny, and the couple who owned the cottage.

The Doctor came out first, followed shortly by his wife. He introduced themselves as John and Christine Davenport. 'Kit Carson. It is very nice to meet you both. I just hope this hasn't put you out too much?'

'Not at all,' said Christine. 'Do come in out of the cold. I'll put the kettle on.'

Kit and Penny followed Christine inside out of the cold and John followed in the rear. She led them to a very nice bright, light lounge, beautifully furnished with some very nice English antique coffee tables and a sideboard, plus a real log fire that was going now. Both Kit and Penny took their top coats off as it was so cozy and warm in the lounge.

John asked Kit how having command of the *Holland* was going.

'Very well thanks. There are just the usual hiccups which are expected in a new boat and crew. On the whole I am very pleased with it.'

'Good… do you want a tour of the cottage whilst Chris is making the tea?'

'Yes please,' said Kit.

John showed Kit around the cottage. He showed her the

two bedrooms, the second of which was slightly smaller, the blinds were drawn as their baby boy was having his afternoon nap. Kit tiptoed over to have a look at him. He was a sweet little thing and was sucking his thumb with a bit of saliva on his bottom lip. He had a typical baby smell – Johnson's talcum powder and milk. Kit crept back to the bedroom door and shut it gently behind her. 'He's gorgeous,' she whispered to John 'We think so too, but we're biased,' he laughed.

'What's his name?' asked Kit.

'David George,' he said proudly, 'after my father and Chris's'.

'You and Clive never had children, did you, Kit?'

'No. We were going to after his first patrol.' She looked wistfully back at the closed door of David's room and continued, 'and probably as you know he never made it back to the Clyde Submarine Base.' She turned her back to him so that John wouldn't see the tears that were welling in her eyes.

'I'm sorry, how tactless of me.'

'That is alright, John.' She turned to him, smiling, and he could see the brightness of the unshed tears.

'Do you wish to continue with the tour, Kit?' he added gently.

'Oh yes please, John.'

Kit followed him back towards the back of the house to a very large kitchen filled with every modern aid there was, and mostly stainless steel. In the middle of the kitchen were a huge wooden table and four chairs. 'Oh, I do love this kitchen. In fact I love the whole cottage, John.'

'Enough to make me an offer?'

'Yes.'

'Do you want to think about it for a couple of days?'

'Well, the couple of days will have to be next Saturday or Sunday to suit you and Christine as we will be doing work ups all week.'

'Yes of course. That will be fine though. Come and have a cup of tea.'

Christine looked up as they entered the lounge and smiled at them. 'Come and sit by the fire, Kit. Would you like tea?'

'Yes please.'

John said to his wife, 'I'll have a cup too please, Chris. When Kit has finished her tea, perhaps she would like to have a look at the garden?' He looked across at Kit who nodded and smiled.

* * *

Driving back to the boat, Penny asked Kit what she thought of the place.

'Actually, I thought it had everything I needed.' She smiled over at Penny then gave the road her full attention. She said no more and Penny knew better than to ask.

They soon arrived back at the base and Kit thanked Penny for giving up her afternoon, to which she answered, 'I just hope that it wasn't a waste of time for you, Ma'am.'

'No. Anyway, thanks Penny.'

When Kit got back to her cabin she phoned her dad up. Her mother answered and she had a chat with her. As usual her mother was immaculately dressed but she asked her if her father was in, to which she said yes.

'May I have a word with him?'

'Of course dear, hang on a moment.' Kit saw her mother look over her shoulder and called her husband to the phone, saying it was Christine.

'Hello darling. How are you today?'

'Fine thank you, Daddy. Did you have any joy with the estate agents?'

'As a matter of fact I did, dear. I went to two and showed

them your flat and they said it was worth £1.5 million. They both said the same thing.'

'Wow.'

'I take it that you are pleased with that.'

'Yes, Daddy. Do you think you could sell it for me please? I'm sorry but I can't get down there to sort it out myself. Do you mind, Daddy?'

'Of course not, it will give me something to do. I need a new project to get my teeth into. Have you seen something you like up there then, dear?'

'Yes I have, Daddy. It's a divine two bedroom bungalow. Solid, made of granite it looks like to me, and a view to die for.'

'That sounds ideal, dear. I hope you can get it.'

'Well, it's not on the market yet so I have first refusal. You and Mummy will have to come up for a holiday once I am organised. It has no doubt been a few years since you have been up here, isn't it?'

'Yes, it definitely is, I can't even remember the last time I was at Faslane. It has probably changed quite a bit since then? No doubt you have quite a bit to do so I'll let you get on.'

'Thanks Daddy, especially for selling my flat. I'll let you know next weekend what I want doing about the furniture there. Love to Mummy. Goodbye.'

'Goodbye darling. Bye.' And he hung up.

Kit just sat there for a while taking in what her father had told her. £1.5 million. A million and half. If I offer John and Christine £400K, I think that is more than fair. That will leave me just under £1.1 million, she thought, more than enough for anything that needs doing, like building a garage for two cars. It is all very well having a sports car but should Mummy and Daddy come up, I can't expect them to use that. Perhaps Daddy, but Mummy, definitely not, with a capital N. She chuckled to herself. Her mother may get a hair out of place. She chuckled again then got up to take a shower.

Showered and changed she went to the wardroom for a pre-dinner drink.

Wiggy was there and Penny, both reading a Sunday paper. They both made to get up as she came in, but Kit signalled them to stay where they were.

Kit was still smiling, imagining her mother in her sports car, and as Wiggy looked up, she noticed Kit's smile and she said, 'C'mon, share the joke, Kit.'

'I was thinking about my mother in my sports car. Although that may not be funny to you, unless you know my mother, as she is one of those women who never have a hair out of place. Whatever the time of day or night it is.'

'Oh, I see,' smiled Wiggy.

Kit laughed again and said, 'You don't have to be polite, Wiggy, for my mother wouldn't understand it either.'

'Oh, alright,' smiled Wiggy again.

'Right,' said Kit, 'who's for a drink? Penny?'

'Yes please, Kit.'

Wiggy gave Penny a bit of an old fashioned look as much to say, 'that is a bit familiar', but let it go as Kit didn't seem to notice.

'Gin and tonic, Wiggy?'

'Yes please, Ma'am.'

'What was yours, Penny?'

'A rum and coke please, Ma'am.' Penny took her cue from Wiggy as she had been calling her Kit, all afternoon, and it came automatically to her now.

Kit was on such a high she wouldn't have noticed in any case.

The Duty Steward brought the drinks over to them and they all thanked her.

'Mm, that's good. What sort of day did you have at Garelochead, Kit?' asked Wiggy.

Kit told her that she was very pleased with the cottage and she was going to put an offer to them next weekend. Naturally she didn't say how much as Penny was with them and it may have got back to John and Chris before she could speak to them herself.

'Good. So you were pleased with it then?'

'Oh yes. I told John that I would put in an offer next weekend. And I have just phoned my father who will be selling my place for me and he has been offered a very healthy price for it. And that was by two independent estate agents. They both gave the same amount, which was very good.'

Penny excused herself and left the mess so Kit was able to tell Wiggy what exactly she could expect for her apartment.

'Wow! Think of what you can do with that extra money.'

'I have, and I think I'll have a double garage built there.'

'Why a double?' asked Wiggy.

Kit explained that she would buy another car as her mother and father would be up on a visit. Although her father would love driving around in a sports car she couldn't quite see her mother in it.

'Now I can understand what you were grinning at when you came in the mess,' Wiggy said.

'I've been thinking that when we have done all these trials and are ready for a patrol we ought to have a cocktail party. What do you think, Wiggy?' asked Kit.

Wiggy thought about it for a minute and smiled and thought it a good idea. 'When are you thinking of having it?'

'How about the last Thursday we are in as that will give everyone a long weekend, except those that are on duty, that is? And we will need volunteers to act as stewards. We will have to work out a guest list but of course those officers that are married or engaged should be able to invite their partners. What do you think?'

'That sounds very reasonable…'

'But?'

'Well I was thinking about the likes of you and me, who as far as I know haven't another half, so to speak.'

Kit could see Wiggy's dilemma, but for herself there would be so much mingling, and meet and greet to do, that she wouldn't have time to worry about a partner. She said as much to Wiggy.

Wiggy eventually answered by agreeing with Kit that as she, Kit, would be too busy meeting and greeting that would be ideal as Wiggy could get on, making sure everyone had a drink and that there were plenty of canapés being circulated by the stewards and making sure the guests weren't bunching up in the entrance to the Wardroom.

Kit and Wiggy agreed that the second Thursday in June would be the evening to have it, providing that "Their Lordships" didn't have different ideas. That agreed, they had another round of drinks, and by this time Penny had returned to the WR. She had felt so guilty as she hadn't rung her parents for ages or written to them and hearing that Kit spoke to her parents nearly every weekend, she felt that it was about time she did so.

CHAPTER 14

Rounds went off fairly well the following Monday. Naturally there were some nooks and crannies that were missed in the initial clean up. The crew hadn't taken into account how tall the Captain really was and she could reach further behind and above things than the crew ever thought of.

Wiggy followed behind with a clipboard making notes so Kit would have them to hand when she made a broadcast after they were over.

Eventually they were over, much to everyone's delight, but the ship's company hadn't heard Kit's report. They didn't have long to wait.

'This is the Captain speaking. As most of you know I have been doing rounds in the Junior Rates' quarters. For the most part they went off okay but it was the little things that were really neglected that in the long run, if neglected further, can cause a lot of problems. Those messes have been informed about it and I expect them to be up to an A1 standard by 1500 today when I do rounds a second time, which in my book is unprecedented, and as I have already said to them, that I expect them to be perfect. Well, as perfect as they can be.

'I know that I am taller than the majority of you but that is no excuse. So by 1500 I expect to find everything perfect. *Holland* is a brand new boat and has only been in our hands for less than a month and already it is like a "Shit Tip", but I know you can make it better. Be proud of her, and remember it is your home, and mine for a while. Thank you.'

Kit looked across to Wiggy who was smiling and Kit smiled

too.

Kit gesticulated with her head for Wiggy to follow her. They went to her cabin. After they arrived there Kit rang for a pot of tea plus two cups.

'Well, how did that go? I was dying to laugh when I was in the control room, especially when I saw you grinning like a Cheshire cat, Wiggy.'

'I'm sorry Kit, but you were looking like thunder and I knew that things weren't really that bad. I just couldn't help it.' She laughed, and Kit laughed too.

'I know, but you know yourself that if you let them get away with it they carry on doing the same thing. What will the next crew think when they come on for the second patrol? They will say, "What a Shit Tip this boat is."' And they both burst out laughing.

At that moment Steward Jones came with the tea. 'Thank you, Jones.'

'I should have mentioned that in my address to the boat, about…'

'The Shit Tip?'

'No. Of course not,' she laughed, 'the bit about the next crew coming on board after them. I'll mention it in my final address this afternoon.'

Kit poured out a cup of tea for them both. 'Sugar?'

'No thanks, Kit.'

* * *

The second lot of rounds went off a lot better and most things that were picked up in the first lot were made good. There were a few exceptions and she let the people concerned know in no uncertain terms that it wasn't good enough and to do better next time. She thought they got the message.

When Kit made her address to the ship's company after she had finished doing rounds for the second time that day, she mentioned about the crew that were to come after them. She said, 'I don't expect them to come to this boat and find this boat just like a 'shit tip'. I expect them to find it as it was when it was first taken over by us. So be proud of her and don't you forget that there are many Americans that will be looking over it as well when we are in Florida after we have done our missile firing. So God forbid if you let me down.

'I can just imagine those Americans saying something like this, "Well how d'ya like that. Those Limey Broads don't give a fish's tit about cleanliness." Kit said this very well with an American accent, and even heard a few chuckles from the crew.

'You may well laugh, but they will think or say something like that, so don't let me down when we are in Florida please as I can assure you that there will be no shore leave for Junior Rates whilst there. So be warned.' When Kit made her final address to the ship's company after she had finished doing rounds for the second time that day, she mentioned about the crew that came after them, and said, 'I don't expect them to come to this boat and find this boat just like I said earlier, a "shit tip". Thank you.'

CHAPTER 15

The trip to Florida went off very well. The Ship's Company must have taken notice of Kit's threats. Just before reaching Florida she did another inspection of the Junior Rates' messes. This time Rounds went off excellently. She couldn't find fault at all.

Even the firing of the missile went off smoothly too with no hiccups at all, for which Kit was very pleased.

Kit saw the firing later that day when she was on board *USS Kennedy*, who had taken a video of the firing. Kit was jubilant that the firing had gone off so well. The Commodore and his entourage came on board to have a look around. When they got to the control room one of the American officers that was with the Commodore asked, 'Why is there a toilet roll hanging by the periscope?'

Kit promptly answered, 'Well, don't you use toilet rolls in the USA then?'

The lieutenant that had asked the question blushed and said, 'Of course we do, but not in the control room.' Kit nearly burst out laughing when she saw Wiggy's face, but she covered it by blowing her nose and left his statement unanswered. What it was used for was occasionally wiping a little bit of condensation from the periscope lens.

After the crew had finished the firing to everyone's satisfaction, Kit made the pipe of shore leave for those off duty. A cheer went around the boat. Kit had ordered shore leave with one stipulation. 'Those going ashore are to do so in their Number One uniform but just medal ribbons as opposed to medals. Have a pleasant time and remember that shore leave will end at 0100 tomorrow am. Thank you.'

The ship's company were very excited about going ashore in Florida and they all looked very happy when they left the *Holland 2*.

The ship's company and all the officers including Kit and Wiggy managed to get ashore during their stay in Florida. The first time the officers went ashore they had all been invited by a Captain to his house for a BBQ. He had a pool so those who wanted a swim took their swimming togs with them.

The captain's wife was a real sweetie and took everything in her stride. Although the captain did all the cooking, his wife must have done all the preparation of salads and breads. The girls couldn't believe their eyes when they saw the size of the steaks. They were huge.

After their dinner had gone down, most of the girls had a swim in their host's heated swimming pool. There were a few exceptions to this as a few of the girls were a bit overweight and didn't go for a swim.

The USN bus arrived at the Captain's house to take them back to the *Holland*.

As they were leaving, Kit thanked the captain and his wife for a very pleasant day out and invited them both to dinner on board HMSM *Holland 2*, two days hence.

* * *

Everything went well with the rest of their stay in Florida and there were very few incidents that had to be punished.

Soon after they had sailed from Florida Kit found out that some of the ship's company had gone horse riding and the chap that took them had taken them through some fairly low rivers, telling the girls that there were sometimes snakes in the rivers.

Like most girls, they were afraid of snakes, so tucked their legs up as near to the saddle as possible!

The trip back to Faslane went off without any trouble too. Kit commented to Wiggy how well everyone looked. Obviously it was having seen some sun and been out in the glorious sunshine of Florida.

They docked in their usual berth in Faslane before which Kit had made the usual pipes. After making the pipe, Kit made her way to the WR and saw Wiggy and Val had beaten her to it. As she entered she said, 'Phew!' She plonked herself down in an armchair and the steward bought her a horse's neck just as she liked it. 'Boy, I needed that. Who did the honours?' Wiggy nodded. So Kit said, 'Cheers.'

CHAPTER 16

The evening of the cocktail party was soon upon them with a vengeance. The last few weeks of the work up had gone very well with no unsuspected glitches that couldn't be sorted.

Kit had been meeting and greeting for a quarter of an hour and the queue to get in had died down now. She was pleased to see John and Christine there and said that she would have a word with them later.

There had been such a hubbub of chatter that she didn't catch everyone's name when they came on board which could be embarrassing.

She was having a quiet moment with Wiggy, when she felt a pair of eyes on her. She looked up and saw there was a rather attractive man watching her who looked vaguely familiar. He was very tall and had dark smouldering eyes that made Kit blush. Wiggy noticed the blush and whispered, 'Are you okay, Kit?'

'I am, but it is just that chap looking over at me and smiling. He looks vaguely familiar but I just can't place him.' She looked away from him and down at Wiggy.

Wiggy looked over to him quickly then away again. 'Do you mean that tall chap with the dreamy eyes?' She smiled.

'Yes.'

Wiggy laughed at Kit's predicament. 'I thought you had a photographic memory.'

'So did I, but it was so noisy in the doorway that I didn't catch everyone's name. And his, I didn't catch.'

'He is the base padre, Steven Thorpe.'

'My God, I'm not surprised he looked familiar as he officiated at Clive's funeral. I'm afraid I wasn't too receptive that day.'

'I'm not surprised,' said Wiggy, 'I wouldn't have been either.'

'I suppose I'd better mingle with him, hadn't I?'

'You sure had.' And Wiggy laughed.

'You are loving this aren't you?'

'Yup.'

Kit turned to make her way over to him and bumped right into him, spilling her drink down both of them.

'Oh, I do apologise. How clumsy of me,' he said in a lovely deep voice.

'Not at all, Steven, I should have looked where I was going. I was just coming over to you to re-acquaint myself.' A Leading Steward came over and offered them both napkins to mop up their spilled drinks. 'Thank you, Leading Steward Jeffries.' Jeffries just smiled at her.

When they had finished cleaning themselves up they started to chat. She said, 'I do apologise for not recognising you when you came in but there was so much noise going on that I could hardly hear myself think,' she said lamely.

'That's alright, Kit. May I call you that?'

'Of course you can.' For some reason her heart was going like the clappers.

'It must be well over six years since we last met and you were in no fit state to remember what went on that day, let alone me,' he said gently and squeezed her arm.

There were quite a few interruptions that they couldn't avoid to have a proper conversation. Kit said how sorry she was about so many interruptions and Steven asked her if she was doing anything on Saturday evening to which she answered, 'No.' Much to her surprise, he asked her out to dinner. Rather surprised at herself, she said yes. At that he said he'd pick her up at the gangway at 1830; she said fine.

He shook hands with her saying, 'That is the problem of command.' He smiled then whispered, 'I'll see you at 1830 Saturday, Kit.' And he left the wardroom.

Kit watched him leave then had a quick glance around to see if John and Christine were still here. While her eyes were skimming around they caught Wiggy's, who had a knowing look on her face. Kit just grinned and carried on looking for John and Chris. She saw them at the back of the WR in front of Penny Soames, so they were partially hidden; in fact, Christine was sitting down.She made her way over to them and apologised for not getting to them sooner. Between themselves they had settled on a price of £400k and the couple seemed pleased with that. All that they were waiting for was John's next appointment to come through. They'd made arrangements for John to leave the keys with her solicitor, who in turn would give the couple a certified cheque. This only being if Kit was at sea. So everything was working out well.

'Hello, John and Christine. Are you alright, Chris?' Kit asked kindly.

Chris laughed and said that her back was aching a bit, which was why she was sitting down for a minute.

'Can I get you a drink?'

'Oh, yes please.' Kit signalled a steward over and asked her to get all four of them a refill.

They chatted about this and that and Kit chided the two doctors on the fact that Chris had a back ache and couldn't they do something about it. Eventually Kit excused herself to go and mingle some more. The mess seemed to have thinned out a bit so there weren't that many to mingle with, thank Heaven. There was Admiral Ambrose and his wife whom she hadn't had a chance to talk with yet, so now was her chance.

'Hello Sir, hello Ma'am, it is so nice of you both to come.'

'We wouldn't have missed it for anything, Kit,' said the Admiral's wife. 'It must be very hard for you being so tall as you will have to keep ducking to stop banging your head.'

Kit laughed and said she was quite used to it, but it came in handy at times, especially when she did rounds.

The Admiral's wife looked a bit confused at this but she let it go. No doubt she'd ask him later.

The Admiral said, 'Kit, we have to go now, so thank you for a pleasant evening. Best of luck with your first patrol. Good night.' This was echoed by his wife.

They shook hands and left the mess.

It seemed that the Admiral and his wife leaving was the cue for all the other guests to leave too. There were always one or two that didn't take the hint.

Kit went over and had a quiet word with Wiggy, who promptly went over to the Petty Officer Steward and told her to shut the bar. It is surprising how soon hangers-on leave when they realise that they can't get any more drinks. Good manners should have told them that they should have left earlier, just after the Admiral left.

Eventually there were only mess members. 'One thing before you leave, ladies,' said Kit, 'is that I'd like to thank you all for making it a successful cocktail party, and also the chefs and stewards for their help this evening and to say that those who are off watch, to have a nice weekend until Tuesday.' There was a spontaneous round of applause by the assembled officers for the chefs and stewards, then those who were off for the weekend left to get changed and off for the weekend.

That left Kit, Wiggy, Penny and Joan Shakespeare in the WR. There were a couple of other officers not going on weekend who had gone back to their cabins though.

Kit sank down into an armchair and heaved a sigh of relief.

'Thank God that is over, one never can have a real talk with anyone.' She took a huge mouthful of her horse's neck.

'One seemed to be doing okay with Steven Thorpe,' said Wiggy.

Kit choked on her drink and mopped up the spillage, giving Wiggy a withering look that made her roar with laughter. When she had recovered from her choking fit, Kit pointed to Wiggy and said, 'I owe you one.' She said this with a grin on her face as she drank what was left of her drink.

This bit of banter between the Captain and the XO went over the others' heads.

Wiggy said, 'Can I get you a drink, Ma'am and anyone else?'

'Yes please, First Lieutenant.' All the other officers went, 'Oooh,' and laughed. This made Kit blush like mad and she promptly picked up a magazine and held it in front of her face. The others took the hint and left the mess.

'You are safe now as everyone else has left, Kit. Here is your drink.'

'Thanks.' She had a very sheepish grin on her face.

Wiggy looked across to Kit and saw that Kit wasn't holding a grudge and said, 'How did your meeting go with Steven Thorpe? You seemed to be chatting to him for ages.'

'Did I? It seemed as though I hardly said anything to him.' She looked at Wiggy candidly.

'Well you seemed to be going like the clappers every time I looked over at you.'

'I did? I can't understand that, really, as I only said a couple of things to him.'

'Perhaps it was him doing all the talking then.' Wiggy smiled at Kit.

'Perhaps.'

'Anyway, how did you both get on?'

'I spilt my drink over the both of us and Leading Steward Jefferies came to the rescue with two napkins.'

'After that?'

'He did most of the talking.'

'Oh, come off it. What did he have to say?'

'You are a nosey bugger, Bennett. For your information, I'm going out to dinner with him on Saturday night.'

'Wow. Good for you.'

'I feel very guilty about it though. It wasn't until I had said, "Yes" and he had left the mess, that's when I started feeling guilty.'

Wiggy thought about it for a while and said, 'You have nothing to be guilty over. It has been over six years since Clive has gone. I am sure he wouldn't have wanted you to be a hermit for the rest of your life, would he?'

'No, and I suppose you are right.'

'You're damn right I am. You go and enjoy yourself. You deserve it.'

Kit gave Wiggy a mock salute and said, 'Yes, Ma'am.'

Then they both laughed.

CHAPTER 17

All Friday, Kit just wandered about the boat looking into cupboards and lockers and making notes of what she found. She had lunch and dinner and seemed like a zombie so much so that Wiggy commented on it. She said to Kit quietly, 'Excuse me saying so, Kit, but it is only a date you're going on, not an invite to Buckingham Palace you know.'

'I wish it was Buckingham Palace, at least there I would know how to comport myself,' Kit said.

'Just be yourself. One couldn't expect anything else of you.'

'One couldn't, could one?' And they both roared with laughter.

'Seriously though Wiggy, I am rather nervous about it. I just wish I had said that I'm busy Saturday.'

'But that would be a lie. Wouldn't it?'

'Yes. That's true.'

'There you are then. You are stuck now. You will probably have a ball, so stop worrying about it. Come on, grab your coat, we are going to the Ardencaple.'

'Right.' And Kit left the mess to do just that.

Wiggy was rather surprised at that so went to get her coat and asked the Duty Steward to phone for a taxi.

Kit and Wiggy spent a pleasant evening in the Ardencaple Hotel. At one stage Val Kennedy and her husband joined them. Ron, Val's husband, seemed a nice chap and had the girls laughing at some of the things he said at times.

They didn't stay with Kit and Wiggy too long and soon went to their room upstairs in the Hotel.

'He seemed a nice chap, didn't he?'

Wiggy agreed with Kit.

The two women went back to talking about the boat then decided to go back to the boat.

The taxi driver was the same one that had picked them up a couple of weeks ago and as he was dropping them off said, 'Best of luck with your first patrol, Captain. Goodnight ladies.'

'How the hell did he know that?' Kit asked Wiggy.

'It's a small world. Perhaps we should've asked him when we were due back to see if it coincided with your sealed orders.' At this, they both laughed.

* * *

Saturday evening, Steven picked Kit up dead on 1830 and she was pleasantly surprised to find that his car was a very well kept vintage MGB GT. Kit could just make out the colour in the gloomy June evening. It was what she called 'electric blue', she just loved it.

'I hope you don't mind going out in this, Kit?'

'No, not at all. I was just admiring the colour and the make. They are both gorgeous.' She smiled at him.

He helped her into the car and at least they had something in common. Steven drove quite fast but always within the speed limit. Kit had an old BMW Z3 and they talked about the pros and cons of both cars. Kit preferred automatics, but Steven preferred a manual.

At least they would have something to talk about over dinner just in case there were any awkward pauses. Kit was curious as to where they were going. She didn't have long to wait for Steven pulled into the Cairndhu Hotel car park. Steven came round to help Kit out of the car. It was just as low as her own car but she found it twice as difficult to get out of the

MGB GT as it was less roomy at the front than hers.

Getting out she stumbled a bit but Steven caught her and steadied her. She turned to thank him and found him closer to her than she thought. To cover her embarrassment she took his arm and they walked in to the Cairndhu.

It had been a few years since she had been there. The last time she had been there was with Clive. She told herself that it was no good getting morbid as nearly anywhere in Helensburgh was bound to bring back memories of Clive.

Steven helped her off with her coat and a waiter took both their coats to a cloakroom. Another one led them to a table in a quiet corner.

Steven then asked if she would like a drink before dinner, to which she answered, 'Please,' and asked for a horse's neck without ice. Steven complied and had whisky and soda, with ice. While the waiter was getting their drinks the Maître D' came and placed a linen napkin on their laps and gave them both a menu.

As they were sipping their drinks, Kit noticed the wedding ring on Steven's finger. She was wondering whether or not to ask him about it as she liked to know how things stood between them. She was feeling very vulnerable as it was and was in two minds whether or not to stay.

Steven noticed where Kit was looking and said to her, 'I am a bit reluctant too about taking my wedding ring off, Kit.'

'Oh. I am sorry too as I didn't realise you were a widower. In fact, I was not aware of your marital status. I hadn't thought about you being married at all.'

'I was married when we last met, but since then my wife has died of breast cancer. I must say that it came as a shock that she actually had it. When we found out it was practically too late. She had a lump on her right breast and it was operated on with the idea of cutting it out, but when she was opened up they found that she was riddled with the cancer and sewed her back up.'

'How awful for you, I am so sorry.' Tears came involuntarily to the back of her eyes which Steven noticed and told her not to feel sad about it. 'She didn't suffer too much and it was over not long after she was diagnosed.' He took Kit's hand and said, 'Don't let it spoil our evening, Kit. I must say that this the first time I've been out with another woman since.'

Kit laughed, 'It is the first time I've been out with another man too.' At this they both laughed.

'I must say that I find that hard to believe, a good looking woman like you.'

'Thank you,' she said with downcast eyes, then looking back up she said, 'It doesn't seem possible that you haven't been on a date before, either, as you too are rather a good looking man as well.'

He took hold of her hand and kissed it, which sent shivers up her arm. Whilst still holding it he asked her if she would like to dance. She nodded and got up and he led her to the small dance floor. She said that she was a bit rusty and he said he was too, so they both smiled and shrugged.

It was a gentle waltz for which they were thankful. When Steven took her in his arms she nearly melted against him. She looked up into his eyes and realised he was taller than she. *Well that's a first. I needn't have worn flat shoes after all*, she thought.

Steven asked her what she was thinking of and she said, 'Shoes.'

'Shoes?' he asked, astounded.

'Yes, shoes,' she said and laughed.

'How unromantic.' He laughed.

Kit explained it to him and he laughed again and said, 'At least it has broken the ice. Let's go back to our table and order some food and a nice bottle of wine.'

'Yes, let's.'

They ordered a very nice meal with a bottle of wine recommended by the wine waiter. Not that it would have mattered what they ate or drank as they were chatting too much to notice what was going into their mouths. It was all so automatic.

Then Steven looked at his watch and said, 'Good Heavens, it's eleven thirty.'

Kit looked at her own watch, and said, 'Oh yes, so it is,' and smiled at him.

He cleared his throat and said, 'Are you in a hurry to get back on board, Kit?'

'What else did you have in mind?'

He was hesitant for a few seconds then he asked, 'Would you like to come up for a coffee?'

'Up where?'

'To my flat in Helensburgh.' He was looking hopefully at Kit who gave him a beatific smile in return and said, 'I'd be delighted.' Steven looked so surprised that Kit laughed and told him she was big girl now, so he paid the bill and got their coats and drove to Helensburgh.

The flat was nice and warm and when he put the lights on Kit was rather surprised at how nicely it was furnished. He went round behind her to help her off with her coat. When he saw her long smooth neck he couldn't resist kissing it. She was rather surprised at that and he apologised for the impulse.

'No, that's okay. It was just that you took me by surprise, that's all.' She was looking at him and he said, 'Oh, well I'm sorry.' He was looking rather sheepish and to put him at his ease Kit went to him and pulled him by his lapels toward her and kissed him on the lips. At this they were both surprised and breathless and then they went toward each other and kissed again and again.

'I've been wanting to do that all evening,' Steven murmured.

'I've been wanting you to do that since Thursday.' He stood back, raised his eyebrows, then pulled Kit onto the settee. He fumbled with the buttons on her blouse, and Kit didn't object, then he managed to get it and her bra off without a problem. He unzipped her skirt and removed her panties, leaving her stockings and suspender belt on. She took them off whilst he was undressing. He didn't take long to get undressed and he turned the lights down before going back to her.

He looked at her on the settee, saw her lovely full breasts and narrow waist. Lovely rounded hips and her very, very long legs. He said, 'Beautiful. You are just so beautiful, Kit.'

She blushed and held her arms out to him. He came to them and proceeded very gently to make love to her.

He entered her and they found their rhythm but it was over too soon even though they both enjoyed it and were quite breathless.

'I'm sorry, I'm a bit out of practice, Kit.'

'That seemed okay to me, but so am I. May I suggest we start again.' She looked up at him above her hopefully. He saw that she was serious and bent his head to her nipples and began to play with them. Kit put her hands on his buttocks and pulled him into her. They both had explosive climaxes that they couldn't believe and they seemed to go on and on.

Eventually he collapsed on her and then lay beside her on the settee.

'What about that coffee, Steven? That's what I came for. The rest was just a bonus. A very pleasant one, though.' She smiled at him.

He laughed and said, 'Do you really want some?'

'Of course.'

'Righty ho.' He went out to the kitchen and got cups and saucers from the cupboard. 'Instant or real?' he asked her.

'Instant will be fine thanks, Steven. Where is the bathroom by the way?'

'Just down the hall at the end.'

'Thanks.' She easily found it and was pleasantly pleased at how immaculate it all was. In fact what she had seen of the flat the whole place was very clean.

When she got back to the lounge she started to get dressed and Steven came out of the kitchen and saw her dressing and said, 'Are you going so soon, Kit?'

'Well, I thought that I had better, as you have a service to give tomorrow.'

'There is no need as there is a relief vicar in Neptune who has already agreed to do tomorrow's service, so if you would like to stay you are more than welcome, Kit.'

Kit thought about it for a minute and said she'd like to stay.

Steven was very pleased and went back to the kitchen to get the coffee. When he came back he excused himself and grabbed his trousers and shirt and went to the bathroom.

Kit leant back on the settee and closed her eyes. She thought why, why did she say yes? She smiled to herself and thought that he was a typical vicar, very persuasive. She chuckled to herself. Then she became serious. *What am I doing here? Why did I let him make love to me? I must have wanted him to. I did want him to as well, and what of the rest of the night?* All these thoughts were going through her head when Steven returned and he was smiling at her, she thought lovingly.

She smiled at him and he sat himself beside her on the settee and poured their coffee. She sipped hers gently. It was black and not too strong, just as she liked it. She turned to him and asked if he had any children to which he answered, 'Yes, one son, twelve years old.'

'I gather he doesn't live here with you though.'

'No he doesn't. He lives with my mother in London.'

'Oh. Whereabouts in London?'

'Near Kew Gardens. Why, do you know London then?'

'Yes. I've just sold my flat in Chelsea and bought a cottage in Garelochead, although I haven't moved in yet.'

'Oh, why is that?'

'Because the couple are waiting for a new posting. He is a Doctor on one of the boats in the base. The arrangement is if his posting comes through whilst I am sea, he is to leave the keys with my solicitor in Helensburgh who in turn will write him a cheque for the cottage.' She smiled at him and he smiled back at her.

'Who is your solicitor?'

'Mr McCloud Snr.'

'He is excellent. You couldn't ask for better than him, although he's a trifle expensive.'

'I thought that myself, but I don't mind as long as he does what is expected of him.'

'He'll do that alright, and more, and he also knows the English law too.'

'It sounds as though you've had dealings with him before.'

'Yes, I have. After Jenny died she hadn't left a will so everything went to probate…' His eyes clouded over at the thought of his late wife.

Kit said, 'Don't talk about it if it makes you sad, Steven.'

He smiled weakly at her, 'That is okay. I've noticed that it is the same with you when you think about Clive.'

'How did you know I've been thinking of Clive?' she asked.

'When I was in the kitchen…'

'The kitchen!' she exclaimed.

'Yes, when you were stretched out on the settee in all your naked glory. You suddenly drew your legs up and blushed and heaved a long sigh of relief, opened your eyes then smiled and closed them again.'

She just laughed and said, 'I will have to be more careful, won't I?' She was still smiling as he leaned over her and kissed her again.

She had tears in her eyes which he noticed and he told her not to be sad.

'Sad, sad!' She told him that she was so happy. 'I had visions of never finding anyone like you, Steven. Just to go about my business of driving the boat and writing up papers and all that sort of thing. Even though I have found you, it is short lived, Steven.'

'How do you work that out?'

'You must know I will be going to sea shortly for two or three months, maybe more.' She looked up at him with a great sadness in her eyes.

He pulled her into his arms again. 'I know that, Darling, but I will still be here when you get back. You can count on it.' He cuddled her and kissed her with a passion that he hadn't displayed before. He leant back from her and said, 'Come on, let's get to bed. I need you again.'

They made love again and again and eventually fell asleep from exhaustion.

CHAPTER 18

Kit awoke about 1030 to the smell of bacon frying and couldn't quite orientate herself. When she did she stretched and smiled and went to get out of bed.

At that moment Steven walked into the bedroom wearing a pinny and nothing else. She just roared with laughter, her breasts shaking with her laughter too.

'So you think I look funny, do you?' She followed his eyes and noticed her nudity. She said. 'Oh.' And covered herself.

Now it was his turn to laugh. 'There is no point in covering yourself as I know very well what you look like uncovered. Rather beautiful.' He leered. 'Especially with that sun-tan.'For a vicar, have you no shame, Sir.'

'For a Commander of one of Her Majesty's submarines, I could say the same thing of you, Ma'am.'

They both laughed and Kit got out of bed to go to the bathroom.

'I've put a new toothbrush in there Kit, a yellow one.'

'Thanks, Steven.'

'Breakfast will be ready in twenty minutes.'

'Okay.' She had a quick shower, cleaned her teeth and went back to the bedroom to look for her clothes. She found her suspender belt and stockings folded neatly on the chair beside the bed, not that she remembered doing it, and her panties and everything else in the front room in a heap where she'd left them last night. She took them back to the bedroom and got dressed.

When she had finished she went out to the kitchen and saw Steven was wearing a pair of jeans and a t-shirt. He turned and smiled at her and asked her to sit at the table.

The breakfast he served was delicious. Two fried eggs, two pieces of bacon, mushrooms and tomatoes and a sausage. There was a stack of toast, white and brown, and fresh orange juice. 'There is tea or coffee if you'd like some?'

'Tea, please.' She thanked him and smiled and got on with her breakfast. After she had finished she wiped her mouth on her napkin and leant back and heaved a great sigh of contentment.

'Had enough?'

'Yes, thank you. That was delicious, Steven. Thanks.'

'What do you want to do for the rest of the day?'

'If you don't mind I'd like to get back on board.'

He seemed quite disappointed at her decision, but said, 'Okay Kit, it's your call.' He smiled at her.

'In case I forget to tell you when you drop me off, I have had a wonderful time, and I do believe that I am falling in love with you. I won't see you for a while,' she reached over and squeezed his hand. 'Don't forget me when I have gone Steven, you know I'll be coming back to you.'

'I know my Love. I can't wait for you to get back even though you haven't gone yet. My thoughts and prayers go with you.' He kissed her hand then helped her up from the table.

'What about the dishes?' she asked.

'No problem. I'll do them when I get back.'

* * *

They drove back in silence. Both were mindful of the other's thoughts and they knew that Steven wouldn't be able to kiss her goodbye when they got back to the boat. The journey was soon over and Steven squeezed her knee just before she got out of the car. He watched her go down the gangplank and salute, and she turned and gave him a smile and a wave before she disappeared on board.

* * *

Back on board she managed to get to her cabin without seeing anyone. She was grateful for this as she didn't fancy a confrontation with Wiggy, at least not yet.

She had another shower and got into a complete change of clothes from her wardrobe. That done, she had a look to see if there were any signals. There weren't, so she stretched out on the bed and thought of Steven and last night.

Last night… it made her blush to think of it, but why shouldn't she? After all, she was a warm blooded heterosexual woman. It was obvious she was ready for some sex. Was she ever ready for it, she could hardly wait for it. And yet, Steven was the first chap she had ever wanted in that way, not that she cared what anyone thought as she knew that Steven was not about to shout it from the roof tops. He was a delightful lover and a very nice man, with a twelve year old son!

Kit never did ask him about his son. She couldn't even remember his name or if Steven mentioned it.

There was a tentative tap on her door. She said, 'Come in,' and in came Wiggy. The QM (Quarter Master) had just told Wiggy that Kit was back on board. Kit didn't want any conversation with Wiggy for the present. It was obvious that Wiggy wanted to chat but she must have got the message from Kit's body language that she didn't want to be disturbed.

'I just popped in to tell you that everything is A Okay, Kit.'

'Thanks, Wiggy. I'll see you at dinner this evening.'

Wiggy got the message and went to her own cabin, thinking about Kit. She was looking a bit tired and Wiggy smiled to herself. Kit must have had a great time for her not to have come back on board last night. Mmh… Good luck to her. She laughed to herself.

CHAPTER 19

At dinner that evening, Wiggy asked Kit if she had had a nice time and Kit said, 'Yes thanks.' Before Wiggy could ask another question Kit countered and asked Wiggy what she had done with herself last night. She said that she and Penny had gone to the cinema in Helensburgh.

There had been a very old double feature on that Wiggy said, 'Considering their age, they were quite enjoyable.'

'Oh. What films were they then?

'Doris Day, and Rock Hudson, in "Pillow Talk" and the second feature was "Lover Come Back."'

'My mother is a big Doris Day fan. Even in this day and age. I must admit that through her enthusiasm for her I've become a fan too.'

Just then the phone rang in the steward's pantry. It was answered by the Duty Steward who said, 'Hold on please. Commander Carson, it is for you.'

'Thank you Jones.' Steward Jones put the phone on the bar for Kit.

'Commander Carson...'

'Hi Kit. Steven.'

'How are you?'

'Fine thanks. I know it will be a bit embarrassing to talk, so if you just answer yes or no, the rest of the mess needn't know who you are talking to.'

'Okay.'

'Right. Tomorrow evening, would you like to come to my flat for a meal?'

'Yes.'

'Good,' said Steven, 'then I'll pick you up 1800. Okay?'

'Yes, goodbye.' Kit put the phone down and went back to the table. Wiggy looked up at Kit but Kit wouldn't meet Wiggy's eyes. Kit just got on with her dinner. Although she hadn't been on the phone long, the gravy had congealed and it put Kit off. She squared off her knife and fork and just sipped her wine.

Wiggy looked over at Kit again and this time she was rewarded with a smile. Kit said, 'Where were we when the phone rang?'

Wiggy answered that they were talking of Doris Day and Rock Hudson movies. 'Oh yes,' said Kit, 'my mother was very shocked that Rock died of AIDS. Apparently the disease was in its infancy way back in the seventies and eighties and it was the first time my mother had heard of it.'

'Is that right?' Penny asked. 'I knew that he'd died of AIDS but I didn't know it was in its infancy then. I know that every-one should wear a condom and not have unprotected sex, even though it is cured now. It is not worth the risk.'

'No,' said Wiggy, 'it's not worth it, however much you trust the other one.' Wiggy looked across at Kit as if she had known that Kit had been to bed with Steven Thorpe.

Kit looked up and agreed with them both saying, 'No, it is not worth the risk, is it?' and thought that she must have a word with Steven when she meets him tomorrow evening. In the meantime she had better sort out some condoms. She must confess that she never gave it a thought as everything had happened so quickly. She blushed at that and hoped that the others weren't looking at her. As far as she was concerned she had enjoyed the act so much that she didn't care, and she was more than sure that Steven was not a candidate for AIDS.

'Anyway, ladies, AIDS isn't a suitable subject to be having

at the dinner table, especially with all the millions of lives it has taken over the years. Don't you agree?'

The whole mess answered as one, 'Yes, Ma'am.'

After dinner the mess settled down, some to play Uckers and a few to read the Sunday papers. Kit was one of those that read a paper. At least she could hide behind it if anybody asked her anything embarrassing.

'I'm off to bed, ladies, as we have a busy day ahead of us tomorrow. Even though the troops will still be on leave until Tuesday, we can still do a little bit towards making a clear way to storing ship for the trip. So see you tomorrow at breakfast. Goodnight Ladies.'

'Goodnight Ma'am,' the rest of the mess said.

After Kit had gone, Penny looked across at Wiggy and smiled, and asked quietly if Kit had stayed the night with the Vicar. 'When I came back on board, the trot sentry said that the Skipper was back and she'd arrived in a blue MGB GT driven by the base padre.' Wiggy raised her eyebrows and Penny just laughed saying, 'Good for her.'

The next morning Kit was bright and early for breakfast and the Steward took her order. She smiled when she heard the Steward shout down her order for the Duty Chef to cook, 'The whole "ish" for the Captain, please Chef.'

Wiggy was the next one in and she had the whole "ish" as well.

Both Kit and Wiggy said good morning to each other and discussed where they should start the troops that were left on board clearing spaces for the amount of stores that they had to take with them.

The stores would start arriving from the suppliers the next day, and a relay of the crew would pass the stores down to the Supply Officer, for the girls to stow away in different parts of the boat. The canteen stuff would be coming from NAAFI on

Wednesday, such as cans of coke, lemonade and ginger beer. Also the nutty would be brought, which would include bars and boxes of chocolate, Bounty, Mars, Munchies, Picnics, and Crunchies, plus boxes of crisps in various flavours and boxes of No. 3 biscuits. These take up a lot of room as the boxes are quite large, especially the boxes of crisps. Roll on deodorants and cosmetics and all the things that the girls would need whilst they are at sea. Things haven't changed much over the years. The reason for roll on deodorants is because the spray-on type have gas in them, as might hair lacquer, which is dangerous to the atmosphere in a dived submarine. Although the air is closely monitored by the doctor it helps to cut down on gases beforehand.

The First Lieutenant and the few officers and ratings that had stayed on board worked really hard and finished by 1600hrs. Wiggy reported to Kit that they had finished what they could and invited Kit to have a look to see if she could think of any other spaces that could be used.

Kit followed Wiggy around the boat and saw what the officers and crew had done so far and was very pleased with their efforts. When she got back to her cabin she made a pipe to that effect. She also ordered a pot of tea for two and at the same time she told the Duty Steward that she wouldn't be in for dinner that evening. She then rang for Wiggy to come to her cabin.

Wiggy came straightaway and was pleasantly surprised when Kit invited her to sit down and offered her a cup of tea. When Kit had poured for them, they both visibly relaxed. 'Do you feel that the crew is ready for this patrol?' Kit asked the other woman. Wiggy thought about it and replied, 'They are as ready as they will ever be, Kit, and they did do well on the trip to Florida.'

'You can't think of anymore we could have done?'

'No…no,' she smiled. 'We've done all we could and I can't think of another thing,' she said with reassurance to Kit.

'Thanks, Wiggy. I'd come to the same conclusion too. We will just have to wait now until we are at sea.'

They finished drinking their tea in companionable silence. When Wiggy got up to leave she turned to Kit and said, 'We'll see you at dinner, Kit?'

'No. I won't be at dinner, Wiggy. I may see you later though.' She turned her back on Wiggy and so as Wiggy left, she said, 'Right.'

CHAPTER 20

Steven was very prompt picking Kit up, and they were soon on the road to Helensburgh. They arrived at Steven's flat quite quickly. They made their way up to his flat where they hugged and kissed with the pleasure of seeing each other so soon.

'I am so glad you could get away to see me.' He kissed her again, this time with more passion. He pushed his hand up under her jumper and fondled her breasts through her brassiere. He slid his hands around her back and undid it. Kit groaned at the pleasure his hands were giving her so she started to unzip his trousers and he was already erect when she released him. He pushed her back toward the settee and raised her skirt and quickly pulled her panties off and entered her. Kit groaned again as they found their own rhythm. She was surprised at how moist she was for him to enter her so easily. She must have wanted him desperately.

'You are simply gorgeous. I can't get enough of you.'

'I can take as much as you can give, Steven.' She smiled at him.

He started to take her jumper off but she stood up to undress herself and he did the same. Their clothes were left in an untidy heap on the lounge floor as he manoeuvred her to his bedroom and they collapsed on the bed. He was soon playing with and caressing her breasts and sucking her nipples. Then he started to kiss her stomach and got lower and lower until he stopped and looked up at her, but she told him not to stop, she was enjoying it too much. He carried on until she was writhing at his ministrations. 'Oh, Steven, don't be long as I am ready for you.'

'Yes, I know you are, my love. I was just enjoying myself.'

'Oh.'

He soon entered her and she clung to him and was having a spasm as he pushed deep inside of her and she had a mighty climax and he followed suit. They were both breathless and were breathing too hard to talk.

Eventually, when they had their breath back, she leant up on one elbow and said, 'Why?'

'Why what?'

'Why are we so taken with each other? I can't think of the right phrase, but last time we met was only the second time of meeting you.'

'Third actually, counting Clive's funeral.'

'I wasn't very receptive on that occasion. I was too upset to even take notice of what was being said.'

'I don't really know, Kit. But I do know what you mean.'

'Anyway, I'm glad we have crossed paths again. It must have been fate or Kismet. All that I know is I needed you just as much, I think, as you needed me. Is that right?'

'Too right it was. Come here,' he said, pulling her towards him and kissing her again.

She just gave herself up to him, kissing him back with as much fervour as he was kissing her. Why worry about the time factor? She pushed him from her then mounted him. So slowly and languorously she did it, that Steven's eyes flew open. As she lowered herself onto him he groaned with pleasure and grabbed both breasts and started fondling them again. He started to move within her and she sank down on him as far as she could go and then she started to climax and it seemed to go on forever. 'Oh Steven, you are beautiful.'

'You are too, unbelievable, just unbelievable.'

Kit's stomach started rumbling, which wasn't very romantic, but they both laughed.

Steven said, 'I was hoping to make love to you after dinner, not before.'

Kit laughed and said, 'You still can, Steven.' He hugged her to him and rolled from under her and said, 'I had better start getting dinner ready then, hadn't I?'

* * *

They were sitting eating a dinner of pasta and beef in a bolognaise sauce. Kit found it rather delicious and a nice bottle of chilled chardonnay complimented the dinner very well. She was glad that Steven didn't believe in having red wine with red meat or white wine with white meat or fish, and she said as much to him.

'I don't go in for that sort of thing. I just go for the one I fancy at the time.' Then he thought about it, saying, 'Didn't you enjoy it then?

Kit laughed and said she enjoyed it very much and that the chardonnay went with the meal very well.

'One thing that I didn't ask you about, Steven, is your son. All I know is that he is twelve and is staying with your parents in London.' She raised her eyebrows in question.

Steven thought about him and Kit saw the love shining from his eyes before he spoke. 'His name is Mark Steven, after me,' and he laughed and continued, 'As you said he is twelve, but very tall for his age. He stays with my parents when he is not at school. He is a very bright lad and the school my parents put him in seems a very good one. When he has his summer holidays he comes to me for a few weeks.'

'That is nice. What do you do when he's here?'

'Go camping or boating you know, outdoorsy things.'

'That sounds fun.'

'Perhaps you will join us in the summer if you are free?'

'I would love to, but won't Mark object to having a woman along?'

'Do you know, I never thought of that? Perhaps you had better meet him first and you should be back by summer time,' he said, smiling at her.

'I should. If we leave as scheduled and only do a three-month patrol, yes, we will be back.' She smiled back at him and added, 'We had better make the most of these couple of days, Steven.' She got up and started to gather up the plates and serving bowls.

'You don't have to do that Kit. I'll do them tomorrow evening when I come in from work.'

'Come on,' she chivvied him along, 'it won't take a minute to sort them out and put them in the dishwasher.'

Reluctantly he agreed with her. She turned to him saying, 'With any luck, I may be in my cottage by the end of summer and I'll be able to reciprocate. Depending if I have my furniture up here, I can always buy a huge king-sized bed until then, eh?'

He chuckled and grabbed her and kissed her and lifted her skirt where she wasn't wearing anything underneath it, and started caressing her and rubbing himself against her. She was experiencing such feelings she had never felt before, wanton and lustful. Steven seemed to bring them all out in her as she never felt like this, not even with Clive. She was still joined to him when he lifted her up and put her on the kitchen table. Steven pushed into her again and again until she came. 'Oh, Steven, that was remarkable. What else did they teach you at that thespian or whatever school do they call it?'

'Not that.' He chuckled. 'It was something else, wasn't it?'

'I'll say. Rather decadent if you ask me, but very enjoyable.'

He pushed into her again and this time it was even better. She was able to grab his buttocks and pull him into her even more. He was rubbing and nuzzling her breasts again, she was crying out and calling his name, then had another enormous climax.

He came too, even more so than last time, and this time he seemed sated, but probably not for long. He withdrew from her and excused himself and went to the bathroom.

Kit eased herself from the table, and put the kettle on and found two mugs and put coffee in them both.

Steven was back before the kettle boiled and had a spare robe, like the one he was wearing, over his arm and held it out to her. 'There is plenty of hot water if you would like a shower, Kit?'

'I'd love one, Steven. Thanks.'

She went and showered and wore the robe that he had given her. When she got back to the kitchen he had made the coffee and was taking a sip from his mug. He looked up and smiled at her saying, 'Is that better?'

'Oh yes, Steven.'

'Have a sip of your coffee. I've put a little something in it. I hope you don't mind.'

'No, not at all.' She took a sip from the mug. 'That is delicious. What is it?'

'Royal Mint Chocolate.'

'I've never heard of it before. It's delicious, Steven.'

'Will you be able to spend the night Kit?'

'Yes. But it will mean leaving very early in the morning as there is a lot to do.'

'Good. We'll leave about 0630 if that is early enough for you, my love.'

She smiled at him and said, 'That will be fine for me, Steven. I hope it is not too early for you?'

'No, that's the time I usually go in. So it won't cause me any problems.'

'Good.' Kit laughed. 'Shall we go to bed now? I'm bushed.'

It was Steven's turn to laugh and he agreed with her.

They went to the bedroom, hand in hand, and she told him that she wouldn't be able to stay tomorrow evening.

'I quite understand, Kit. Tell you what, I'll make us a booking at the Cairndhu Hotel and we'll have a nice dinner before you go off.'

'That will be lovely. Thank you.'

They went into the bedroom and took off their robes and climbed into bed. Steven cuddled Kit but both of them were soon asleep. After all, it was 2315, and way past their normal bedtime for a weekday.

Steven awoke Kit at 0600, apologising for the late hour. She rushed around and gathered her clothing before going to the bathroom to have a quick wash and cleaning her teeth. She was ready by ten past six. She said to Steven, 'I'll be able to have a shower back on board and some breakfast, Steven.' 'I am so sorry that everything is rushed, Kit. For the first time in my life I forgot to set the alarm. I, like you, must have been bushed. I am sorry,' Steven said, rather shamefaced.

Kit just kissed him and said, 'Don't worry about it. It's not as though we are sailing today. I'll be alright.' All this was said as they were rushing downstairs to the car.

They got to Faslane in record time, only a couple of minutes late. As she was leaving him she said she'd see him this evening. He said he'd pick her up at 1830.

She rushed down to the boat just as Wiggy was coming up the gangway. Kit thought, *Shit. This is all I need*. She smiled at Wiggy and said 'Good morning, see you at breakfast,' and rushed past her. She got to her cabin without bumping in to anyone else. She took a deep breath to calm down and stripped off her clothes and noticed the bruises on the base of her spine. She chuckled to herself as she remembered every detail of how she got them. It was the first time she had ever had sex on a kitchen table, and twice at that. She chuckled again and this time she went straight to her shower.

When she finished her ablutions she dressed in uniform and went straight to the wardroom for breakfast.

There were quite a few of the other officers in there to whom she said good morning, and as one they looked up and said, 'Good morning Ma'am,' and carried on with their breakfast.

Kit was pleased that Wiggy hadn't come down yet. The Steward came and asked her what she wanted to eat, and Kit said, 'The "ish" please, Leading Steward Jeffries, and a large pot of tea. Thanks.'

Jeffries went away with her order to the Chef and was soon back with a large pot of tea as requested.

Kit poured a cup of tea and it was just like nectar. She definitely needed it and thoroughly enjoyed it. By the time she had poured her second cup her breakfast was ready. She had nearly finished it when Wiggy returned. She told Kit that she had put a couple of confidential envelopes in her in tray but she had a Top Secret one which she handed to Kit. 'Thanks, Wiggy.' She looked down at her plate and decided she may as well finish her breakfast as there wasn't much left. When she had finished she poured another cup of tea and excused herself from the table and took the Top Secret envelope and her tea with her to her cabin.

She sat at her desk and made herself comfortable before breaking the seal. She read it and re-read it and smiled. She piped for the XO to come to her cabin. Wiggy was quite prompt getting to Kit's cabin. Kit showed Wiggy the letter from Commodore Clyde, saying that the sailing of *Holland* had been put back for a week. It would be sailing now for Coulport for arming at 0730 on Tuesday sixth July and then on patrol from there.

Wiggy read it and re-read just as Kit did. 'That is a nice

respite, and it gives you a couple more days with the Rev. Thorpe.'

Kit just said, 'Mmh,' and looked away from Wiggy, then said, 'it will give the crew another weekend at home too.'

'Will you stay with Steven over the weekend too?'

Kit looked at Wiggy shrewdly then made up her mind to be honest with the XO and told her, 'Yes. I hope so,' and smiled at Wiggy.

'The best of luck to you, Kit. He must be something special.'

'I think he is,' she said and smiled again. 'I'd better have a look at the confidential letters.' Wiggy made as if to move, but Kit said, 'No, hang on a tick, there may be something important in them that may need your attention.'

Kit opened the first one and turned to Wiggy saying, 'Oh, that is nice.' She looked at Wiggy and handed her the signal that was enclosed, still smiling. When Wiggy read it she smiled too, saying, 'That is so nice, and it couldn't happen to a nicer girl.'

One of the killicks had just been recommended to be made up to a Petty Officer as from April 20th. 'Is she on board at the moment, Wiggy?'

'She should be, Kit. Shall I go and find her?'

'No. I'll make a pipe for her to come here,' and she promptly did so.

The girl, Leading Seaman Janet Jennings, came and timidly knocked on her skipper's cabin door. She was shaking like a leaf, wondering what she had done wrong. It made her feel worse when she went in to find her DO (Divisional Officer) and the XO there with the Captain. The Captain was smiling but it was her DO that spoke. 'Congratulations, Leading Seaman Jennings. You are now a Petty Officer backdated to 20th April.' She shook Jennings' hand, as they all did. It was rather bewildering for the girl, then a cloud passed over her face.

'What's wrong, Jennings?' asked Kit.

'Well, it usually means a draft doesn't it? I so much wanted be part of the first all-female crew, as well, Ma'am.'

'That is alright, Petty Officer Jennings, you can still be a part of it. Go along and see the duty SA and get your new uniform and she will know what to give you and if she hasn't got some of it she can go inboard and get it, just tell her to ask the Supply Officer for a chit for any discrepancies.'

'Yes, Ma'am.'

'In the meantime I'll ring Lieutenant Osgood to give her the authority to take action. Request men will be held at 0830 this Friday so you will have some sewing to do before then. Congratulations again.'

She shook the Captain's hand and for the first time the girl smiled.

'That was nice,' said the girl's DO.

Kit smiled and told her to carry on. When she left she rang for a pot of tea with two cups. 'We may as well have a cuppa and relax a bit, especially as we have a couple of days' grace.'

CHAPTER 21

Kit ran up the gangway and Steven was on time as usual and waiting for her. He leant over and kissed her as she strapped herself in. 'Really Steven, that was bit OTT, but nice though.'

'There was no one looking and I couldn't resist it,' he said, pulling away from the jetty. 'Anyway, I am proud to be going out with you, Kit.'

'Thank you Steven. I'm proud to be going out with you too. Did you manage to get a booking at the Cairndhu?'

'Yes I did and it is usually quiet on a Wednesday as well.'

'Good. That is just what I fancy, a nice quiet evening with you, my love.' She looked over at him fondly. Then she looked at his hands, his hands that could do such wonderful things to her body. She had to stop thinking like that in case she started to caress him whilst he was driving; that would make charming headlines. "Commander and Royal Naval Vicar found in a compromising position in crashed vehicle."

She didn't laugh out loud but just smiled at her thoughts. They were soon at the Cairndhu and Steven came around to help her out of the car. He kissed her again and she leant back and looked into his eyes and she could see real lust in them. 'At least wait until after dinner.' She smiled at him. He looked hopeful.

She just laughed at him and grabbed his arm and he led her into the hotel. They left their coats in the cloakroom and then they were shown into the restaurant. They were given a table quite a way from any others, for which Kit was pleased.

Steven ordered for both of them and a drink whilst they

were waiting for dinner.

The waiter brought the drinks over and said, 'The couple over there sent the drinks over. I hope they are alright, Sir.'

'Yes, thank you,' Steven said.

Kit looked over at the couple and saw it was young Sue Osgood with whom Kit assumed was her fiancé, Peter. Kit and Steven raised their glasses to them in thanks. 'Who are they?'

'The female is my Supply Officer and the chap, I assume, is her fiancé.'

'The secret is out now then,' and Steven laughed.

'Yes, it sure is. I didn't see any other cars in the car park. They must be staying the night here then.'

'Lucky them.'

Kit looked up at Steven and told him, 'Keep it under your hat, but we are not sailing until next Tuesday now.'

'Does that mean you can come back to my place tonight and come for the whole weekend, Kit?'

Very quietly she said yes.

'Oh I am so pleased. Come on.' He held his hand out to her.

'What? Before dinner again?'

'No, a dance.' And he laughed.

She just laughed up at him and got to her feet. 'Do you know what? I didn't realise there was any music playing as I've been so entranced with you, my dear.'

It was his turn to laugh now, 'Yeah.' And he hugged her closer.

This gesture didn't go unnoticed by Sue Osgood. She spoke to her fiancé, Peter. 'Is that the Captain's husband she's dancing with?'

'No, it's the base padre.'

'Well, that is a bit naughty of her,' she said indignantly.

'Didn't you know, Susan? She is a widow and he is a widower.' Sue's eyes flew open at that. 'I didn't know that.

Well good luck to them is all I can say to that.'

Kit and Steven enjoyed their dance and sat down and finished their drinks. Magically, the wine waiter appeared and asked if they would like another drink, but Steven said, 'No thank you, but we'd like a bottle of Shiraz please.' He turned to Kit, who nodded. 'And do you know what that young couple is drinking?'

'They have just changed to Chardonnay, Sir.'

'Well, get them another bottle of that please.'

'Yes, Sir.'

Kit smiled at Steven just as their entrées arrived. They were duck paté.

It was delicious and the main course was something to die for. The Shiraz was an exceptional year too. Kit was sated and she said as much to Steven who said, 'Not too sated for making love, I hope?'

'Of course not, but I will have to let that delicious dinner go down a bit though.'

'Problem solved. We'll go back to my place and have some coffee.'

Kit laughed, saying, 'I remember what happened last time I was invited back for coffee.'

'I promise to behave myself, at least until we have had the coffee.'

'Yeah right. For a vicar you are not very reverent, are you?'

'No, my love.' He leered at her.

She just laughed and said 'Come on then'. On the way out they said goodnight to Sue and Peter. They mouthed goodnight and thank you.

Steven paid the bill as Kit stood in the car park and took deep refreshing breaths of air until Steven arrived. He was there in a couple of minutes and they got into his car and made straight to his flat.

True to his word he made the coffee first. 'Do you want some Royal Mint chocolate in it?'

'No thanks, just black please.'

'Okay.'

They drank their coffee sitting on the settee. When Kit had finished hers she put the cup down on the little side table, sat back and sighed.

'What was that for?'

She knew what he meant and told him, 'It was a sigh of contentment for an excellent meal and company. Thank y…'

Kit didn't get any further for Steven crushed her lips with a burning kiss. He pushed her dress up and pulled her panties down. She managed get her dress off without too much trouble and also to remove her slip and bra without stopping Steven who was doing lovely things to her bottom half. She was completely naked by this time, except for her stockings and suspender belt.

He got up to remove his own clothes but that didn't take a minute. While Steven was taking his clothes off Kit managed to take her stockings and belt off too.

Steven soon returned to the wonderful things he was doing to Kit. He stretched up and was soon caressing her breasts as well as doing lovely things with his tongue and lips. She was soon climaxing and then he entered her.

'Oh my God. That is unbelievable, Steven.' And she climaxed again and again. When they had finished she asked him, 'Why are we so hungry for sex?'

'I don't really know Kit. Fair enough, it has been some time since either of us has had any, but when I'm at work I think of what I'd like to do to you. I never thought like that when I was married.'

'That is exactly how I feel. Just as you. We are sex mad,' she chuckled, 'but it is so nice that we are so compatible.' At this she pulled his head down and started kissing him.

He pulled her to her feet and steered her to his bedroom and they made love again and again until they were overcome with exhaustion.

Steven managed to wake up early, early enough for Kit to get a shower and some breakfast before leaving.

He drove her back to the Clyde Submarine Base and made straight for Kit's boat. Before she left he said to her, 'We must make the most of these few days together. On Friday, will you be able to stay for the weekend, coming back on Monday a.m.?'

'I thought you would never ask.' She laughed.

'If you can get away this evening, would you like me to cook for you?'

'That will be very nice.'

'Good. I'll pick you up at the usual time. Casual will be fine, Kit.'

They kissed goodbye and Kit made her way onboard.

As she was going down the gangway, Wiggy was coming up. Kit thought, *Shit. That's all I need.* Fortunately Wiggy just smiled and said, 'Good Morning Ma'am.' Kit smiled back and said, 'Good morning,' but thought *Thank Heavens for that*.

* * *

The morning went quite quickly and Kit managed to clear her in-tray. Wiggy came along to her cabin and knocked and entered at Kit's bidding.

'Everything alright, Kit?'

'Yes thanks, Wiggy.' She smiled at the other woman and said, 'I was just about to make the announcement to the crew about our sailing orders. If you would take a seat while I do it, then we can have a chat.'

'Of course.' She sat down whilst Kit made the Pipe.

'Good morning ladies. This is to let you know that we will not be sailing until 0730 next Tuesday. I will want you all on board by 0600 that morning. If you have difficulty getting up may I suggest that you come back Monday evening. We will close up for leaving harbour stations at 0700. If any of you miss the boat – the gang planks being removed at 0601 – you will be severely dealt with by me when you arrive at Coulport. I will take no excuses. Thank you and good luck to us all. Leave will start at 1400 Friday until 0600 Tuesday.' She closed the switch, and turned to Wiggy with a smile saying, 'How was that?'

'Okay, do you want me promulgate it on Daily Orders for today?'

'Yes please. What will you be doing this weekend?'

'Not much, just pottering around and taking it easy.'

'Right.' Kit thought that she may as well be honest with Wiggy so she told her. 'I'll be staying at Steven's this weekend, returning on Monday a.m. The address will be in the leave book where I'm staying.' She may as well tell Wiggy the truth.

'I thought as much. You are really taken with him, aren't you?'

'Yes, I'm afraid so, Wiggy. I think I'm falling in love with him.'

'Oh how nice. That is good news, Kit.' She looked at her watch and said, 'It is nearly time for lunch. Coming?'

Kit smiled and said, 'Okay.'

The two women made their way to the wardroom and sat down to a really nice lunch that included spinach. All the women took some spinach and Kit turned to Sue Osgood asking, 'Is there much of this fresh spinach left, Sue?'

'Not much Ma'am. I was thinking of getting one more delivery on Monday to take with us.' She looked up, very pleased with herself.

Kit smiled at her and said, 'Thank you Sue.'

Sue plucked up her courage and spoke to Kit. 'I would like your permission to get married in late September please, at the base church. Do you think your friend Reverend Thorpe would officiate for us please?'

Kit choked on her mouthful, and Wiggy just smiled. To cover her embarrassment, Kit covered her face with her napkin and coughed and laughed at the same time. She kicked Wiggy gently on her ankle then removed her napkin from in front of her face and coughed again, then spoke seriously to Sue, saying, 'I am sure that the Reverend Thorpe will be delighted to officiate for you and Peter, Sue. Just ask Peter to ask him while we are on patrol. I'm sure that in a family gram Peter will let you know the answer. It will give you something to look forward to.'

'Thank you, Ma'am.'

'You are welcome.' Kit dare not look at Wiggy otherwise she'd burst out laughing again.

After lunch she asked Wiggy if she would come to her cabin. When Wiggy got there she took one look at Kit and burst out laughing. Soon both women were killing themselves laughing. They both had tears in their eyes. It was no laughing matter really, as Sue had asked in all seriousness about whether Steven could officiate; it was just the suddenness of the question.

When they had both run out of laughter and calmed down, Kit asked Wiggy if she would like a G and T. Wiggy widened her eyes and nodded in the affirmative. Kit got the gin, brandy and dry ginger from a cupboard and a tonic and ice from the small fridge at the back of her cabin.

'When Steven and I were in the Cairndhu, young Sue and presumably, Peter, her fiancé were there too. So in that respect as, Steven said "The secret is out." Although I'm sure she hasn't shouted it from the roof tops, at least not yet.'

'Well, I haven't heard her say anything yet and I'd put a curb on it if I did. What you do in your off duty time is nothing to do with us until such a time you make it our business.'

'Thanks, Wiggy.'

'You are welcome.' And they burst out laughing again at the memory of Kit saying the same thing to Sue Osgood.

'I'm going walkabout around the boat when we have finished our drinks, just to see how things are going.'

'Okay, Kit. I assume you don't want me along. So I'll see you later then. I presume you are meeting Steven later, so if I don't see you, I'll see you tomorrow.'

'Okay, Wiggy.'

* * *

Kit went down to the missile compartment. Chief Petty Officer Hawkins was talking to Seaman Graham. When Kit said, 'Good afternoon, Chief Hawkins and Seaman Graham,' they came smartly to attention. Kit said, 'At ease. How are your twin daughters, Chief?'

'They are growing in leaps and bounds now, Ma'am.'

'You must be very proud of them.'

'Oh, I am, and my husband is too.'

'Of course.' She turned her attention to Seaman Graham. 'And how are you, Seaman Graham?'

'Fine thank you, Ma'am.'

'Have you thrown any more wobblies lately?' She laughed, squeezing the young girl's shoulder as she walked away.

Graham just watched her go with what seemed like adoration in her eyes. The Chief said to her, 'She is something else. Isn't she?'

The girl turned and smiled at her Chief saying, 'She sure is.'

Kit carried on round the boat, giving words of wisdom and

encouragement where needed or just chatting in general. She had finished by 1545 so she decided to have a quick shower and relax until it was time to meet Steven.

CHAPTER 22

Steven was waiting for her as usual and they drove straight to his flat.

On arrival he kissed her longingly. He stood back from her and said, 'Dinner won't be ready for another hour. What shall we do until then?'

'You randy specimen.'

'That didn't answer my question, did it?'

'What do you suggest, we play cards?'

'Well we could…' He got no further as he kissed her again and took her blouse off after carefully unbuttoning it. He then removed her bra, saying what gorgeous breasts she had and kissed both of them. He pulled her slacks down and her panties came down with her slacks. She stepped out of them and there she was in all her naked glory.

Steven stood back and studied her. 'This is the first time I've really had a look at you, you are truly beautiful. What is that small scar alongside your naval?'

Kit looked down although she knew exactly which scar he meant and said, 'It is where I had a Hysterectomy not long before Clive was killed in that car crash. We were going to start a family after his next patrol, but then I started having problems, you know,' and she blushed. 'Female problems.'

Steven took her in his arms. 'I am sorry, my love. We won't be able to have any children then.'

'Would that make a difference?' Kit asked, looking worried.

'Of course not,' he assured her, 'we can always adopt if we felt we needed children.' He smiled.

'We're getting a bit ahead of ourselves, aren't we?' she said.

'Not at all darling, I was going to ask you on Saturday but I am asking you two days' early instead. Will you do me the honour of becoming my wife, Christine?'

She didn't hesitate for a second, 'Oh yes Steven. Yes, I'd love to.'

'Good,' he said, pulling her back into his arms and kissing her very deeply. She unzipped his trousers and as soon as she released him he was ready for her. He removed the rest of his clothing and pulled her back into his arms. 'Oh Kit, Kit, I'm so pleased you said yes. We can discuss the time and place after your next patrol.' 'Of course we can. But not for a moment as I can think of better things to do than having a discussion whilst standing naked in the middle of your lounge.'

He laughed and led her into the bedroom. He sat her on the edge of the bed and spread her legs then knelt down in front of her. He then did unbelievable things to her. He then stood up and turned her legs onto the bed and then mounted her but sat back on his heels and started fondling her breasts. She was ready again for him and he must have read her mind as he pushed fully into her and they both came together with such power again that they couldn't believe it. 'My God!' Steven exclaimed. 'This is unbelievable.'

Kit agreed with him. 'I'm always amazed at how much power and strength we manage to muster each time.'

Steven just chuckled and pointed heavenwards.

'Really,' she said a bit indignantly, but smiling. 'You can't be serious, can you?'

'If it was meant to be, it was meant to be. So don't knock it.' He laughed at the expression on her face.

'Hadn't you better get back to the kitchen before whatever it is you are cooking spoils?'

'I suppose I had. But that was a nice interlude. Wasn't it?'

She smiled and hugged herself and said, 'I wholeheartedly agree with you. Very.'

He reluctantly left her to get dressed and go back to the kitchen.

After she had been to the bathroom and then got dressed she went to the kitchen and asked if there was anything she could do. He asked her to lay the table.

She did so and went back to the kitchen and watched him work. He was very adept at what he was doing. She asked him what was cooking for dinner and he told her, roast pork with all the trimmings. 'That sounds delicious,' said Kit and he answered by saying that he hoped it was. She sat down at the kitchen table and continued to watch him. He went to the fridge and got the bottle of white wine out that they had started a few days ago. He also got a couple of glasses out too.

'Will you pour for us, Kit?'

'Of course.'

She took a sip from her glass and said, 'Mmh. That is still delicious even though it is a few days old.'

'There is another bottle in the fridge that we can have when that's gone.'

'Great.'

Dinner was soon ready and they sat down. Steven carved and the aromas that were coming from it were truly lovely.

Steven said grace and then they toasted each other. He picked his glass of wine up and said, 'To us both, forever.'

'To us both, forever.' She echoed him with moist eyes.

'Dig in.'

And she laughed at him saying, 'That's exactly what my Dad says when he has finished carving.'

'I suppose I should ask your father for your hand in marriage.'

'I wouldn't worry about that as Clive never did, so I don't

expect he'll worry about that at my time of life. My mother will want to arrange a big wedding, but I don't know about you. That isn't exactly my scene.'

'Well, I was thinking of a small wedding at the base church.'

'Oh, that will be fine. But who will officiate?

'We'll worry about that nearer the time.'

'We could tell my parents when I have finished my handover and then go and tell your son and parents afterwards. What do you think, Steven?'

Steven thought about it and said that it was a good idea.

'I'm so glad then if it is alright with your son we can bring him back with us then decide about the holidays.'

'Yes, okay.' He smiled at her then excused himself for a couple of minutes. When he came back he gave Kit a little package. 'Go on, open it.'

Kit hesitated for just a moment but at Steven's urging, she opened the package. She took out the little box that was inside the packet. Inside the box was a beautiful diamond and emerald engagement ring. She looked up at Steven with tears in her eyes. 'It is so beautiful, Steven. Thank you.'

She took her wedding ring and engagement ring off that Clive had given her and put them on her other hand.

Steven took the ring from her hand and slipped it on the third finger of her left hand. It fitted her perfectly.

'I love it. I just don't know what to say.' Tears were rolling down her cheeks by this time.

Steven leaned over and wiped her tears away with his napkin. 'Come. We'd better go and consummate it, my love.'

'Oh yes.'

He was very gentle with her the first time they made love after dinner but the second time she made love to him and she was quite aggressive and he loved every minute of it.

'That was just beautiful, my love.'

'Not as beautiful as you are, Steven.'

'I have some cognac if you would like a glass, Kit.'

'That sounds absolutely delightful.'

'I'll go and get a couple of glasses.'

He came back with two large balloon glasses.

Kit opened her eyes wide at the size of the glasses. 'Have you an ulterior motive on my person? Going by the size of the glass and the amount in it, it sure looks as though you have.' She laughed at him.

'Of course I have ulterior motives on your person. What a stupid question. I always have designs on your beautiful body.' He leered at her and she just laughed.

They took large sips of their cognac and then he leaned over and started kissing her breasts. They both put their cognacs on the side, and Kit gave herself up to his kissing. Naturally it turned to love making again. Kit rolled over on top of him and mounted and guided his erect penis into her. He groaned at that and was able to do a thorough job on her breasts, in between his groans of desire.

Kit was really enjoying it herself and it was not long before she came, followed by Steven, less than a minute later. She collapsed on him afterward and gave him a big kiss. They were both breathing heavily but that didn't last long.

She got off him to go to the bathroom. As she went, Steven asked her how she got those bruises on her lower back. Kit said, 'From the kitchen table.'

'What do…' then he laughed out loud as he fell in.

'It is just as well I had a medical check-up before going out with you as they would have been very hard to explain away. I couldn't have said, "I have been fucking the base padre." But fortunately it was before I did.'

'Kit, really!" he exclaimed and laughed.

'I'm sorry, Steven, that just slipped out.' She laughed as she went to the bathroom, and she could still hear him chuckling.

She went to the lounge on the way back to the bedroom and picked up the bottle of cognac and took it back with her.

Steven looked surprised but pleased.

'I forgot to tell you that I will finish for the weekend at 1400 tomorrow, so if you care to give me a key, I'll let myself in as I can come in my own car. That is, assuming you can't get away at that time.'

'I'm not sure of my programme until I get into work, but I'll give you a key just in case and a phone call at lunch time.'

'Good,' said Kit and went and had a shower.

By the time she came back, wearing the dressing gown, he had re-made the bed and was about to start on the dishes. Kit told him she'd do that for him.

Kit finished stacking the dishwasher but didn't start it and tidied the dining room and was sitting in the lounge sipping her brandy by the time Steven came out of the bathroom. He too was wearing a dressing gown.

She had topped his balloon glass up and he raised his eyebrows and smiled at her.

Soon after, they went to bed. He kissed her and the next thing she remembered was Steven waking her with a cup of tea at 0545.

CHAPTER 23

When she got back on board she went straight to her cabin. She looked at her new engagement ring and smiled. She looked over to the photo of Clive that still sat on her desk. She spoke to him out loud as if he was still alive, 'I am sorry Clive. I still love you and always will, but I now love Steven too. We will be getting married, probably in September or October.'

Kit changed into uniform and went to the wardroom. There were quite a few officers there who made to get up as Kit entered, but Kit signalled them with her hand to remain as they were.

Leading Steward Jeffries came to ask the Captain what she would like to eat. Kit replied, 'The whole "ish" please Jeffries and a cup of tea, thank you'.

'Congratulations, Ma'am,' smiled Jeffries.

'Thank you.' All the others looked up to see what Kit was being congratulated for, but by this time her hands were back in her lap. As they couldn't figure it out they got on with their breakfasts.

Wiggy was the last to arrive and she said, 'Congratulations, Ma'am.'

'Thank you Wiggy. But who told you?'

'I overheard the stewards talking about it when I passed their pantry.'

The others looked up again with questions in their eyes, and Wiggy looked back at Kit who shook her head.

'The Captain got engaged last night, ladies.'

'Congratulations, Ma'am,' they said as one with a smile.

'Thank you, ladies.'

'I know it is a bit soon,' smiled Joan Shakespeare, 'but have you decided on a date yet, Ma'am?'

'Not yet, Joan, but it will probably be in September or October.'

'May I ask who the lucky chap is?'

'Steven Thorpe, the base padre, Penny.'

'Ladies, let the Captain get on with her breakfast, please,' Wiggy suggested.

Kit finished her breakfast and excused herself. On the way out she asked Wiggy if she would join her in her cabin when she had finished her breakfast.

Wiggy joined Kit soon afterward. Once again she congratulated Kit. 'That came as a bit of a surprise. You have only been going out with him for a couple of weeks.'

'Yes, I know. But it just seemed right to both of us. It is a bit difficult to explain. It just felt right, Wiggy, that is all I can say.'

'I understand, really I do, Kit. May I have a closer look at the ring please?'

Kit held her hand out so that Wiggy could get a closer look at it. 'It really is beautiful you know, and it looks an antique too,' Wiggy said in awe.

'Would you like some coffee?'

'Yes please, Kit.'

Kit rang for coffee and two cups and while they waited chatted away about the patrol that was pretty imminent, namely Tuesday.

'Do you think any of them will do a bunk before then, Wiggy?'

'That's funny you should ask me that as I was thinking the same thing only last night.'

'Well?'

'I don't think so, but you can never tell, can you.'

'You can never tell,' Kit repeated. 'We'll have to wait until Tuesday morning to find out, won't we?'

Wiggy just laughed and said, 'Yes'.

'Right, what's on the programme today?'

'We have Request Men and Defaulters at 0830.'

'Are there many defaulters?

'No, not many and I can handle them okay. You have just two request men. After that nothing that really needs your attention.'

'Can you be free to come here for a drink at 1145, just before lunch?'

Wiggy thought about it and said, 'There's nothing that can't be put off. I'd love to come back for a drink. Thank you Kit.'

'I had better get ready for Request Men. It won't do for the Captain to turn up scruffy, will it?'

'Huh. I've never seen you look scruffy in any rig you have worn, Kit. And no doubt you will be the smartest there.' She finished her coffee and got up to leave saying that she would see Kit in a couple of minutes at Request Men and Defaulters.

Kit smiled at the older woman and said, 'Thanks.'

* * *

Request Men went off very well. With Kit wearing her No. 1 uniform, with medals, she looked ultra-smart. Although the two Request Men were wearing their No. 1s as well and looking smart, they weren't a patch on their Captain. Kit had the type of figure and height to look good in anything.

As soon as it was over, Kit went back to her cabin and changed back into working rig, and even wearing that she looked smart.

Kit decided to read the files that were in her in-tray. There wasn't much to do there so she decided to go on another walka-bout again.

The walkabout finished at 1130 so she got out a couple of glasses and put ice in the ice bucket and started to pack while she waited for Wiggy.

Wiggy arrived promptly at 1145 and Kit pointed to the chair that she had only vacated at 0815. 'G and T, Wiggy?

'Yes thanks.'

Kit poured the drinks, adding ice and lemon to Wiggy's and hers straight up with nothing in it except dry ginger. They touched glasses and took a sip and visibly relaxed.

'Boy, I needed that.'

Wiggy said she did too. 'Are you staying with Steven this weekend?'

'Yes, I am.'

'You really have it bad for him, Kit?' she gently suggested.

Kit blushed and said, 'Yes, I'm afraid so.'

At that moment the phone on Kit's desk rang. 'Excuse me,' she said as she picked it up. 'Commander Carson?' She smiled and said, 'Okay I'll use mine then, that is probably better in any case.' She carried on listening then said, 'See you later.'

'Talk of the devil.'

'Steven?'

'Yes,' she said. 'Would you like another one Wiggy?'

'Yes please, Kit, as long as you are having another one.'

'Yes, I'm having another one before lunch.'

'Good.'

* * *

After lunch, Kit finished off her packing and went to the garage where she kept her car in the Base. It started first time for which Kit was pleased. She drove back to the boat and knocked on Wiggy's cabin door. Wiggy was most surprised to see Kit standing there.

'What are you doing here?' she smiled, 'I thought you had gone.'

'No, I'm just going. I came to give you the number just in case anything urgent crops up.'

'Oh, I see.' Wiggy went to her small desk and wrote the number that Kit gave her down saying, 'I hope nothing comes up, but if it does I just hope I can handle it without having to disturb you, Kit.'

'I'm sure you will be able to handle it. Anyway, I'll be back late Monday morning. See you then Wiggy. Goodbye.'

'Bye, Kit. Don't do anything I wouldn't do.' And laughed.

Kit laughed with her then made her way to her car and onward to Helensburgh.

Chapter 24

Kit arrived at the flat and let herself in. She went around it and tidied it up, made the bed and opened a couple of windows.

She had a look in the cupboard to see if Steven was short of anything essential and there didn't seem to be anything urgent, but she went out to the shops anyway.

What she did buy were a couple of bunches of flowers. Then she went to the supermarket and bought a few bits and pieces that weren't essential but nice little treats, and some more wine.

She went back to the flat and found a couple of vases and arranged the flowers into them then put one vase in the lounge and the other in the hall. She had found a duster and the vacuum cleaner and gave the flat a quick tidy up, not that it needed it for as usual it was immaculate.

Kit made herself a cup of tea and sat down and relaxed, enjoying the tea. One thing she couldn't figure out was Steven and her own great need for sex. Not that she was complaining, but the amount of times in one evening?! She was quite content with the once or twice that she and Clive had most days of a weekend, those far away days in their flat in London and a couple of times a week when they were not too tired. And she was sure that Steven was the same with his wife. What would have made it difficult for Steven was having a young son around, and that would really have cramped his style.

She avidly invited his attentions, she didn't mind at all, but *why?* Why were they both so sex mad? Why? She had only known him for a couple of weeks and here she was in his flat and betrothed to him and once married, a ready-made family, namely in the form of a teenaged son. It was quite an undertaking and she was wondering whether she was up to it.

She heard Steven's key in the lock and her heart gave a big flip. At that moment she knew she was up to it. He came into the lounge and saw her sitting on the settee with a beautiful vase of flowers that seemed to act as a halo on her.

He kissed her as she stood up. 'I've really missed you, Kit, even though it has only been nearly a day.' She laughed with him.

'I know what you mean. Would you like a cup of tea?'

'Yes please. I'm really looking forward to this weekend.' He followed her out to the kitchen and as she bent over the fridge he went up behind her and grabbed her by the waist, pulling her to him. He kicked the fridge shut and kissed the back of her neck and his hands went around to her front and up her jumper. Kit leaned back into him and she could feel his arousal and it too aroused her. She sighed as he managed to push her bra up and fondle her breasts. 'What a nice welcome home, my love.' He turned her around to face him and kissed her very deeply, then he concentrated on her breasts. She undid her bra and pulled her jumper over her head. She was wearing a short flared skirt that she managed to remove without disturbing him. Her panties were a bit more difficult so she left them on for now.

He manoeuvred her into the lounge and on to the settee. He stopped to take her panties off and to strip himself. His arousal was rampant and he was standing in front of Kit and so she stretched out for him. She took his penis in her hand and gently rubbed it up and down. By this time both their arousals were about to burst. Steven bent down to her just as Kit opened her legs. He entered her and their climaxes were instantaneous, leaving both calling each other's name.

By the time they had their breath back Steven had sat on the settee and held Kit in his arms. 'Oh I do love you so, Kit. What did I ever do without you, and what am I going to do whilst you are away?'

She looked up to his eyes and she saw they were shut. He had sounded so sad and sincere and as she looked closer she saw a small tear roll from under his right eyelid.

Very gently she told him, 'Please don't be sad, Steven. I will be going away with lovely memories and hopefully you will still want me when I get back in three months' time. We have until Monday morning too, so don't worry, my love.' She kissed his tear away and hugged him closer to her.

He kissed the top of her head and said thank you and she just smiled.

'What do you want to do about dinner?' he asked.

'I hadn't given it a thought, to be honest.'

'What say we go out tonight, but tomorrow we'll go out and get some shopping and I'll cook for us. How does that sound?'

'That sounds great, but I have a better idea. You cook Saturday's and I'll cook Sunday's dinner.'

'You have a deal,' laughed Steven. 'Now let me get at you.' He pulled her down onto the carpet and held her hands above her head. Then he straddled her and started kissing her breasts. Kit found it a wonderful sensation. She said as much to him, and then she felt him getting harder and pushing against her. She then opened her legs to him invitingly and he entered her and her legs went up around his waist and he managed to go even further into her. 'Oh yes, Steven, that is the most.' They were both bucking and Kit was writhing in ecstasy as she said, 'Oh Steven, I can't wait.' And she had a prolonged climax and he soon followed suit.

They lay panting on the carpet and he rolled from her and went to the bathroom. She stayed there until he came back and he pulled her to her feet.

She too went to the bathroom and by the time she got back he was pouring them both a drink. She got dressed and went and joined him in the kitchen. 'That's lovely,' said she, taking a sip of the horse's neck.

Steven misunderstood her. 'Do you want to do it again?'

'No. I mean yes, but no.' Steven, having got hold of the wrong end of the stick, looked quite disappointed.

This made Kit laugh and she said, 'I meant the drink, silly.'

He laughed too at his gaff. 'I was quite worried for a minute.'

After a couple more sips he asked her where she would like to go for dinner. They decided on the Ardencaple Hotel.

Steven booked for 1900 and as it was only 1645 that gave them plenty of time to talk and have a couple more drinks. Well, that was the idea but they were soon making love again.

* * *

Kit went and had a shower first and Steven had one while she was dressing. She wore a loose fitting navy blue dress, cinched at the waist by a broad white belt. It was sleeveless with a low V neck back and front which really showed off her lovely breasts.

Steven whistled as he walked into the bedroom. 'You'll be the best looking woman in the restaurant.' He kissed her neck.

'Thank you, kind sir.'

'Whose car are we going to take tonight?'Kit looked down at her high heels.

'Oh we can go in mine or we can walk,' he suggested.

'I don't know about you, but I fancy a walk and the forecast is good.'

'Okay then. We had better get going as soon as I am ready then.'

* * *

They took a pleasant walk along the Gareloch seafront to the Ardencaple Hotel at Rhu and arrived there not long before their booking.

They were shown to their table straightaway. The waitress asked them what they would like to drink. That didn't need any thinking time and the waitress was soon back with a horse's neck for Kit and a whisky and soda for Steven.

While they were having a quiet moment, Val and Ron Kennedy came in to the restaurant. Kit looked up and smiled and introduced Steven to them both. Ron already knew Steven. 'It's nice to see you again Steven.'

'Congratulations to you both, and I hope you both will be very happy,' said Val.

'Thank you, Valerie and Ron, for your good wishes; it's most kind of you. Would you care to join us for dinner?' asked Steven.

They looked at each other and both and in unison said, 'Yes please.'

Steven stood up and pulled a chair out for Val, next to him, and Ron sat beside Kit.

'I gather that you're the first Commander of an all-female crew, Commander.'

'Yes. That is true, but please call me Kit.'

'Thank you Ma'am,' he laughed. 'I mean Kit.' And they both laughed again.

A very pleasant evening ensued with a lot of wine drunk and a lot of laughter, until Steven said to Kit it was time to go as it was quite a walk back.

Kit suggested that they get a taxi back to which Steven agreed. Kit rang and was told it would be at least twenty minutes and she said that would be okay. 'It will be twenty minutes so may I suggest that we all have a nightcap?' They all agreed to that and it was cognacs all round.

They had just finished their cognacs when the waitress came and told Kit and Steven that their taxi had arrived. They said goodnight to Val and Ron. Ron stood up and helped Kit with her chair and her jacket, and she gave Ron a lovely smile and said goodnight again.

After they had left Ron said, 'What a lovely couple they make.'

'Yes,' said Val, 'and she is a smashing boss too.'

'Shall we go to our room, darling?' Ron suggested.

'Yes, we may as well, dear.'

Ron called for the bill and was most surprised to find out that Steven had paid their share.

'That was very kind of Steven.'

'What was?' asked Val.

'Steven, paying our share of the bill.'

'That *was* nice of him.'

'Anyway, we may as well go to our room.' He held his hand out for Val, then thanked Maggie, the waitress for looking after them, and made their way upstairs to their room.

As soon as they got upstairs and in their room, Ron started to undress Val.

'What do you think that Kit and Steven are doing now?'

'Exactly what we are doing, my love.'

'Oh they can't be, not Kit.'

'What makes you think she is so pure? You should have seen the way that Steven was watching her, practically undressing her with his eyes.'

'Was he really?'

'Yes. Now let's not worry about them. Let me make love to you, Val. I've been wanting to all evening.'

CHAPTER 25

Steven and Kit were soon back in his flat and he grabbed her to him as soon as the door was shut. 'I've been wanting to kiss you all evening, Kit.' And he kissed her very thoroughly and Kit responded to him.

He helped her off with her light jacket then took her by the hand and led her to the bedroom.

It was only ten fifty and they had the rest of the weekend before them so they got undressed and put their dressing gowns on and went back to the front room and Steven poured them both a very generous measure of cognac.

Kit opened her eyes wide and said, 'Have you designs on my person again, after you have got me drunk? Not that it will take very long.' She laughed.

He laughed too. 'I'm not planning on waiting that long, my love.'

'You randy so and so, at least let me enjoy this drink please.'

'Okay.' And he leered at her and it made her splutter.

'That is one way of getting me to finish my drink quicker,' she laughed.

'Oh come here.' And he pulled her to him, took the glass from her hand and opened her dressing gown at the top, exposing both breasts. He leant down and kissed them. 'God they are beautiful, as are you, my love.'

'Thank you. I do enjoy you kissing them.' And she just sighed and sat back and let him carry on. He didn't need any encouragement.

* * *

Apart from going out to get the shopping on Saturday they hardly left the bedroom. It was a weekend of lust and a weekend of sadness.

They got through until Sunday and then had a serious talk about their future. Steven said that he would come round to Coulport to meet her when she got in. No doubt he would hear of the boat's arrival through the grapevine. He couldn't wait for that day.

'What will happen then Steven?'

'I will bring you back here and make mad passionate love to you.'

'I won't be able to contain myself, waiting for that day.'

'I'm afraid we will both have to, darling.'

'By then, I may be able to move into my bungalow. I can't wait to start furnishing it, with input from you of course.'

'I'd be delighted to help you.'

'Good,' she said, and kissed the top of his nose. Then she got up to cook the dinner and left Steven to his Sunday paper. It was just like it used to be with Clive.

She went into the front room a couple of times and found Steven asleep on the settee, the scene of their many sessions of lovemaking. She smiled to herself and went back to the kitchen. After shutting the door so as not to disturb Steven, she got on with preparing the vegetables. The beef was cooking away very nicely in the oven and Kit looked in the cupboard for some flour to make the Yorkshire puddings. She found some eventually, and proceeded to beat the flour and eggs together into a nice smooth batter with the aim of letting it rest before cooking. She managed to find another smaller roasting tin to cook it in. It was a pity that she couldn't find a bun or muffin tin which she much preferred.

When everything was prepared, she sat and read *The Sunday Times*.

After skimming through the *Times* it was time to cook the vegetables and put the Yorkshire pudding in the oven.

She went into the lounge to lay the table. Steven was just stirring.

Kit went over and kissed the top of his head which smelt lovely and clean from the shower that he had had that morning. He reached up for her, but she managed to get away, saying, 'Dinner will be ready in twenty minutes, darling.'

'Okay my love. I'll come and open the wine.'

'I've got a bottle out in the kitchen, a Shiraz if that is okay with you.'

'Sure is. It will give the wine a few minutes to breathe,' Steven suggested.

'No giving it a kiss of life, Steven.' She laughed.

Everything was ready in about twenty-two minutes so Steven carved the joint of beef. A bit of blood ran out and Steven said it was just as he liked it.

It was while they were eating dinner that Steven dropped his bombshell.

Kit put her knife and fork down, wiped her mouth on her napkin and said, 'Are you serious. Is that true?' She was horrified.

'I've only just remembered.'

'You mean to tell me that you have been making love to me completely unprotected, when there is a possibility that you may have contracted AIDS through a contaminated blood transfusion your wife had?' She was furious.

'I'm sorry. But you can see that I haven't got it, Kit. I've had all the tests and they have come up negative,' he said with pleading eyes.

'You may not have it, but there is no guarantee that you

are not a carrier of the disease, is there? How could you?' she shouted at him. There were tears in her eyes. 'I have loved and trusted you with all my heart and you, you… have betrayed that love and trust.'

She was sobbing now and the anguish he could hear in her sobs made him weep too.

'I am so sorry Kit. I didn't think, as they said I was clear, I literally took them at their word. I never knew that as I had made love to my wife after they found out about the contaminated blood and having had all the tests I could still be a carrier of it. I honestly did not know that Kit. Believe me, Kit.'

She looked up at him and could see that he was sincere in his denial. 'Where does that leave me, Steven?'

He just shrugged and pleaded with his eyes.

Now she was really angry. She stood up and pushed her chair back with quite a force that it fell over, and stormed off to the bedroom.

He could hear her banging around in there and he just sat and waited to see what she was going to do. He didn't have to wait long as she came out with her packed bag and gently put the front door key on the table in front of him. He looked down at it then up at her and saw that she was about to walk out on him.

'Please don't go, Kit. I love you.'

She looked at him with utter disgust in her eyes. 'I am sorry, Steven, that it has turned out as it has. I still love you but I cannot go on seeing you under these circumstances. Goodbye.' She turned on her heel and left the flat.

He just sat there astounded at the swiftness of her departure. He heard her engine start up and went to the window and looked out only to see her little BMW Z3 disappear round the corner and out of sight.

CHAPTER 26

Kit drove back to the Base but she stopped in a layby on the way to wipe away her tears and to pull herself together. She spent about ten minutes sorting herself out before she felt she was ready to carry on driving. She had looked in the mirror and checked her eyes before starting off. She was glad she had her dark glasses in the glove compartment.

When she got back to the boat she managed to get to her cabin without seeing anybody. As it was only 1800 she decided to have a shower and wash her hair.

That done, she phoned the Stewards Pantry to ask if there was the chance of a sandwich and a cup of tea. The answer came back straightaway. 'Will a beef and salad one be alright, Ma'am?'

'Yes of course, thank you Jones.' Kit hung up the phone.

She had a look at her in-tray and there wasn't much that needed her immediate attention so she decided to leave it until Monday.

Jones soon came with the sandwich and a pot of tea. Kit decided against the tea and poured a horse's neck instead.

She saw the horse's neck off with just a couple of swallows and poured another one. She took a deep breath and sighed before starting on the second drink. What to do? She had better speak to Penny Soames and ask for her advice on what to do about it.

She was thinking of Steven. How could he be so irresponsible, or perhaps, in his case, naïve? She didn't think he knew the dangers involved. *It was a pity I didn't take any contraceptives with me*, she thought. *I must admit it came as a bit of a surprise when we made love the first time. Oh Steven, Steven, how could you be so naïve?*

Just then there was a knock on the cabin door. She said, 'Come in.' It was Jones, who had come for the tray. 'Thank you, Steward Jones. Could you tell me which officers are on board, please?' Jones told her what she had asked and left with the tray.

So Penny was on board. Kit didn't hesitate. She went to Penny's cabin and knocked on the bulkhead. Fortunately it was Penny who drew the curtain back. It was pretty obvious to Kit that Penny was surprised to see her boss there. She gave Kit a smile, but before Penny could say anything to her, her Commander said, 'If you have a few minutes to spare, do you think you can come to my cabin, please?'

Penny answered without hesitation, 'Yes, of course, Ma'am. I'll put some shoes on first.'

Kit said, 'Thank you,' and went back to her cabin.

Penny soon arrived, having combed her hair. Kit smiled at her and showed her a seat. It was obvious that Penny was curious as to what her boss wanted. She was even more intrigued when she was offered a drink. 'A vodka and tonic please, straight up. Thanks.'

Kit didn't beat about the bush, she just started straight in. 'Penny, do you remember a couple of weeks ago we were discussing AIDS in the mess and you said in this day and age there should be no problem or words to that effect because it was more or less cured,' and Penny nodded. 'Well, is that really the case?'

Penny thought about it and said, 'Yes, I remember it very well, er, have you a problem with that Ma'am?'

'I'm not really sure, Penny. You know I'm engaged to Steven Thorpe, the base padre, and he is a widower.' Penny nodded and Kit continued, 'His wife died of breast cancer, but before she died she had a contaminated blood transfusion. Steven and she made love...' Kit was very embarrassed at having to ask the younger girl's advice but Kit had nowhere or no one to turn to, '...and they didn't find out until later that it *was* contaminated with the AIDS virus. Er, um I may be doing the Rev Thorpe an injustice, but he said he was clear, having had all the blood tests, and he is not contaminated.'

'Does that create a problem, Ma'am?'

'Well he may be clear, but doesn't that mean he could still be a carrier?'

'Excuse my asking,' an embarrassed Penny asked Kit, 'but have you had unprotected sex with him, Ma'am?'

Kit looked down at her feet then up to the young girl and answered her honestly. 'Yes. I have. And this conversation is not to be bandied around anywhere except within these cabin walls.'

'Of course not. As young as I am, I have signed and understand the Hippocratic Oath, Ma'am.'

Kit seemed to have got the younger girl's back up, but smiled at her. 'Of course, and I am sorry as I didn't mean to imply that you would, but I'm a bit uptight at the moment.'

'I quite understand, Ma'am. In answer to your question the answer is no.'

Kit heaved a sigh of relief, and smiled at Penny.

'Would you like me to do a blood test on you Ma'am in any case?'

'Now?'

'There's no time like the present, and I can get it off first thing tomorrow and mark it urgent and hopefully we will have the results late tomorrow or early Tuesday morning.'

'Of course. Do you want me to come to the sick bay?'

'No. If you don't mind, I can do it here.'

'That will be great, Penny. Thank you.'

Penny went to the sick bay to get the necessary equipment she needed for a blood test.

While she was gone Kit refilled Penny's glass and her own. She sat drumming her fingers on the desk; she was so relieved that she sat there smiling. She was still smiling when Penny came back.

A knock on the door and Kit said, 'Come in, Penny.'

Penny came in with the hypodermic needle wrapped up with a white cloth and all she needed kept in an enamel kidney dish.

'Shall we get on with it, Ma'am?'

'Yes, of course. I'm not very enamoured with needles though.' She laughed.

'To tell the truth, neither am I and I'm a doctor.' She too laughed.

Kit looked away as Penny found a vein and put the needle in Kit's arm. Once the needle was in she looked at what Penny was doing. She had drawn a tube of blood and was putting it in a plastic bag and was addressing it to the Naval Hospital in Neptune.

'Are they equipped to deal with that sort of thing, Penny?'

'Oh yes Ma'am. I think they are just as good as any of the major hospitals in Scotland and in many instances even better.'

'Thank you. You have taken a load off my mind.'

'I'm pleased to hear that, Ma'am. I'll just go down to sick bay and type a letter, telling them the urgency, but don't worry, as no name will be on the blood test.'

Kit leant over and squeezed Penny's hand. 'Finish your drink before doing anything else.'

'Yes, Ma'am.'

'Please, call me Kit. You have been very helpful to me on two occasions now, so it is the least you can do for me as there is no one else around.'

'Okay Kit,' she smiled at her Captain. 'Steven must be a very special chap for you to have fallen so deeply in love with him in such a short time.'

'Yes he is. I had met him before a little over six years ago, although I don't remember much about that day except it was very sad. He officiated at my late husband's funeral, and I didn't meet him again until the cocktail party.'

'I'm very sorry Kit.'

'Don't be, Penny, for he made me feel that there's life after death, so to speak. Do you know what I mean, Penny?'

'Yes, Kit, I do. At least, I think I do... I must go and put the blood test in the fridge before we can carry on with this conversation, Kit.'

'I have a fridge here if you would like to put it in there until later.'

'That will be ideal. Thanks.'

Penny had just put the blood sample in the fridge and regained her seat, when there was knock on the door. It was Wiggy.

Kit invited her in too. 'A G and T, Wiggy?'

'Yes please, Kit. The trot sentry told me you were back. I didn't expect you back until late a.m. tomorrow.'

'That was the plan, but I remembered that I haven't rang my mother and father for a fortnight so I came back early to do it, especially as we'll be off on Tuesday,' she lied glibly.

Penny bent to her glass and took a swig to hide her smile.

Kit looked at Penny who nearly burst out laughing, but she managed to hide her mirth very well.

Kit carried on talking to both women and they had a pleasant evening. Fortunately Wiggy left first so Penny was able to retrieve the blood sample without causing Kit any embarrassment.

The result to the blood test came through at 1530 Monday afternoon. It was negative. Both Kit and Penny were very pleased with the result, especially Kit. She said to the younger girl, 'I think I owe the Rev Thorpe an apology.'

'How are you going to do that, Kit?'

'I think some grovelling will be called for, Penny.'

'Well, the best of luck, Kit.' Penny smiled.

'Thank you.'

Kit managed to get hold of Steven in his office. 'Hello, Steven.'

'Hi, Kit.'

'Are you free to speak?'

'Yes, I am. What's up?'

'I am so sorry. I made a terrible blunder…' He started to interrupt but Kit said, 'let me finish please, Steven before you say anything. I said some horrible things to you Sunday, but they were out of ignorance. You were perfectly correct when you said you were clear and that you *were not* a carrier of the disease. You were right and I was wrong. I had a chat with young Penny, our Doctor. She also took a blood test to make sure and of course it was negative. I'm sorry, Steven. Can you ever forgive me?' By this time, there were tears rolling down her cheeks.

Steven said, 'Of course I forgive you my love. I am just glad you found out the truth before you sail, otherwise it would have been a torturous three months for you.'

'Thank you so much, Darling. How can I make it up to you?'

'I could pick you up now and we could go back to my flat for a couple of hours. What do you say to that?'

'Oh, yes please, Steven.'

'Right, I'll pick you up in half an hour.'

'Okay. I'll be at the top of the gangway.' And she hung up.

Kit rang Wiggy to tell her that she would be going ashore for a few hours and that she'd let her know when she returned. Then she rushed around and got changed. She got to the top of the gangway just as Steven was turning his car around. As they were turning back round young Penny was just coming back from somewhere and when she saw Kit and Steven she gave a huge grin and saluted them.

'Who was that?'

'Penny Soames, our Doctor.'

'God bless Penny Soames.'

Kit laughed and said, 'It's so nice to be with you again. I thought we had had it after our dust up on Sunday.'

They were soon at his flat and as soon as the door was shut he pulled her to him and kissed her saying, 'I thought I had lost you too, Kit due to my ignorance.'

'It was my ignorance too. So between us we are just two ignorant souls. At least we have found out before it was too late.' She kissed him too and started to undo his tie. He already had her blouse undone and had manoeuvred her to the couch. They were soon naked and he was doing things to her that were really nice and doing it very gently too. At first he was kissing and fondling her breasts, then his head and hands moved down. Soon they were both ready and he entered her very gently. Kit pulled him further into her and soon they were calling each other's name and she was practically screaming with ecstasy. It was soon over. Kit took a deep breath and said, 'Oh Steven that was simply heavenly. I do love you.'

'I love you too, my love. I'm just glad that we sorted all that trouble out before you went away. It would've been awful, not knowing whether we would be back together or not, at the end of your patrol. The suspense would have been killing for both of us.'

'I'm sure it would. Thank heaven for Penny. She came up

trumps for one so young.'

He was playing with her breasts again. She always seemed to enjoy it.

'I can't stay too long, Steven, I'll have to get back soon.'

'Mmh,' he said through his nibbling, 'just once more before you go my love.'

The nibbling had gotten to her and she just said, 'Mmh,' as he had, and lent back on the settee and let him do as he wished with her. Whatever he did to her was always nice and sometimes it was ecstatic, making her squirm with desire for him, like now. 'Oh Steven, now, now. I want you now.'

He entered her and it was exquisite and he was fondling her breasts too. They soon came with such a force that it surprised them both.

'Wow,' Kit said, 'that was absolutely fabulous. What a way to go.' She smiled at him.

He smiled back at her. 'It's a pity you have to go back so soon, I was hoping we could have something to eat.'

'I'm sorry Darling, but I'm afraid that I must get back.' She leant down and kissed him, putting everything she had into it.

When they came up for air he said, 'Are you sure you must go?'

'No. I mean yes. I have put too much on the XO's shoulders and I told her that I'd be back in a couple of hours. So I really must go, Steven.'

'Okay, I give in. If you wait a minute, I'll get dressed and take you back to the boat.'

Kit laughed. 'Surely you weren't expecting me to go back without getting dressed?'

'You will create a precedent, Darling.'

She laughed again saying, 'That is not all I'll create if I go back like this.' She looked down at herself and laughed at her own nakedness.

'What is wrong with it? It seems perfectly natural to me.'

'You are biased though, so if you give me a couple of minutes to get ready, we can go.'

In a couple of minutes she was ready, as was he.

They drove back to the boat in silence. When they got there he leaned over and kissed her. 'Goodbye my love. My prayers will go with you, and for a safe return.' He kissed her again and she left him without saying another word.

She couldn't speak as she was too choked up, and if she had stayed just a little bit longer she would have been in tears. Kit wouldn't have liked to go back on board in tears.

Kit made it to her cabin and managed to get there without being seen. In that respect she had been very lucky. She made a phone call to tell Wiggy she was back and that she'd see her in the mess for dinner.

After a very refreshing shower she got back into uniform. It was just 1755 so she had made good time, after seeing Penny, on the way to Steven's flat. She would have loved to have stayed with him for longer but she owed it to Wiggy to be back on board.

When she arrived in the wardroom, Penny, Wiggy, Joan and Val were already there and were having a drink. Penny got up and asked Kit if she would like a horse's neck to which Kit answered in the affirmative. Penny winked on her way to the bar and Kit smiled at her.

'Everything okay, Ma'am?' Wiggy enquired.

'Yes thank you, Wiggy. Excellent.' She smiled. 'Thanks for holding the fort for me these past couple of weeks.'

'My pleasure, I can assure you.'

Kit looked up and was about to tell her to "get a life" but thought better of it as it seemed a bit cruel and it wasn't in her nature to be cruel. She obviously enjoyed her work so she wasn't going to upset the poor woman who had turned out to be an excellent XO. She made a mental note to put her in for early promotion to Commander when she wrote her papers up.

'Thank you,' she said again.

Penny brought Kit her drink and sat down as the stewards were just coming in to take their orders for dinner. That done, they all sat down in their allocated places at the dining table, and waited for their orders.

Lively chatter ensued and at one point Kit asked if they would care to join her in a glass of Shiraz. They all said yes, so Kit ordered three bottles.

Val Kennedy spoke up and said to Kit, 'I liked your fiancée, Ma'am.'

'Thank you, Val.'

'He has dreamy eyes.'

Kit blushed and said, 'Yes, he has.'

Wiggy, bless her heart, changed the subject, asking them all if their respective departments were all ready for sea, as she could tell that Kit was getting embarrassed talking about Steven.

Kit looked at Wiggy and signalled thanks with a slight nod of her head.

They all said that they were all ready and their talk returned to normal subjects and the conversation went on for quite a while. Kit wanted to write a letter so she excused herself saying, 'We have an early morning tomorrow, ladies, so don't make it a very late night. Goodnight.'

'Goodnight, Ma'am,' they all said.

Kit went back to her cabin and wrote a letter to Steven.

CHAPTER 27

The morning that HMSM *Holland 2* left the Clyde Submarine Base, it was a nice sunny day.

Kit conned the boat around to Coulport. On the way round, when they passed Rhu Narrows there were two chaps waving; one Kit knew was Val's husband, Ron, but she wondered who the other one was. She took her binoculars that were around her neck and focused on the other chap. It was Steven. She laughed and waved back to him. He then blew her a kiss. She made as though she had caught it and waved back, then concentrated on conning the boat.

The boat arrived at Coulport about two hours later. Kit had taken it easy getting round to there, letting various officers who were OOWs take turns in conning the boat for a bit of practice.

When the boat was secure alongside to Kit's satisfaction she went below. Even though the weather had improved since she had arrived back in Scotland nearly three months ago, it was still chilly and damp on the bridge. That is why one always wore oilskins on the bridge even when it wasn't raining, like today, which made a change. There was always an occasional shower of sea water, or goffer as it was nicknamed, that managed to splash anyone on the bridge.

Kit went ashore as soon as the gangplank was in place. There then ensued a few frantic days of arming the boat with missiles and torpedoes. Kit had got that all in motion before going back to her cabin. She wanted to rewrite her letter to Steven. She ordered a pot of tea from the stewards and started the rewrite.

My Darling,

Please forgive me for all the harsh and hurtful things I said to you on Sunday. It was borne out of ignorance on my part. I am so sorry.

I know you have forgiven me, but I felt I had to write and say my piece.

I really have enjoyed my time with you these last couple of weeks and look forward to picking up where we left off!

Hopefully we will be able to wear out a settee or bed of mine when I return, for my little bungalow may be vacant by then.

Always remember that I love you my darling, and look forward to the day when I return to you.

With all my love, hopefully forever.

Kit. XXXX

Kit put it in an envelope and sealed and addressed it to Steven, and marked it personal. She put it in her out-tray for she knew there was one more collection of mail today at least.

She looked at her watch and saw that it was time for lunch, so she went to the wardroom.

There were quite a few of them there and Kit smiled at them all and said, 'Good day, ladies. I hope all your departments are all closed up and ready for sea tomorrow?'

They all replied as one, 'Yes, Ma'am.'

When all the officers were there, Wiggy excused herself for a minute or two, and came back with a big box and put it down in front of Kit.

Kit looked down at it, then up at Wiggy, who was smiling and at the others who were smiling too. Wiggy said, 'Go on, open it then.'

Kit opened the box and found a smaller one inside and there was a bigger one besides. In the smaller one were two beautiful crystal brandy goblets. She was speechless. They were absolutely gorgeous. Then she opened the other one, which was quite heavy. It was a large blue presentation box and inside, amongst padded blue silk, was a crystal decanter and six large crystal glasses suitable for any drink that had a mix in it or for just a straight whisky.

'Well I don't know what to say. They are absolutely beautiful. In fact they are gorgeous. Thank you.'

Wiggy added, 'All the officers contributed to the present. It is all Edinburgh Crystal and we all hope that you and Steven will make good use of them and are very happy.'

'Oh, we definitely will. On behalf of Steven and myself, thank you, all of you.' Kit was a bit embarrassed at the gift. She definitely wasn't expecting anything, let alone a present. A present that was so beautiful too.

Chapter 28

The first patrol of the *Holland 2* commenced on Thursday. It was a bit nerve wracking for everyone concerned, especially for Kit and Wiggy. They were a bit tense until the boat had dived.

Once they were on their way everyone seemed to relax.

They were fully armed with sixteen Trident missiles, and Tomahawk missiles that can be fired from the torpedo tubes, as well as conventional Torpedoes. Should any other hostile nation have picked up the *Holland's* whereabouts, whilst on patrol they were fully armed to take care of the situation.

Hopefully that occasion wouldn't come about as there was a twenty-four hour listening watch and the Sonar operators were all fairly senior, with a Petty Officer, two Leading Seamen and four Junior Ratings all of whom had been doing it for years.

As the *Holland* was a bit smaller and more compact than most boats, that seemed quite enough sonar operators for its size. Their hearing must be impeccable, and even though they wear earphones it is surprising what they hear. They can differentiate between a shoal of shrimp or prawns, and tell if they are mating, as well as tell which other submarines are nearby, by the noise the screw made. All highly technical if you didn't know about sonar.

For the first few days everyone was on a learning curve, but thereafter everyone settled down and got on with the job at hand.

In all close confinements there are usually minor arguments about this and that. Usually, Wiggy managed to sort them out but occasionally they came to the Captain's ear, and God help them then. The girls concerned were then given snap kit musters. The little minor arguments soon died down after that as no one liked kit musters, and/or even extra duties.

On the first Sunday at sea, Kit decided to hold a church service, and anyone who wanted to attend in the Junior Rank's dining room could do so. Most boats carried a small portable organ and she had ascertained beforehand that Joan Shakespeare could play one so she would play the hymns.

When all who were coming to the Service arrived, and Joan had stopped playing, Kit started the service first by everyone singing the National Anthem, followed by Kit greeting and making welcome all those present. She said a few words, followed by a short prayer, then the first hymn which was, I VOW TO THEE MY COUNTRY. After that there was the first reading of the Bible, which was ably read by Wiggy then followed by the Navy Hymn, "Eternal Father, strong to save, whose arm doth bound the restless wave, etc…"

After another reading from the Bible, which was done by Penny Soames, there followed the Submariners' Prayer.

(All together)
O Father, hear our prayer to Thee,
From your humble servants beneath the sea,
In the depths of oceans as oft we stray,
So far from night, so far from day;
We would ask your guiding light to glow,
To make our journey safe below,
Please oft time grant us patient mind,
Then the darkness won't us blind;
We seek protection from the deep,
And grant us peace when we sleep,
Of our homes and loved ones far away,

We ask your care for them each day;
Until we surface once again,
To drink the air and feel the rain,
We ask your guiding hand to show,
A safe progression sure and slow;
Dear Lord, please hear our prayer to Thee,
From you humble servants beneath the sea.
Amen

The service ended with Joan playing a rousing version of Beethoven's Ninth Symphony as almost everyone trouped out.

Kit thanked all the officers who attended and those who took part in the actual service, and Joan for playing the organ.

CHAPTER 29

The *Holland* had been at sea for four weeks and Kit was browsing from section to section on her consul as she usually did once a day. She had looked at the sick bay and saw Penny writing up some notes and Kit smiled at the girl's dedication, then moved to the next section, but something made her go back to the sick bay. What had she seen that made her go back? A shadow of something… She made a sweep very carefully looking at each section. Yes, there it was, coming under the door. Smoke. Smoke! She rang Penny and told her to get out of there as she could see smoke and hung up to raise the alarm. She raised the alarm.

'Fire, Fire, Fire. Fire party close up at the double at the sick bay. This is not, I repeat, *not* an exercise. Fire in the sick bay.'

Before she had a chance to ring Wiggy, she was at the scene of the fire. Kit herself went there too.

Once she was there Kit was glad to see that Penny had gotten out straightaway.

The duty watch was there, wearing breathing apparatus, and the Killick in charge with two other seamen were in the sick bay trying to see the source of the fire. They had taken portable fire extinguishers with them.

The Killick came out, removing her mask. The first thing she said was, 'The fire is out now. It was a short circuit to the steriliser that set it on fire, Ma'am.' She reported this to Wiggy who seemed to be at the fore.

'Very good, Leading Seaman Humphreys. What are the other two doing in there?'

'Clearing up the mess, Ma'am.'

'Very good,' Wiggy said to the rest of the duty watch, 'Well done. You may secure now. Thank you,' she said, dismissing them. They all shuffled off.

Penny turned to Kit saying, 'Thank you Ma'am. How did you know?'

'You could say that Big Sister is watching you.' The parody was wasted on Penny but at least Wiggy understood it and laughed. Penny laughed too but not understanding it, and said thank you once again and went into the sick bay, followed closely by the XO and the Captain.

The amount of mess was negligible but the steriliser was a complete write off.

'Is there another steriliser, Penny?' Kit asked the doctor.

'I am afraid not. If I need to sterilise anything it will have to be done the old fashioned way – with boiling water.' She smiled.

'Anyway, I'll send a "greeny" down here to fix the damage, rewiring it and so forth,' Kit said and walked off.

With Kit gone, Penny turned to Wiggy and asked, 'What was all that "Big Sister" stuff?'

'You obviously haven't read George Orwell's "1984". It was a book that came out early last century, a bit futuristic for its day, and was about Big Brother watching you, but the Captain changed it to sister for our benefit.'

'Oh, I see. But I still can't see how the Skipper knew of the fire, Wiggy.' Penny, poor kid was still totally confused.

This was still pretty obvious to Wiggy who decided to put the girl out of her misery. She told her about the consul that Kit had in her cabin that showed every working space. She usually looks at all the work places once a day, she told Penny.

'I am sure glad she happened to be looking at my section when she was. Is she able to see into the living quarters too?'

Wiggy laughed at this and said, 'Of course not. We are all allowed some privacy.' She was still smiling at the Doctor, who was still looking worried. 'She can't hear anything either when she looks in on the various sections, so don't worry your head about it.' She smiled gently at Penny.

'Thank you Wiggy. I'd better start cleaning up the mess now. Not that there's much. Thank you, Wiggy.'

Wiggy went to Kit's cabin and knocked and went in at Kit's command.

Kit had already ordered a pot of tea and two cups for she knew that Wiggy would soon be there.

'Hi. I was expecting you. How is young Penny?'

Wiggy said, 'Fine,' as she pulled the chair up to Kit's desk and added, 'I had to explain to her the Big Sister bit though.' She laughed. 'She did seem a bit confused by it all.'

'I thought she was. I hope you put her out of her misery?'

'She did ask if you could see into the cabins, but I told her no, as everyone is entitled to a bit of privacy, and also that you couldn't hear anything either.'

'Thanks, Wiggy. Would you like a cuppa?'

'Yes please, Kit.'

They sat in companionable silence as they drank their tea until Wiggy asked Kit, 'I suppose I was correct in saying that your consul is only tuned in to places of work.'

'Yes of course. Imagine what it would be like if I could look anywhere. It would be a pervert's paradise. The workplace suits me just fine.' And both women laughed.

* * *

After the fire in the sick bay, there were no more hiccups until a few weeks later. Actually, it was during the night, when everything was quiet and the only people around were the duty watch, when all hell broke loose.

The duty MEO, Joan Shakespeare, was taking a wander around the boat when she heard from behind her a loud snap of metal and another snap and bang, and suddenly a gush of water soaked her. It was salt water and it was freezing. *God almighty*, she thought as she shone her torch to where the water was coming from. It was coming from the pipe overhead that fed the toilets with sea water. Joan wasn't sure exactly where the break was. She rushed back to the control room and told the OOW what was happening and went and got her tool kit, then rushed back to mid ships where the water had already wreaked havoc in the surrounding area. Soon the duty watch had arrived and started mopping up. As fast as they mopped there was still as much water as there had been before. The flooding had been going on for about forty-five minutes before Kit and Wiggy arrived and some other sailors were standing around getting in the way.

Kit stopped everything and told everyone who was not on the duty watch to go back to their cabins until they heard otherwise.

She asked the MEO what the situation was. The MEO said, 'Bad Ma'am. If I could get more light in here I may be able to find whereabouts the pipe has broken and hopefully fix it.'

'Right,' said Kit. To Wiggy she said, 'Go to the Naval Stores and ask them for a LED light torch and bring it here straightaway, please.'

By this time both Joan and Kit were soaked. Wiggy was soon back with the torch and shone it on to the salt water pipe.

'That's better,' said Joan as Wiggy shone the torch along the whole length of the pipe. 'It looks,' said Joan, 'that it has broken right through, just there.' She pointed to where both Kit and Wiggy could see where Joan meant.

Kit asked if Joan could fix it. She said she could but it would take some time as she would have to get an oxyacetylene torch and some extra piping to be able to do it.

'Very well,' said Kit, 'Get to it please, and let me know when you have finished it please.'

'Of course Ma'am.'

'I'll be in the wardroom until it is fixed, and don't hesitate to let me know if the problem worsens, Joan.' Kit said this with a smile although she was worried sick about the problem.

'Yes, Ma'am.'

Joan managed to find the valve that turned the water off, which she did, which made things a lot easier.

Kit went and got changed first before going to the Wardroom.

When Kit got to the WR with Wiggy, she put the light on and got a magazine from one of the tables and started flicking through it. Quite soon after getting there the hatch was opened and Ldg Steward Jeffries put her head through and asked if she could get them anything. Kit looked across to Wiggy and Kit turned back to Jeffries and asked for a large pot of tea please.

Kit and Wiggy sat there drinking tea and munching McVities half-covered chocolate biscuits. Kit had told Wiggy to go to bed and she would tell her when it was over. But Wiggy decided against going to bed. Kit was secretly pleased at the older woman's decision.So they sat there for another hour, until the MEO came and told them the news.

They both looked up at her expectantly.

'All fixed, Kit. I've just left the duty watch clearing up the mess.'

'Well done Joan, and thank the watch. Is there much damage and water around?'

'Not now, as we managed to mop it up and put it into buckets. There was gallons and gallons of it. Between us we managed to pour it down the sink of the ships laundry, ready for pumping out tomorrow.'

'Okay Joan. Go and get into some dry clothes. I'll just pop along and see the OOW and give her the news too. Before you go, would you like a cup of tea and a biscuit? The tea is wet and warm but I expect it will taste better than the salt water.'

'Yes. It sure will. Thank you, Kit.' She sank down into an armchair and began to relax.

Kit went to survey what damage had been done by the burst pipe the following morning. Not that the boat looked any different than at any other time but the clocks were still set on UK time. The mess wasn't as bad as she thought it could have been, nothing that a good polish to the deck and a dehumidifier couldn't cure. Overall she was very pleased with the repair job that was done by the duty watch.

CHAPTER 30

The rest of the patrol of the *Holland* seemed to go smoothly. The night before the *Holland* was due at Coulport, all the Officers had assembled in the Wardroom at Kit's request with the exception of the OOW and the OOD. Kit addressed all those present that she was very pleased at how their first patrol had gone, the first of many she hoped, and with the same officers too.

'I realise that some of you will be promoted and will go on to other jobs or boats, and I say the best of luck to those of you that do. But I would like to say to all of you that this first patrol of HMSM *Holland 2* is a first. You will be able to tell your children and grandchildren that you were on the first all-female crew of a submarine anywhere in the world.' There was a spontaneous cheer at this. 'And I am very proud of you all,' she continued. 'Thank you all and please charge your glasses as the drinks are on me.'

Wiggy said, 'We couldn't have done it without you at the helm.' The others agreed, saying 'hear, hear'. 'This was your first command and I've been on boats before where the skipper is also new, but I have never felt so secure as with you being in charge. It is not easy being in command but I would say with hindsight, you are the best I've ever served with.'

Kit was at a loss for words. She blushed and said, 'Er, um, I just don't know what to say to you Wiggy…'

'Just drink your drink,' said Wiggy, laughing, and the rest of the officers were laughing too.

The rest of the evening turned into an impromptu party and

they all got to bed a bit worse for wear.

The next morning Kit conned the boat alongside at Coulport. It was good to be back.

Kit greeted the new Commander who was the captain of the crew that was to take over when Kit had finished doing the handover. 'Hello Tina. It's good to see you. I'll soon have my kit together and out of here when we get around to Faslane.'

'How did it all go, Kit?'

Kit laughed and said, 'There were a few hiccups but nothing serious. They have all been ironed out and you should have a boat that is all tickety boo.'

Tina Anderson knew she had a hard act to follow so she just laughed and said, 'Thanks.'

'Come to what is going to be your cabin,' Kit said, leading the way.

'Wow,' Tina exclaimed, 'it's fantastic. And a real door too for added privacy.'

Kit smiled at her enthusiasm and asked if she would like the grand tour.

'I would, but I realise that you have things to do so I will take a rain check on that and wait until you get to Faslane. Will that be okay, Kit?'

'Yes, of course. I'll see you off the boat and get on with getting ready for the handover.'

'Thank you Kit. See you in Faslane.' She saluted on leaving the boat then got into the Service car the Navy had provided.

Wiggy had come up on deck and said, 'She's a bit keen, isn't she, Kit?'

'She sure is. I could have done without that visit. I'm just glad that she declined a tour round the boat though.'

'I know it is not my place to say so, but I think she had a bloody cheek.'

Kit just guffawed. Then she said to Wiggy, 'While they are

disarming the boat, come along to the wardroom for a drink.'

Wiggy didn't decline, just raised her eyebrows. Kit smiled saying, 'The sun must be over the yard arm somewhere.'

* * *

The disarming took two days and Kit had given leave to those who had nothing to do with the disarming so it was a skeleton crew that was going to take the boat round to Faslane.

CHAPTER 31

Kit had seen Steven at about 1730, the first evening in. She wasn't quite ready to leave the boat as there were still things to do and she went to the jetty to tell him just that and she would see him at 1830. He looked very well and she had to stand there without touching him or giving him a kiss. Fortunately he understood her predicament and realised all this so said quietly, so no one else would hear, 'Welcome home my love. I can hardly keep my hands off you, roll on 1830.'

Kit laughed and said, 'Not here on the jetty in full view of everyone I hope?'

'Of course not.' And she could hear him chuckling as she went back on board.

Wiggy saw that Steven was waiting on the jetty and said to Kit that she would finish up what had to be done and to get herself changed and go and have some fun.

'Wiggy, you're an angel. Thanks. See you tomorrow.'

Kit rushed and had a quick shower and was off the boat in less than half an hour. Steven couldn't believe his eyes and he got out to open the door for Kit to get into the car. There was no one in sight of them and once Kit was in the car, Steven leant over and gave her a resounding kiss.

'Boy, I needed that. Let's get this show on the road,' Kit said.

'So did I,' Steven agreed.

He drove fast as usual but safely to get to his flat in Helensburgh. As soon as they were in the flat with the door closed Steven was all over her. He had her clothes off and his

165

too within five minutes.

She said, 'You don't…'

He said, 'Ssh…'

He did unbelievable things to her body and they were soon on the settee and he was kissing her breasts, kissing her all over. She was writhing at this and when he entered her it was as though it was out of this world.

'Oh Steven, Steven, yes, yes… Oh yes…' Then she had an amazing orgasm. Then he collapsed on her, groaning at his own orgasm.

'You were fantastic,' she said and added, 'I don't know how I managed these last couple of months without you, Darling.'

'Me neither,' said he, cuddling her and nibbling at her nipples. He knew she liked that and it didn't take Kit long to get going again. She was always ready for him. And she was, very soon after he'd started his nibbling, amongst other things.

When it was over she said to him, 'What will happen after we are married, and I change my name to Thorpe? That will mean "Kit" will have to give way to Christine again.'

'Mmh, I see what you mean, but you can change your name to Carson-Thorpe, dear. But thinking about it, Kit is already a diminutive of Christine.'

Kit looked at him in surprise as this dawned on her. 'I'd forgotten that.' And she laughed.

After that they went to bed for some more lovemaking. The first time she took the initiative by climbing on top of him. As she sank down on his already erect penis, he groaned with pleasure. He was soon pushing Kit's hips up and down but she was going faster than he, so he left her to it. He was squeezing both her breasts and her hands went up to his. She was leaning back and groaning then she sank forward having an almighty climax, and then collapsed on him, breathing heavily. 'Oh, oh. That was… I don't know how to describe it, apart from being Heavenly.'

'The Good Lord meant us all to enjoy it, Kit.'

Kit gave him a funny look as much to say, *Isn't that blasphemy?*

He shook his head without saying anything either. She climbed reluctantly from him, still breathing heavily.

They lay there talking for a while and at one stage Kit said, 'I wonder if my cottage is ready for occupation? I hope so. I'll have to ring the solicitor tomorrow.'

'That will be lovely if it was, my love. Think of the fun we'll have furnishing it.'

'Yes. It will be great. I also have to ring Mother and Dad to let them know I'm back. But until then, we still have some loving to catch up on if you have any energy left, Steven.'

'For you, I always have energy.' He looked down at his lower parts and said, 'Look at that, just talking about it has made him raise his head.'

Kit looked down and saw what he meant. She laughed saying, 'It is a pity to waste it, so I'll get on top again.'

'Oh no you don't.' He rolled her over onto her stomach and lifted her into a kneeling position and entered her from behind. She was on her knees and he was able to play with her breasts too. It was a new one on her and she was most surprised, but she liked it. He couldn't get as far in as she would like it to go but nevertheless she still came fairly soon after he entered her. It didn't take him long either. When he withdrew they both lay in silence for a while. Until Steven said, 'You didn't like it that way, did you?'

She looked up at him. 'It took me a little by surprise, but I did like it,' she assured him. 'I've never had it that way before though,' she added, smiling at him.

'Don't look sad, Steven. I assure you that I did like it that way. Now I don't know about you, but I'm ravishing, I mean ravenous… I'd just love a sandwich if you have the makings of one?'

He smiled, 'I have more than that and I came home with all good intentions, but if a sandwich is acceptable, your wish is my command, my love.'

'I have noticed that your shower is rather large so we can both have a shower at the same time and then we could both make the sandwiches.' Her eyes were sparkling as she said this.

Steven said, 'That is rather a decadent suggestion, nevertheless a good one, so let's get to it.' He took her hand and led her to the bathroom.

It started all innocently until Kit dropped the soap and bending down to get it she accidentally brushed against him. He grabbed her, turned her around towards himself, and kissed her very deeply and his tongue went in her mouth. She pressed herself against him and he lifted her and with all the soap on their bodies it was very easy to enter her. Her legs went around his body and pulled him to her. They held the position, not moving for a while, just kissing until he wanted more and started moving within her.

'Oh Steven, that is great.' It wasn't long before they both climaxed.

After they had finished showering they both got into their dressing gowns and went to the kitchen to make a sandwich.

Steven poured them both a drink; Kit's usual, and a whisky and soda for himself.

They took the sandwiches and drink to their favourite seat in the lounge. They talked about Kit's cottage and what furniture it would need and what to get sent up from London. Kit had some really lovely pieces that she wanted to bring up from London to put in her cottage and said she was really looking forward to it.

Steven and Kit chatted on in this vein until it was time to go to bed and as Steven set the alarm for 0530, Kit said, 'What an unearthly hour to have to get up. Yuk.'

Steven laughed. 'It is only for one more day hopefully, and the boat will be back in the base.'

Kit stretched and yawned and she said, 'Yes…' and she was asleep. Steven smiled and pulled the covers up and over her, kissed her gently, then settled down himself.

Chapter 32

Steven drove them around to Coulport. It was fairly gloomy even for that time of day, 0600. When they arrived it was 0630. Kit leaned over and kissed him goodbye, saying, 'It will be a more civilised hour tomorrow as we are bringing the boat back to Faslane. If you have a spare key on you, I can come in my car.'

He fished around in his pockets and came up with one and gave it to Kit. He kissed her and said, 'See you later, darling.' And he leered at her.

She got out of the car and smiled at him and went on board, and Steven drove off.

On board she rang Wiggy to let her know that she was back on board and that she would see her at breakfast. She had a quick shower and got back into uniform.

At breakfast she ordered the 'ish and her usual pot of tea, after saying good morning to all who were there, including Wiggy. Wiggy smiled at Kit and said that no disasters happened in her absence and everything was okay. They should finish disarming about 1115 or thereabouts.

Kit smiled at Wiggy and said, 'Thank you very much, Wiggy.' By this time the pot of tea arrived, followed shortly by the breakfast. She poured a cup of tea and took a mouthful. She thought, *That's better*, then got stuck in to the breakfast.

When breakfast had finished she went to her cabin and packed away her civvies clothes and what needed washing she put into a plastic bag.

It was soon after that that Wiggy tapped on her door and

said there were two Mod Plods to see her in the control room.

Kit went along to see them, wondering what the hell they wanted. She didn't have long to wait. The Sergeant said, 'Commander Carson?' Kit nodded in the affirmative and the Sergeant continued, 'Could we have a word in private please Ma'am?'

'Of course, come this way to my cabin.' The Sergeant and a female constable followed her. When they got there, Kit invited them to sit down. The Sergeant removed his hat and spoke very slowly and precisely. Kit didn't say anything at first, then she said, 'Thank you.' Then she stood up and showed them back to the control room, then walked very stiffly back to her cabin.

After the Ministry of Defence Policemen had left the boat, Wiggy went to Kit's cabin. She knocked gently and went straight in without waiting for Kit's command.

Kit had her back to the door and Wiggy said, 'Kit?' Then Kit turned around. There were tears rolling down her cheeks with an utter look of devastation on her face. Wiggy went straight over to her and knelt before her and took her in her arms. It took Kit a while to tell Wiggy what had happened. Between sobs she told her.

'My God. You had better get round to the Naval Hospital straightaway. Do you want me to drive you there?'

'Yes please, Wiggy, but give me a couple of minutes to sort myself out please.'

'Of course.'

Wiggy made sure the control room was clear, and waited for Kit to come from her cabin. She was wearing dark glasses although she had cleaned herself up the best that she could. The XO and the Captain got off the boat as soon as they could. Wiggy told the Trot Sentry that she was just driving the Skipper round to the base and that she should be back as soon as possible.

Wiggy unlocked the car and opened the other door for Kit. Once both ladies were in, Wiggy adjusted her seat forward and Kit took hers back as far as it would go.

She drove safely round to the base and the only hiccup they encountered on the way round was at the crash site, and that was when Kit saw Steven's lovely little blue MGB GT, a complete write off, lying on the side of the road, a mangled heap. 'God almighty, he was lucky to live through that. I just hope his injuries are not too severe.'

'So do I Kit. But I'll have to drop you off and drive straight back to Coulport. You just stay there as long as it takes. Don't worry about the boat, I'll bring it back safe and sound, and there are plenty of others there to give me help if I need it. I'll send Penny round to sit with you Kit.' She squeezed Kit's arm, giving her reassurance. Kit felt Wiggy's strength and love go into that squeeze. The love and respect for a fellow officer in trouble.

Kit said, 'Thank you for all you have done, Wiggy, I'd be at a loss without what you have done for me and I am very grateful. Thank you. I owe you one.' She gave Wiggy a weak smile and said she'd see her later.

CHAPTER 33

When Kit got out of the car at the Naval Hospital, she put her hat on and pulled her jacket down and walked in through the double doors and went straight to Reception and told them who she was and who she wanted to see. She waited while the nurse made a phone call.

She told Kit where she needed to go and who to report to when she got there. Kit said, 'Thank you, Nurse,' and made her way to the lifts. She went to the fourth floor as directed and a Surgeon Commander met her there. 'Commander Carson?'

'Yes, but Kit will do fine, Commander.'

'In that case I'm Keith Dalby, how do you do, Kit.' He proffered a hand and Kit took it and shook it in her usual firm way.

'You know who I've come to see, but before I go in, perhaps you can tell me how Reverend Thorpe is please. I saw the wreck of his car on the way around here. It is a wonder he's still alive.'

'He has the constitution of a horse. He has surprised everyone. He has a broken leg and a fractured wrist and cuts around the face and head...'

'So it is all superficial then?' said Kit, relieved.

'I'm afraid not, Kit. He hit his head on the windscreen and he is still unconscious.'

'Is that bad, Keith?' Kit asked, looking worried.

'It can be if we don't operate soon. Who are his next of kin? On his docs it says his wife is, but I know he's a widower.'

'I am his fiancé but I know his parents live in London and look after his son. All I know is that they live in Kew somewhere so I can't help you there I'm afraid. Now, can I see him, please?'

Keith took her along to Steven's room. When she got there she nearly fainted, and if it wasn't for Keith, she would have gone down. He helped her to a chair.

'Sorry. It was just the initial shock of seeing him like this.'

'That's okay, Kit. I'll get the nurse to bring you a cup of tea.'

'Thanks.'

After Keith had gone, Kit had a good look at Steven. His poor face was covered with sticky plaster. Over his left eye was a bandage that extended over his head. His left leg and arm were both in plaster casts. She spoke to him, not expecting an answer, but to her amazement he was conscious and he answered her.

'How are you feeling, darling?'

'That is a pretty useless question, Kit. How do you expect me to feel? I feel pretty lousy.'

'I'm not surprised really. The Doctor said you were still unconscious due to the bang on the head.'

'What does she know about it then?'

'She's a he and a Commander to boot. Keith Dalby.'

'Well, how was I to know?' Steven said moodily.

Kit looked at him and for the first time she saw a glimpse of another side to him. Not a very nice side either. It could be the pain he was in though. So she gave him the benefit of the doubt.

She was sitting on his right side so she was able to hold his hand and she kissed it and he smiled at her and said, 'I'm sorry, I didn't mean to take it out on you, darling. I just feel so bloody helpless.'

She laughed, saying, 'I'm not surprised being trussed up like a turkey on a plate at Christmas dinner.'

'Thank you, my love. I really needed that bit of info.'

'Didn't the doctor tell you anything?'

'I don't remember anything until you spoke to me and before that nothing about how I ended up here, Kit.'

'You don't know that you crashed your car. I'm afraid that it's a complete write off. I saw it on the way round here and I'm surprised that you are still alive. Anyway, you are and that is the main thing as far as I'm concerned. You have a broken leg and a fractured wrist, both of them are on the left side, as well as various cuts and abrasions to your face. But I don't know why you have that bandage over your eye and head although the Doc says you had a blow to the head and he was worried about it.'

'Oh my poor car.'

'I'm afraid it is a mangled heap of metal now, Steven.'

'How did you find out about me?'

'I had a visit from the Mod Plod. Naturally I was upset and Wiggy drove me round here and she is bringing the boat from Coulport for me. I owe her so much, Steven.'

'I'll have to remember to thank her when I get out of here.'

'You won't be going anywhere if you don't get some sleep, Reverend,' an authoritative voice said from the doorway.

They both looked over to the door and there was Keith Dalby standing there with his arms crossed and leaning on the door jamb. He walked over to Steven and shook hands, saying that he was glad he was awake. 'We were so worried about you still being unconscious that we were going to ring your parents to get their permission to operate, but no one knows their address. Not even your fiancé, Commander Carson, knows it.'

'It must be on my documents, Doctor Dalby.'

'You didn't update them when your wife died.'

'I'm sorry. I must have had something else on my mind at the time.'

'Well let's have a look at your head.' He turned to Kit and said, 'You'd better wait outside if you are bit squeamish.'

'No, it's alright Keith.' Steven looked at Kit when she called the doctor "Keith". It was a very old fashioned look and it made Kit laugh.

'That's better, my love, at least you haven't lost your sense of humour.' Steven reached for Kit's hand and squeezed it.

'I thought I had lost you earlier.'

'If you are sure, Kit?'

She nodded, so Keith carried on unwrapping the bandage from Steven's eye and head. His whole eye area was swollen up and severely bruised and Kit was surprised by a neat row of stitches running from his cheek to the eye, which then continued from above the eye into his hairline. He was lucky that his eye seemed to be alright. Kit thought that she must have a word with the doctor when she left the ward.

The doctor shone a torch in both eyes. Steven winced when the doctor did this and the doctor said to Steven, 'Did that hurt?'

'Yes, but only the left eye.'

'I expect there will pain and headaches quite a bit on your left side I'm afraid, but you were damn lucky, Steven.'

'As long as I know what is going on and you keep me informed, I promise to behave myself.'

Kit just smiled but the doctor said that they would be taking Steven down for an x-ray on his head just to see if they would need to operate.

'Okay.'

'Seeing as how you are wide awake and talking quite lucidly, there will probably be no need.'

'Oh I do hope so,' Kit said, and Steven concurred. They took Steven on a trolley down to x-ray and Kit waited where she was.

* * *

Steven seemed to be gone for hours, when in fact it was only fifteen minutes. Penny Soames arrived soon after and asked how Steven was. Kit explained his condition, leaving nothing out. Penny said that the x-ray was obviously a precaution as he wasn't unconscious now, so hopefully everything would be alright.

That seemed to put Kit's mind at ease and she said to Penny, 'Thank you, but are you sure?'

'Yes Kit. 99.9% sure.'

Kit heaved a big sigh of relief and sat back in her chair more relaxed than she had been since hearing of Steven's accident. 'I do hope you are right, Penny.'

They waited in silence for Steven's return, just saying the odd word or two, Penny's of encouragement for Kit.

When Steven returned he was all smiles and Kit smiled too. 'Penny was right. Oh, by the way, this is Penny Soames, Steven.'

'I am very pleased to meet you, my dear.' He was charm personified.

'I am very glad to meet you too, but not under these circumstances, Reverend.'

'Please call me Steven, Penny.'

'How did the x-ray go, dear?'

'Keith seemed very pleased with the results, Kit, but I am sure he will tell you that himself.'

'Well, if you would excuse me, everything seems to be okay here so I had better make my way back to the boat.' Penny left, smiling.

Kit looked at her watch and saw that it was only 1045 and she said, 'I didn't realise that was all it was. I'll be able to watch the boat come in from Coulport. The Doctor said you need some sleep, my love, and I can use the time whilst you are sleeping and I'm waiting for the boat to ring the solicitor.' She bent over him and kissed him saying, 'I'll see you soon.' But he was asleep.

On her way out she stopped and spoke to the doctor. She asked about Steven's eye. 'Will it be alright, eventually? It looks a right mess at the moment.'

'That is only the bruising that looks bad, but once that's gone down it will look okay. The scar going up his face and across doesn't penetrate the eye so there is no problem with his eye. He was very lucky in that respect.' Keith smiled gently at Kit, and thought to himself, *I wish I had a woman like this that was that worried about me, and one so damn good looking too.* And he sighed.

Kit noticed the sigh and looked at him then away again. When she had her hat on she smiled at the doctor and said, 'I assume the head x-ray was okay as nothing has been said about that.'

'Oh yes, there is no problem with that at all, but he must get plenty of sleep though.'

'In that case I'll be back early this evening to see him as I've a submarine to take care of too. Goodbye.' She thrust her hand toward him which he took with both hands and shook hers, saying, 'I will see you later?' as she walked toward the lifts. She was rather surprised by the way he shook her hand with both of his and the look on his face after he had sighed. She just shrugged and promptly thought of what to do next.

Kit went down to the jetty to await the *Holland*. If she stood at the top of the stairs she could just see it coming round the bend of the Loch from Coulport. It would be at least another half hour, so she had time to ring her solicitor about the cottage. She rang and his secretary put her straight through after she had ascertained who was speaking.

'Good morning, Mr McCloud,' said Kit, 'have you any news for me regarding the cottage?'

'Yes, Mrs Carson. The keys are ready for your collection at any time you want them. Welcome back. I trust you had a pleasant trip.'

'Thank you, and yes I did. I'll come and collect the keys later this afternoon. What time do you close please?'

'Six o'clock, Mrs Carson.'

'Splendid, I look forward to seeing you later. If I can't I will give you a ring. Goodbye for now.'

'I too, Mrs Carson, so until later then. Goodbye.' And he hung up.

CHAPTER 34

The boat was alongside tied up by 1330. Wiggy had conned it alongside and had made a very good job of it too.

Wiggy had seen Kit standing on the jetty and waved. Kit waved back with a broad smile on her face. Wiggy saw the smile and gave a thumbs up and then got on with securing the boat.

When the gangplank was secured and the securing party had gone back on board, Kit went up the gangplank.

As soon as Kit was on board she went straight to her cabin and rang the steward to ask if possible for a pot of tea. The answer came back 'Of course, Ma'am.'

'Thank you, Jeffries.' She gave Wiggy a ring and asked her when she had a spare minute to come along to her cabin. Pretty soon after her giving Wiggy a ring the tea was there. When Ldg Steward Jeffries brought it there were two cups on the tray already so Kit said, 'Thank you, Ldg Steward. I see that there are two cups on the tray so at least that will save you a trip of going back for another one,' and Kit smiled at her and said again, 'thank you.'

Wiggy soon came along, knocked, and at Kit's command, went in. The first thing she asked of Kit was, 'How is Steven, Kit?'

'I have spoken to him and apart from a broken left leg and a fractured left wrist and cuts and bruising around the face, he seems okay.'

'Oh, I am so glad for you. When I saw the state of his car I thought the worst.'

'So did I. Here, have a cup of tea.' Kit heaved a huge sigh of relief after her first sip. 'When I left him he was asleep. The doctor said that's the best thing for him at the moment. There was one bit I was worried about and that was his face…'

Wiggy raised her eyebrows at this, but Kit went on. 'After the Doc took the bandage off his head that covered his left cheek and eye it was bruised and puffy and a scar running from here to here,' Kit indicated with her finger. 'It went across the eye so I thought the worst. I must say though that the stitching was very neat. I had a word with the Doctor after Steven had fallen asleep and he said that the eye would be okay. It looked worse because of the bruising and puffiness, or words to that effect.'

'I am so glad for you both. What's going to happen now?'

'I'm not sure. Anyway, I have rung the solicitor re the place in Garelochead and John and Chris have gone and he has the keys, so if you don't mind holding the fort again I'd like to leave here at 1700 and collect the keys and get some things from Steven's flat for him.'

'No problem with that Kit, go for it.'

'I just hope I can reciprocate at some time for you.'

'Don't you worry yourself about a thing. You just get yourself and Steven sorted. You can cook me a slap up meal when you've settled into your cottage.'

'You're on. When Steven is a bit better you can come up then.'

As an afterthought Wiggy said, 'Why don't you go at 1500, Kit, as there is nothing for you to do until tomorrow and even then if there is still a problem I will be able to cope okay. So I will leave you to it.'

'Wiggy, you're an angel. I'll buy you an orange for Christmas.'

Wiggy was chuckling when she left Kit's cabin and went

back to the control room. She was still smiling broadly as Penny came into the control room, looking a bit flushed.

'Phew,' she said, 'I was halfway to Coulport when I saw you coming through Rhu Narrows so I did a U turn where I could, and rushed back.'

'Okay Penny. You will be glad to know that the Captain is back and that Steven was sleeping when she left him.'

'Oh, I'm so glad.'

'Go off and do what needs doing in your section and I'll see you at lunch,' Wiggy said kindly.

The lunch was just a quick meal that all the officers that were on board enjoyed, just soup and a roll and sandwiches and a little fruit.

Kit went to it and enjoyed what she had and excused herself so that she could get to see the solicitor and some things for Steven.

She had a quick shower and changed into civvies and left the boat. She walked to the garages and got into her little Beemer. The engine turned over straightaway and she was able to get to the solicitor by 1530.

Kit was greeted by her solicitor who said, 'It's very nice to see you again, Mrs Carson. Would you like some tea, my dear?'

'No, thank you.' She smiled at him.

'Very well, let's get on with it. When the cottage was vacated I took the liberty of going to the cottage to see if the young couple had left all the chattels that were named on the list.' He smiled at Kit and said, 'You will be very glad to hear that the place is immaculate too.'

'I am so glad. Thank you. If you will send your final bill to me C/O the cottage I will settle up with you as soon as I get it. It has been a pleasure doing business with you and I will deal with you again if I may, should I need to.' She put out her hand

and he stood up and shook it.

'The pleasure has been all mine, I can assure you,' he said, taking her proffered hand. He took the keys from a key board behind him and wished Kit all the luck in the world.

She sedately left Mr McCloud's offices although she was in a hurry to get and see the cottage, but she went to Steven's flat first to get what she thought he needed. She then went into Helensburgh to try and buy him a couple of night-shirts. He would need them for a while as he wouldn't be able to get pyjamas over his cast.

Surprisingly she managed to get a couple in one of the Gentleman's outfitters there, as well as some boxer shorts.

That done, she looked at her watch and saw that it was only 1655 so she went to a little cafe just down the road from the outfitters and ordered a cup of tea and a toasted sandwich of tomato and cheese.

As it was too early to go to see Steven she decided to go to the cottage instead.

She was pleasantly surprised at how well John and Christine had left the cottage, and to find it immaculate too, just as Mr McCloud said it was. She set to work on what she would need to get sent up from London and what she would need from local suppliers.

She decided to get the king-sized bed locally and the bedding of course for Steven may be out of hospital before her father could arrange to get things sent to her.

Having decided what things she needed to buy locally, she looked at her watch and decided it was time to visit Steven.

He was looking a lot better than when she had left him this morning. He was awake too and smiled at her as she walked in. She leant over to give him a kiss and he grabbed her breasts. 'Really, Steven, we are not at home here, so be careful.' Kit blushed and smiled.

'But you liked it, didn't you?'

Kit was still smiling and she had to admit that she did but to be careful in future and went on to tell him that she had been to the cottage and told him that she had made a list of what to buy locally and what to get her father to send up.

She showed Steven the list with the hope of getting some input from him. He studied it and made a few suggestions. Kit agreed with most of them but some she disagreed with. The ones she disagreed with she said were pointless buying locally because she had them packed and her father would send them up. Steven saw the logic in this.

'How long before you are let out?' she asked.

'A couple of weeks, all being well. What did you have in mind?'

'Well, I have three weeks' leave owing to me and hopefully the stuff from local sources and what my dad will have had sent up will all be installed by then, and you won't be able to manage stairs very well, so I was going to suggest you come to the cottage. That way I will be able to bring you backwards and forwards to the hospital for the check-ups you're bound to need. What do you suggest?'

Steven thought about what she had said and said, 'What!? And live with you in sin openly?'

'What does it matter in this day and age? Anyway, the neighbours won't know our marital situation. But if you like we could get married in here first.'

'That sounds a better idea, my love.'

Kit smiled and kissed him again. He tried to grab her breasts but she was too quick for him. She laughed when he said, 'Spoil sport.'

Just then, Keith walked in and said, 'Good evening, Kit, and Steven. How are you feeling this evening?'

'A lot better than I did this morning. It must be something

you put in the water.' He laughed, and Kit smiled at this.

Keith smiled and said, 'You look a lot better than you did this morning, I must say. It must be the visit from this lovely lady,' and he naturally indicated Kit, who blushed.

'Did she tell you that she was my fiancé?' asked Steven.

'No, she didn't.' Kit was still blushing as Keith looked over to her and smiled, 'Congratulations are called for then.' And he smiled at them both, even though Kit had told him that she was his fiancé earlier.

Kit said that the only complication was that Steven may not be able to negotiate the stairs to his place, whereas she had just bought a two-bedroomed cottage that has no stairs. She suggested that he move in with her and that way she would able to look after him.

'That sounds like a good idea to me, but…'

'We won't be married by the time he is let out and it wouldn't be a good idea to just move in with me as Steven said, and I quote, "living openly in sin with me".'

'I can see no problem with that.'

'WHAT?' They both said together, looking surprised.

Keith chuckled and said, 'Couldn't you get a special license and get married from here before going to Kit's cottage?'

'That is what I had already said to Kit.'

'Well, what's your problem then?'

'Nothing,' Kit added. 'It will take some organisation though.'

'Well, I'll leave you to it and come and see you later, Steven. Goodnight, Kit.'

Kit said goodnight to Keith and looked at Steven who was grinning like a Cheshire cat.

'Well, you will have to ring the vicar and your parents and son and I can organise the hotel accommodation and a reception of sorts in here. What do you say?'

'A brilliant idea, I can do all that from here.'

'Right, tomorrow is Saturday and I can order the things from Helensburgh and phone Mum and Dad this evening, asking Dad to send the things I ask him to, and tell them that we are getting married fairly quickly.' She laughed and said, 'My mother will have a fit and something to say about that. It will definitely take some diplomacy on my side.'

'I will probably have the same problem, especially with my son.'

'I'd better get back on board and start organising things.' She leant over and kissed him goodnight.

He fondled her breasts again but this time she didn't complain. She just sighed and blew him a kiss as she left.

CHAPTER 35

Kit went back on board and straight to the wardroom for a drink. She had her usual and soon after Wiggy came and joined her. Kit ordered Wiggy a G & T. 'I presume that you haven't changed your tipple, Wiggy?'

'No. Thanks Kit. How was Steven tonight when you saw him?'

'Oh a lot better thanks, Wiggy.'

'That's good. I'm so happy for you.'

Kit smiled at her friend and said, 'Come over here and sit down please.'

Wiggy did what was asked of her, looking intrigued. She cocked her head as if waiting for a question. She didn't have long to wait.

'Wiggy, I want you to do one more favour for me please.'

'Of course.'

'You haven't heard it yet,' Kit laughed at her friend's eagerness. 'Will you stand up for me when I marry Steven, please?'

'Oh yes, Kit. When and where?'

'Within the next couple of weeks, and in the Naval Hospital. I can't give you the exact date as that depends on the doctor there.'

'But why the Naval Hospital?'

Kit laughed again, saying it was a long story.

Wiggy laughed with her but was still curious as to Kit's intentions, so in the end, Kit had to tell her.

After Kit had explained the reasons and what she had to do and plan, Wiggy still laughed but she could understand

Steven's and Kit's dilemma, especially as Steven's son would hopefully be there. 'And you don't want to shock the "Natives" either,' Wiggy said.

Kit smiled. 'I am so glad you said yes. Things will be a lot easier with the handover out of the way on Tuesday. I presume that you will move inboard?'

'Yes, and you will go to the cottage?'

'Yes, I'll be able to commute from there.' She smiled.

'If you want a hand with anything, I'll be at a loose end until after the wedding, and then I'll go home on leave.'

'That would be great. I may take you up on that.'

'Okay. Would you like a drink?'

'Yes please.' Kit looked at her watch. 'Why don't we go to the Ardencaple for a couple there?'

'Well, that would be a good idea, but isn't it a bit late? I make it 2147,' Wiggy said, looking at her watch.

Kit looked at her watch again and saw that it had stopped at 1855 and she laughed and said, 'I think I'll have that drink here after all.' And she smiled at Wiggy. She took from her handbag the list of what was wanted in town. She asked Wiggy's advice where to buy the things she needed.

Wiggy took the list and studied it for a few minutes and then suggested that she go to Dumbarton for most of it.

Kit thought about that and said that sounded a good idea. 'Do you fancy a day out there in Dumbarton tomorrow, Wiggy? I don't know it at all.'

'Yes, why not?' she smiled at Kit. 'If you like, we could go in my car and maybe we can bring some of the things back with us.'

'That sounds a brilliant idea.' That decided, they both made arrangements to go there after breakfast.

* * *

There were a few others at breakfast, including Val Kennedy and Joan Shakespeare, and there was quite a bit of lively chatter. Kit had decided not to tell the others that she was getting married until she found out the exact dates herself so only Wiggy knew.

Both Kit and Wiggy had a good breakfast to sustain themselves until lunchtime. Once they had finished they went and got ready and then set off for Dumbarton.

It was lucky that Wiggy had an estate car as there was quite a bit that Kit would need from Tuesday until the rest of the stuff arrived, either from Dumbarton or her dad. The odds and ends she would need to tide her over needn't be too fancy. One thing she would need was a fold up or a camp bed and a sleeping bag. She had already transferred money over from her savings account to her current account.

When they arrived there, they managed to find a parking billet with no problem as it was still quite early. Fortunately it was near the main shopping area.

Wiggy knew Dumbarton quite well and all the good shops too so Kit let her lead the way. Kit had only been there once with Clive to the cinema so she didn't know it at all.

The two women had a ball buying things for the cottage. Wiggy suggested things that Kit had never thought of that she would need to get on with, and other things like a small fridge and bedding for the enormous bed that would be delivered on Wednesday. They told the store what they would take with them and what was to be delivered.

They were told to bring the car around to the back and the store-boy would help them load the stuff in the car.

'Can you think of anything we may have forgotten, Wiggy?'

'No, Kit. You can get anything you may have forgotten in Helensburgh. You pay the bill and I'll go and take the car around the back.'

'Okay.' Kit turned to the man who had served her and told him what she was taking with her and what they could deliver on Wednesday. She was shown through to the back door just as Wiggy was arriving with the car. The store-boy opened the back of Wiggy's car and began loading the stuff. Kit gave him a very generous tip for his trouble then they drove back to Helensburgh.

On the way back she looked at the clock on the dash-board and turned to Wiggy saying, 'How about lunch at the Ardencaple? My treat.'

'That's a good idea as it will give us some strength to unload the stuff.'

So Kit and Wiggy stopped for lunch at the Ardencaple Hotel. During the course of the lunch time session, Kit was looking all around her and she turned to Wiggy and said, 'Did you know that Clive and I spent many a weekend and night here?'

'No, I didn't. You must miss him a hell of a lot?'

'Yes I do. Everywhere I go in Helensburgh brings back a memory of sorts. He was taken from me far too soon.' Wiggy squeezed her hand, but Kit continued, 'You and those who knew him must think I am acting like a fifteen year old with Steven, going too fast.'

'I did at first, I must admit that, and even though it has been only a short time now, it is so obvious that you are both head over heels in love with each other.'

'Thank you, Wiggy. I just feel so guilty that I have left everything on your shoulders, capable as they are.'

'Don't you worry about that. I have needed the extra work as it has helped take my mind off things with my ex.'

'I have often wondered about him but I didn't have the nerve to ask.' It was obvious to Kit that Wiggy was about to open up so she gently prodded by asking, 'Do you still see anything of him?'

'Not now, thank Heaven, although I did see him not long before you joined the boat.'

'Oh.'

'He was in the Navy too, but he got chucked out as he was embezzling the wardroom funds. As I said, it was just before you joined the boat. He was the mess president and the wine member, and apparently they did a spot audit and that was how he was caught out. He'd borrowed some money from the funds and was going to pay it back at the end of the month. There was a Court Martial over it and he was discharged SNLR.' She shrugged.

Kit had been listening intently to what Wiggy was saying and she said, 'I read about that in the *Daily Telegraph* when I was on leave prior to coming up here to take over *Holland*.' She shook her head in disbelief. 'So that was him, the little shit. Excuse me, but that is how I feel about him for doing the dirty on you. It sounds like he was one of them all along. But it strikes me that you found out just in time when you did. You were lucky.'

'Thinking back on it all, I suppose you're right, but it still hurts to think that I was duped. I feel more shamed than sorry for myself.'

'You must do,' Kit said kindly. 'Who knows, you may find someone else that is far more suitable for you. You are still a young woman. Come on, let us finish our coffee and get this stuff unloaded.' And Kit quaffed hers back, followed shortly by Wiggy, who said, 'Thanks Kit, for listening and for lunch.'

'My pleasure.' Kit paid the bill and they left shortly after.

They drove in companionable silence until they got to Garelochead and Kit's cottage.

When they arrived there Wiggy said to Kit, 'Is this it?' Kit just smiled at her. 'It's just beautiful.'

'I think it is too. Come inside before we start unloading the car.' Kit unlocked the front door and went in followed by Wiggy. 'Just have a wander around.'

'It is even better inside and that kitchen is something to die for. Now I know why you ordered the pine table and chairs, I thought a lot about that. I presume you are having a dining table and chairs sent up from London.'

'Thanks. There is quite a bit I want my dad to send up. I must ring him tonight to ask him to do just that. Also I must tell my mother about Steven and me getting married…' Kit laughed and added, 'I haven't even told her that I got engaged before we left on patrol a couple of months ago.'

'Whoops.' Wiggy laughed with Kit.

'Well let's get on with this,' Kit suggested.

They went to the car and started to unload it. The only difficult thing was the refrigerator but they managed eventually to unload it and put it in the kitchen. The rest there was no problem, and Kit could move it around to suit herself.

After everything was unloaded and put where Kit wanted it they made their way to the boat. Kit thanked Wiggy for her help and they both went to their cabins, deciding to see each other at dinner.

As it was only 1500, Kit decided to go to the Naval Hospital and visit Steven. With luck the doctor may have decided when Steven would be fit enough to leave the hospital.

When Kit walked in, all smiles, Steven was grinning from ear to ear too. 'I am so glad to see you too, Darling.' She leaned over to kiss him, avoiding his hand that was about to grab the usual piece of her anatomy.

'It's good to see you too. I must say that you look a lot better than you did yesterday, too.'

'It must be the thought that we will be married soon.'

'I presume the doctor may have told you when he is going

chuck you out, Steven?'

'He sure did, so that we can get married a fortnight tomor-row. Will you be able to arrange accommodation for my parents and Mark, plus your parents as well?'

'I can't see why not. I suppose you have told your son and parents about what has happened and that we are getting married in two weeks' time?'

'I was going to tell them tonight when I ring them. Have you?'

'No, as I was waiting to hear when you were getting out first.'

'Right.' He smiled at her.

She went on to tell him that she and Wiggy had been into Dumbarton shopping and what she had bought for the cottage. He added that she could always take things from his flat but she declined, saying that she would get her father to send things up and hopefully they would have arrived by the time they were married.

He asked her what she would wear to the wedding. She told him that she hadn't even given that a thought. She added that she would have a talk to Wiggy about that. And she asked him if he had any preference. He told her that she looked beautiful in anything she wore and he was sure she wouldn't disappoint him.

She told him that she would have to buy another car. He looked surprised at that and asked her why. Kit laughed and told him that her BMW was slightly bigger than his MGB GT, but with his leg in a cast he wouldn't be able to get in it.

Steven asked her what sort of car she would buy and could he pay anything toward it. She said no as she had plenty left from the sale of her apartment in Chelsea. He was a bit worried about the amount she was spending. "Don't worry," she assured him and she went on to tell him how much she had left after buying the cottage. He whistled. She also told him that she was going to buy another car in any case for when or if her parents came up for a holiday. It looked as though her parents would be up sooner than she planned but only for a short time this time and they wouldn't be using the car in any case.

'What about when they all come up here, if they come for the wedding that is?' Steven said, looking worried.

'Don't you worry about that as I am sure I will be able to cope.'

Kit didn't stay too long, for she was having dinner with Wiggy. She would have to ring her parents too. She didn't mind speaking to her father but she was dreading having to talk to her mother. But she had to do it.

When Kit arrived back on board it was only 1730 so she had plenty of time to ring her parents. She took a deep breath and dialled their number. Fortunately for her, her father answered.

'Hello Dad. How are you?'

'Hello darling. I'm fine. How did the first patrol go then?'

'Very well, thank you. I can move into my little cottage on Tuesday when I finish the handover.'

'That is great. What do you want me to send up?'

Kit had a list a mile long and she asked if her father would be able to get the stuff moved and up there as soon as possible.

'Of course, Christine. Are you sure that is all you need for now?'

'Yes I am. Is Mother there, Dad?'

'No, she went to the theatre with her friend, Helen, and won't be back until a lot later. Is there something you need to tell her especially?'

Kit laughed, saying that her mother would have a fit anyway.

'Oh, why is that?' asked her father.

'I am getting married in two weeks' time and was wondering if you and Mum could come up here for it?'

194

'We wouldn't miss it for the world. Who's the lucky fellow?'

'He's Steven Thorpe, a widower. He is also the camp Padre. I met him before we went on Patrol at our farewell cocktail party. Apparently he also officiated at Clive's funeral. He had to remind me of that because I wasn't very receptive that day.' She laughed.

'I'm not surprised, darling.'

'Anyway, he isn't feeling so lucky at the moment.'

'Why is that?

Kit went on to tell her father all the details and also a bit about Steven and that he had a twelve year old son living in Kew with Steven's parents. She went on to explain that hopefully she would be able to get them all booked in at the Ardencaple Hotel.

'That sounds fine to me, dear.'

'I just hope that Mummy will feel the same way as you, Dad.'

'Don't you worry about her, I'll tell her when she comes in,' he chuckled. 'I can just imagine her face.'

Kit laughed as well and said, 'So can I. I'll get Steven's parents' names and phone number when I see him and I'll give Mother a ring tomorrow. Okay?'

'Okay, Christine. I'll look forward to speaking with you tomorrow. Goodbye dear.'

'Goodbye Dad, and thanks.'

Kit sighed a big sigh of relief.

CHAPTER 36

Kit went to the wardroom and found Wiggy there already. 'Hi Wiggy.' She looked up from the paper she was reading and said, 'Hello Kit. How did everything go? I presumed you went to see Steven after we came back.' She smiled at Kit. 'How is he?'

'Oh, he is fine thanks. He asked me a good question though. What am I going to wear for the wedding? I told him that I didn't have a clue and said I'd consult with you.'

'Have you decided on a date yet?'

'Yes, two weeks tomorrow.'

'Wow! I presume that he's being chucked out then? Well, we'll have to move then. What do you suggest, Kit?'

'I haven't a clue. I suppose, being summer, dresses will be appropriate. What do you think, Wiggy? Personally I'd rather wear jeans and t-shirt.' She chuckled.

'Yes, that's true. Where do you suggest we go for them?'

Kit thought for a while and shrugged. 'I have no idea. At the moment, I've still got to tell my mother. I told Dad earlier and he said he'll tell Mum when she gets in. I told him that I would ring again tomorrow. I'm dreading it.'

Wiggy laughed saying, 'Rather you than me.'

Kit laughed with her. 'It's all go.'

Just then the steward came and opened the bar prior to dinner.

'Usual, Wiggy?'

'Yes please, Kit.'

'Stay there Ma'am, and I'll bring the drinks over. One G & T and one horse's neck coming right up.'

'Thank you, Jones.' Kit smiled at her.

* * *

Meanwhile, Steven was ringing his parents and son. His mother answered the phone.

'Hello Mum, how are you?'

'Oh Steven, hello son. Very well, thank you, and how are you?'

He went on to tell her about the accident which he played down and then went on to tell her, 'I'm getting married again in two weeks' time.'

'Well that is a bit sudden. Is she… er, um…'

'No, she isn't pregnant, Mother. I've known her since May, but I knew her before when I officiated at her husband's funeral six years ago.'

'So she is a widow.'

'Yes, she is, and very beautiful if I do say so myself.' He chuckled.

'You always could pick 'em, Steven.'

'Anyway, will you, Dad and Mark come up here for it?'

'Of course, dear.'

'Good. I'll tell Kit when she comes to see me, so she can book you all in to a local hotel. Is Mark there, Mother?'

'I'm afraid not. Dad managed to get tickets for Lords, England versus New Zealand, and he has taken Mark there.'

'Well I'll ring again tomorrow, Mum, and speak to Mark then.'

'Okay, Steven, I'll hear from you tomorrow then. Goodbye dear and take care.'

'Goodbye, Mother.' And he hung up.

* * *

The phone in the wardroom rang and Kit answered it. 'Commander Carson.'

'Hello darling. How's it going?'

Kit smiled and said, 'Fine thanks. Have you told your parents and Mark?'

'I've spoken to my mother but Dad and Mark were at a cricket match, but Mother said they'd come. Have you spoken to your parents?'

'Well sort of. I spoke to Dad and gave him a long list of what I wanted him to send up for the cottage. My mother was out, but Dad said he'd tell her and that they'd be here for the wedding. So it is all go.'

Kit took a sip of her drink. 'That still leaves us with the problem with what to wear for the wedding...'

'I am sure you will sort out something and that you'll be beautiful in anything you choose my love.'

'I'll sort something out. Between Wiggy and me, we'll get it sorted. So don't worry about it.' Steven hung up after a few minutes and Kit went back to join Wiggy.

'There is a rather good dress shop in Helensburgh that will probably do the trick. If you like we could take a trip down there tomorrow sometime and see what they have in the window. Who knows, they may even be open?'

'Yes okay. We'll do that. And this evening, if you feel like it, we can go to the Ardencaple. What do you reckon?'

Wiggy took a sip of her G & T and said, 'That's a good idea. Yes.'

'Good, that's settled then. Shall we go in for dinner?'

Wiggy just nodded and stood up.

* * *

Dinner over, some of the women went in to have another drink. Penny was with Kit and Wiggy when they asked the steward to order them a taxi. Penny raised her eyebrows at this and Kit noticed and said to her, 'We are going to the Ardencaple, would you care to join us?'

'Yes please. That sounds great, Ma'am. Thank you. I'll go and get my bag and a cardigan. Excuse me.'

'She's a good kid, isn't she?' Kit smiled, after Penny had left the mess.

'Yes she is, and for one that seems so young, she seems very efficient too,' Wiggy added, also smiling.

Penny was soon back with her handbag, and sat down just as the steward told Kit that the taxi was waiting at the jetty for them.

'That was quick,' said Wiggy. 'Let's to it, ladies.'

The three of them trooped above decks and saw it was their usual taxi driver. 'Hello ladies, welcome back. Now let me guess. The Ardencaple?'

All three women laughed and asked him how he had guessed.

'You could say I'm psychic.' They laughed again. Kit was sitting at the front, having the longer legs, and the driver asked her how their first patrol had gone.

'Very well thanks. You are very well informed,' Kit said to him as they were turning into the car park of the hotel.

'It is surprising what you hear sitting here. Did you know that I even heard that a great grandfather of yours way back when, built the first *Holland*?' he said.

'There must be some very loose tongues in the Naval Base?'

'Yes Ma'am,' he chuckled as Kit paid him.

They went into the lounge bar and found a table straightaway. It seemed very quiet for a Saturday which was unusual.

'Would you excuse me for a few minutes whilst I go to the Reception please?'

Penny looked across to Wiggy, but Wiggy just smiled.

Kit was soon back and she said to Wiggy, 'All fixed. Three rooms, well two doubles and a single.' She smiled at them.

It was obvious that Penny didn't have a clue what Kit was talking about, so Kit decided to put her out of her misery.

'In case you are wondering what that is all about,' Penny nodded, 'Well Steven and I have decided to get married a fortnight tomorrow, the day he is released from the hospital.'

'Well that is great, Kit. Congratulations. I'm very pleased for you both.'

'Just in case you were wondering why it is so quick, it's because we are moving into the cottage as it hasn't any stairs, and we don't want to shock the neighbours by not being married.'

'Yes, I see what you mean, Kit. It is just as well that you bought the cottage when you did otherwise things would have been a bit awkward for Steven.'

'It sure would, Penny. You will have to give me John and Chris' address when you have it please.'

'Of course, Kit. I don't even know where John has been posted to. But I'll let you know as soon as I have it.'

'Thanks Penny. Now, who would like…'

Kit's question was answered before she uttered the remainder by the drinks appearing just like magic. 'Who bought these then?' Wiggy said she did, and cheers.

They all raised their glasses and chinked them together saying, 'Cheers.'

Then they were all talking at once. When they realised it they all stopped and laughed.

Kit asked Penny if she would like to come to the wedding, to which Penny answered with a resounding, 'Oh yes please.'

'I haven't got the times yet, but when I do I'll let you know. I'll be sending out proper invitation cards when I can get into

Helensburgh to buy some, so the rest of the officers haven't been told yet.'

'I still have to ring my mother to tell her the news although my father will have told her. I'm dreading it,' Kit said.

'Who is going to be Steven's Best Man?' Wiggy enquired.

'That's his part of the ship. I have enough to do without doing that too.' Kit laughed. The other two women smiled at her and Wiggy asked if there was anything she could do to help. Kit thought for a while and said that a bit nearer the time she would have a better idea and in the meantime thanks and she'd bear that in mind.

'Now, who'd like another drink?' Kit asked.

The other two said yes and Kit called the waitress over and ordered the same again. The drinks arrived in record time and Kit took a long pull of hers and said, 'Ah that's better, I needed that.' And she sighed.

They carried on drinking and discussing the wedding when Kit suddenly thought of something to ask Wiggy. 'I've just thought of something you can do for me, Wiggy, if you don't mind,'

'Yes, anything.'

'You haven't heard what it is yet.' Kit laughed at Wiggy's eagerness. 'Could you act as a driver for me, like taking the parents to the hospital on the day of the service, and bringing my dad up to the cottage please?'

'Yes, of course I will.'

Penny said, 'Excuse me butting in, but wouldn't it be better if I pick the parents up and Wiggy bring your dad up to the cottage?'

Kit thought about it for a short while and beamed at Penny saying, 'That is a brilliant idea, Penny, if you are quite sure you don't mind.'

'I don't mind at all, it will be my pleasure.' Penny smiled at them both.

'Great. Drink up ladies. Same again?' and they both nodded.

CHAPTER 37

On Sunday morning, Kit rang her mother. She answered on the second ring. 'Hello Christine, your father told me the news. Congratulations, my dear. We are both looking forward to it.'

When she paused for breath Kit said, 'Good morning, Mother. How are you this fine Sunday morning?'

'Very well, thank you, but it is raining here.'

'Oh what a shame, mind you, I haven't looked outside here, so it is probably raining here too.'

'What is this chap like that you going to marry, Christine?'

'He is lovely, Mum. Tall, dark and handsome, even if I do say so myself.' Kit saw her mother chuckling on the screen. 'Is Daddy there, Mother?'

'Yes, I'll put him on. Hang on.'

Her father was soon on the line. 'Hello Christine. How are you?'

'Fine thanks, Dad. And you?'

'Very well, thank you. I managed to get hold of a removal firm, Pickfords, and they are picking the stuff up tomorrow and will deliver it Wednesday p.m. if that is okay, Christine?'

'Dad, that is great. It couldn't have been better. It fits in just right. That is when the other stuff is coming as well, except that will be here in the morning.'

'I'm glad that everything is working out for you, dear.'

'Thanks, Dad. How did Mother take the news about the wedding?'

'I'll put her back on.'

'Hello again, Christine. I must say that it came as a sudden surprise, but a pleasant one. It is not right for a woman as young as you to be on her own. I am very pleased for you. Daddy said it is the base vicar who officiated at Clive's funeral; is that right, dear?'

'Yes, Mother. I met him again not long before we sailed and we got engaged pretty soon afterwards.'

'Why didn't you say so sooner, before you left?'

'I would have, Mum, but everything happened so quickly and there wasn't time.'

'Oh. Well alright. I hope he will be alright for the wedding though dear.'

'I think he will, but not one hundred per cent. I must hang up, Mother as I am going into Helensburgh fairly soon. Goodbye Mum.' And she hung up.

'Phew,' Kit said out loud and heaved a sigh of relief that that chore was over and done with. She got up and went along to Wiggy's cabin and knocked on her door. At her answer of 'Come in,' Kit went in.

'Oh, hi Kit. Come on in. I won't be a minute. Sit down.'

'Thanks.' Kit sat down and looked around the cabin which she noticed was quite a bit smaller than her own. Overall though, it was immaculate.

She had to chuckle at Wiggy's duvet cover. Normally the crew were issued with regulation sleeping bags which were burnt when the boat came back. But both Wiggy and herself had their own duvet covers, which were also got rid of at the end of a patrol. The pattern on it was of 'Spider Man', which was very colourful. Her own had 'Tweedy Pie,' a canary, and 'Sylvester,' a black and white cat that always saw Tweedy Pie as a quick meal.

They could have had regulation sleeping bags but thought that duvets were far more practical and easier to sleep under than having to struggle into a sleeping bag.

Wiggy turned as Kit chuckled and asked her why and Kit told her she was laughing at the duvet covers, Wiggy's and her own. It seemed peculiar that they both had their own duvet covers whilst the crew had regulation type sleeping bags.

'I expect you have seen mine, Wiggy?'

'Yes,' she said. 'I thought yours was very amusing when I first saw it. That made me chuckle to myself too.'

'Anyway,' Kit said, 'are we still going into Helensburgh, window shopping?'

'Yes, I won't be a tick.' Wiggy grabbed a jacket and her handbag and said, 'Let's get this show on the road.'

'Shall we go in my car, Wiggy?'

'Yes, okay.'

They went up to the garage where Kit kept her car and it started straightaway. Wiggy climbed in and adjusted the seat then they got on their way.

They were soon in Helensburgh and were surprised to see that most of the shops were open. Kit parked the car in the railway car park which as it happened was free. Something for nothing!

Wiggy and Kit wandered around for a while just window shopping before making up their minds as to which shop to try first. They went to the second shop they'd looked at to try their luck there. Kit found a beautiful pale blue creation that was slightly too long even for her, but the shop assistant said she would get it altered by the following Saturday. But the dress was as though it was made to measure. Kit agreed and said she'd pick it up then. The dress itself was a very simple one in style and cut, which was just as well as she wasn't one to go in for frills. To top it off she bought a plain navy blue straw hat and handbag. That was Kit sorted apart from shoes; now it was Wiggy's turn.

This proved a bit more difficult, probably as she was quite a bit shorter than Kit, plus she didn't know what colour to go for, but was the same size as Kit, a fourteen. Kit said she could have whatever colour she wished as long it wasn't the same colour as hers. Anyway, she, Kit, was paying for it so she reiterated to have what she liked.

Kit and Wiggy went through the racks again with a fine tooth comb but there wasn't anything that Wiggy fancied so they gave up and just bought Kit's dress, hat and bag.

Both women didn't like frills at all, just neat, plain well-cut dresses. The next shop they went to had just what they wanted for Wiggy; a nice lemon colour, very similar in style to the one Kit had just bought.

She tried it on and it fitted her to perfection. Kit said she looked beautiful in it and that all she needed was a nice white hat, shoes and a handbag. Fortunately the shop also sold shoes so they were both able to get what they needed there, including white gloves for Wiggy and navy ones for Kit.

All told, it took about three-quarters of an hour to do their shopping, so they put their purchases in the car and went for a cup of tea. Sitting drinking, Kit said as most shops seemed to be open she would try to buy some decent invitation cards.

They went to an arty-farty stationery shop and bought some very tasteful invitation cards. That finished, they made their way back to the base.

They were soon there and just in time for lunch. They carried their packages down to their cabins, both very pleased with their purchases.

They met up in the mess and Wiggy ordered them their usual tipple.

'That was easier than I thought,' Kit said to Wiggy.

'I must admit that I was surprised that the shops were open at all. I've never been there on a Sunday so was pleasantly surprised. And to top it all we got what we needed straight off.'

Kit laughed, saying, 'I just hate buying clothes as well so was glad to get it over and done with.'

'So do I, but I must admit we have made good choices, don't you think, Kit?'

'Yes, I agree.'

They were both quiet for a minute as the mess started to fill up.

'After lunch I'm going to see Steven, then come back for a ziz until dinner.'

'That sounds a good idea to me,' Wiggy said in answer to Kit's statement.

The meal was just a salad and ham off the bone with pickles and bread and butter, followed by a Pavlova and fresh fruit.

Kit excused herself and went to her cabin to tidy herself up prior to visiting Steven.

CHAPTER 38

Kit arrived at the RNH at 1415 and went straight up to Steven's room.

Steven was very pleased to see her and that was pretty obvious by the way he kissed her. He pulled her down onto the bed and gave her a thorough kissing. She was so taken by surprise that she struggled to pull herself up from the bed, which as it happened was just in time, with seconds to spare before Keith Dalby walked in. Kit was a bit flustered and was blushing like a fifteen year old and turned her face toward the window. Steven just burst out laughing and Keith asked them what was so funny. Kit was too embarrassed to answer but Steven just said it was nothing, but was still smiling. Keith had a good idea what had happened and turned to Kit saying, 'Anytime he misbehaves, Kit, you just tell me and I'll sort him out.'

Still flushed, Kit turned to him, smiling sheepishly and said, 'Thank you, Keith. I am pleased that there is one gentleman around here at least.' At this, Steven roared with laughter and when Kit looked at him he roared with laughter again so much so it made him choke and Kit said, 'Serves you right.' She handed him a tissue out of the box on his bedside locker. When he had finished his coughing fit he turned to Kit and sheepishly apologised. 'I am sorry my love, forgiven?'

'Yes of course.' And she squeezed his good hand.

This gentle touch of Kit's didn't go unnoticed by Keith. He cleared his throat and turned and addressed Kit saying, 'Do you know what this chap has done?'

'Nothing would surprise me, Keith.'

'Well, he has asked me to be his best man.'

'I am so glad, Keith. Perhaps you will be able to keep him in check then.'

'I'll do my best, Kit.'

'Thank you.'

Kit turned to Steven and asked him for his mother and father's phone number to give to her parents with the idea that they could make some arrangements between them for getting up there. She told him that she had booked three rooms at the Ardencaple Hotel. She also asked him for a list of who he wanted to invite and had he asked a vicar to officiate?

'Yes, everything is in hand, dear.'

'Good. Just what time is it all happening, and where?'

'Keith said that there is a lovely little Chapel on the ground floor that holds about sixty people. I've booked the other base padre for 1400 if that is okay?'

'Oh, that will be lovely. I'll have a look on my way out.' Kit turned round to speak to Keith and found that he had gone. So she shrugged and turned back to Steven and asked, 'Do you want me to bring in a suit for you to wear and shoes too, etc?'

'Yes please. I'll make a list of what I will need for you to bring in. Thanks.'

Kit stayed a bit longer, making notes and asking him questions and just chatting in general.

At one point Steven asked what she had decided to wear for the wedding.

'Oh I had thought of buying some new jeans and a t-shirt.'

Steven was horrified and Kit had to laugh at the expression on his face. In the end she put him out of his misery. 'No, I've bought a new dress, as has Wiggy, with all the accessories.'

'Thank God for that. You had me worried.'

'My mother would have killed me if I dressed like that for a special occasion, let alone for my own wedding.' She laughed.

'She would have to stand in line after me to do that.'

'Seriously, have I ever let you down, Steven?'

'No you haven't, Kit. So I am pleased.' He pulled her to him and said, 'I do love you, you know.'

'And I love you too. And I'll try not to let you down, ever.' She looked at him fondly with love shining out of her eyes, and then leaned over to kiss him goodbye, saying that she would be in this evening.

'Goodbye my love,' he said.

Kit left him and went down to see the chapel Steven told her about. It was beautiful, really beautiful. Whilst there she sat in a pew and had a quiet think about her life and what it was going to be like with Steven. She came to the conclusion that her life would be fine with him. The only hiccup would be with the son, Mark. How was he going to take to the new woman in his father's life? That could only be decided on the day of the wedding. In the meantime, she still had a wedding to organise. She said a quick prayer for Steven and left and made her way back to the boat.

CHAPTER 39

Kit went back on board *Holland* and did what she said she was going to do, have a ziz. She took off her outer clothes and lay on top of the bed in just her bras and panties. She took a deep breath and was asleep.

She slept quite deeply until 1810. She looked at her watch and thought, *Oh shit. I didn't mean to sleep that long.* She went and showered and got into fresh clothes then went to the wardroom. It was about 1845 when she got there so dinner hadn't been served. There were a few of the officers in there but not as many as usual as most of them were on weekend. She said, 'Good evening ladies.' They all stopped talking and made to get up but Kit signalled them back down and they as one said, 'Good evening, Ma'am.'

Wiggy was there and asked how Steven was. 'He is getting better all the time, Wiggy.'

'I am so glad, Ma'am. Did you tell him what we bought today?'

Kit laughed and said, 'Yes, some new jeans and a t-shirt. He nearly went ballistic.' She chuckled.

Wiggy laughed too and said, 'I'm not surprised. That's mean.' Still laughing, she said, 'Can I get you a drink?'

'Yes please. The usual please.'

* * *

The handover went very smoothly on Tuesday. Kit had done final rounds with Wiggy after breakfast. She'd warned the girls to make sure they had packed everything. She told them this on Monday when she addressed the whole ship's company. She had said words to the effect that she was very pleased with how the first patrol had gone and that she looked forward to serving with them again, if not those that were moving on, she wished them luck but hoped she would serve with them again in the not too distant future.

When the handover was complete, Kit and Wiggy left the boat. They both heaved sighs of relief. 'Thank God that is over,' Kit said.

'I must say that the new Commander is a bit too keen for my liking,' Wiggy mumbled.

Kit laughed at this. 'Yes she is, and even before we left on the first patrol if you remember.'

'Oh yes. She came round to Coulport the day before we sailed and the day we arrived, very keen. Anyway, I'd better make my way to Neptune wardroom. Will I see you later?' Wiggy asked Kit.

'You can come up to the cottage for a coffee or tea later. I haven't bought anything in the way of food yet but I'll pop down to Helensburgh and top up the cupboards later this afternoon.'

'Okay Kit, thanks. I'll be there at about three if that's alright?'

'Yes that is fine. See you about three. Bye.'

They both went their own separate ways.

When Kit got to the cottage she opened all the windows to air the place off. She went out of the front door and just stood there admiring the view and taking a deep breath before going back inside.

She had popped up there the night before and turned the electric on so she knew there would be hot water when she got there. One thing she must do was to get a telephone installed as soon as possible. She phoned Telecoms on her mobile and spoke to a very obliging chap who said that he would send someone up first thing in the morning to reconnect her.

She decided to do a bit of hand washing. Kit had noticed that Chris had left a small amount of dhoby dust (soap powder) in a box under the sink and a few pegs too. So she got on and did it.

After she had pegged her stuff out she set to with getting her bed, which was a fold up type, made. This didn't take very long as she had bought a sleeping bag and an extra pillow for it, from Dumbarton.

Kit had noticed a little corner shop on her way to the cottage, so she decided to go and buy some tea, coffee and biscuits. When she got there she was rather surprised at the things that were available to her. So she got some eggs, bacon, cheese and some frozen chips and a bottle of milk, some bread and butter and salt and pepper, some HP and Tomato sauce. That done she had a word with the proprietor who said that she also could get joints of meat if ordered early enough in the day. So Kit ordered a small joint of beef for tomorrow, paid for her purchases, and made her way back to her cottage.

Fairly soon after Kit had got back and put her shopping away, Wiggy arrived. She put the kettle on after she had ascertained whether Wiggy wanted tea or coffee, put an assortment of biscuits on a plate and apologised for paper serviettes.

Wiggy laughed and said she wasn't expecting silver service. This made Kit laugh too as she dunked her biscuit in the cup of tea.

'One thing that I haven't thought about is where to have a reception. And time is getting on in fact, less than two weeks now. Any suggestions, Wiggy?'

'The Ardencaple, or the wardroom in Neptune.'

'Mmh... I think the wardroom in Neptune will be able to cope better at such short notice. Who is the Wardroom mess manager these days?'

'Commander Pip Jones.'

'Is that a he or a she?'

Wiggy laughed and said, 'A she.'

'Right, I'll give her a ring later.'

Wiggy didn't stay very long as she realised Kit had things to do, but she volunteered to come up to the cottage on Wednesday to give Kit a hand with anything. Kit accepted her offer and got on with writing the wedding invitations. That done, she cooked some egg and chips, washed up and then had a shower and went to visit Steven.

She spent a very pleasant couple of hours with Steven and told him that she had booked a small room in the Wardroom in Neptune for the reception.

Steven insisted that the reception went on his Mess Bill and Kit didn't argue with him. She told him that Wiggy was coming up to the cottage to give her a hand with anything that needed doing.

'That Wiggy must be something special to want to help you so much.'

'She is, but as she said herself she has nothing else to do until after the wedding when she goes on leave…' Kit shrugged. 'I told her a couple of days ago that I owed her one and she said she'd like a slap up home cooked meal when we are organised.'

'That sounds easy enough.'

Soon it was time for Kit to leave and she kissed Steven goodbye, avoiding his groping hand, and left.

CHAPTER 40

The wedding was soon upon them. Kit's parents and Steven's with young Mark arrived on Friday afternoon. She went down just before they arrived at the Ardencaple, in Kit's father's car.

Her father introduced her to Mr and Mrs Thorpe and his son, Mark. She thought that there may be difficulties with him but after shaking hands with her he said, 'Are you really a commander of a submarine?'

'Yes I am, Mark.'

'Is there any chance I can go to see your submarine please?'

'I'm afraid not as I have just handed it over to another crew just last week.' She could tell he was disappointed but she asked him how long he was up here for. He conferred with his grandparents and they said they would be there until the following Friday. 'Well,' Kit said, 'I'll try and fix you up with a visit onto a submarine.' She smiled at the lad.

He was over the moon with that, so much so that he hugged Kit and said, 'Oh, thank you very much.'

Kit was rather embarrassed at his eagerness and especially the way he hugged her so she just smiled at him and tussled his hair. 'I'll see what I can do.'

They all went into the hotel and were shown their rooms whilst Kit waited downstairs in the dining room. She told them all that she would order them all some tea and stickys, and she would see them all in fifteen minutes.

During tea, Kit told Steven's parents and Mark that she would come back at five forty five and take them up to visit Steven. Her father asked if she would like to borrow his car, but she said no, thank you, as she had bought another car and she would come in that. 'Perhaps, when I come back we could have dinner together?'

'That is a good idea, Christine,' her mother said.

'Right, I will see you all later. Bye for now.'

* * *

Kit went back to her cottage and tidied it up, not that it was very untidy; in fact it was immaculate.

She wandered around her domain, thinking of Steven's parents and his son. She was pleasantly surprised by what a well-mannered boy Mark seemed to be, though she was still feeling embarrassed at the hug. Mrs Thorpe was a real sweetie too, elegant and beautifully turned out, whereas Mr Thorpe reminded Kit of her own father. Although he hadn't been in the Navy he was ex-Army, and retired as a Major with the Royal Artillery. He had the same sort of outlook on life and a typical military bearing, a ramrod straight back. Just like her father.

It was fortunate that they all seemed to get on so well. Kit supposed that being cooped up in the car for quite a few hours with strangers was a test of each other's patience and character.

Kit rearranged some of the furniture to her liking and looked at the settee in the lounge and smiled. She thought of the things that Steven and she would get up to on it. Then she thought that Steven may want his son to stay with them after they were married. He hadn't said that he would to Kit, and Kit would have to think long and hard about that if she was asked. She wandered in to what was going to be their bedroom and looked at the king-sized bed that was waiting for them on Sunday. She couldn't wait to get him in bed, even though she may have to do all the work. She chuckled out loud at that.

As the time was getting on she decided to get showered and

changed, ready to take her future in-laws to see Steven.

They were all ready when she arrived at the Ardencaple and young Mark sat up front with her whilst Mr and Mrs Thorpe sat in the back. They all chatted together and it didn't take Kit long to get to the base. She got out and swiped her card and pulled over as the Mod Plod signalled her to. She had to fill in passes for the Thorpes and explained where she was taking them to. They saluted Kit and signalled her to proceed.

When they got to the hospital Kit went in first and kissed Steven and explained that his family was with her and that she was just going to the Wardroom at Neptune to have chat with Wiggy and she'd be back in an hour. They kissed again and as usual she had to avoid his groping hand and she said, 'Soon darling, soon.'

'I can't wait,' he said.

She told the others that she would be back within the hour and to have a nice visit.

Kit found Wiggy sitting alone in the wardroom, reading a magazine. Wiggy was most surprised to see Kit standing there and she said, 'What are you doing here, Kit?'

'I've just bought the future in-laws to visit Steven. I was wondering if you would care to join us all for dinner at the Ardencaple. You will have to meet them all eventually so why not now?'

'Okay. What time?'

Kit looked at her watch, made a quick calculation and said, 'I have to pick them up at the hospital in an hour's time, so say about an hour and a half. I'll give you the keys to my car and we'll see you there when we come out, alright?'

'Alright. I assume the car is your new one and that it is parked outside the hospital?'

'Yes. Here are the keys. I'll see you later.' And Kit was gone.

Wiggy sat in a daze then went to her cabin to get ready then went to the hospital car park. She found Kit's car without much trouble and got in. She read a magazine that was in the glove compartment and settled down to wait.

They all arrived in about ten minutes after Wiggy got there. She got out of the car when she saw them coming and Kit introduced her to the Thorpe family. 'This is Mr and Mrs Thorpe and this is Steven's son, Mark.' She looked at Wiggy and turned to the Thorpes and said, 'This is Shelagh Bennett, my Executive Officer. She has kindly agreed be to my Matron of Honour on Sunday.' They all shook hands and got into the car. Kit had already phoned ahead to book a table for seven at eight thirty.

Kit's mum and dad were in the bar and she introduced them to Wiggy, as Shelagh of course, but Wiggy told everybody to call her Wiggy as that is what she was used to.

The waitress came up to them and said, 'Mrs Carson, your table for seven is ready for you in the dining room when you are.'

'Thank you Maggie. We'll be in, in a couple of minutes.' She looked at the others and asked if any of them needed to use the toilets before going in to dine, and they all said no, so they went in.

The meal was a very lively affair with everybody chatting to each other. Even Mark was chatting away to Wiggy and asking her what she did as an Executive Officer. He was full of admiration of her and he said, 'Gee Miss Bennett, thank you very much. Mrs Carson is going to try and fix me up with a visit on one of the submarines.'

Kit looked across at Wiggy when she heard her name mentioned by Mark. Wiggy took the initiative and said, 'Mrs Carson will be a bit busy next week…' She saw the disappointment on Mark's face. 'But I'm sure that between us we may be able to fix something up.'

'Thank you, Miss Bennett.'

'Wiggy, please.'

Mark laughed and said thank you again.

'Mark,' Kit smiled over at him and carried on when she had his attention. 'On a submarine there are a lot of things that are top secret and are not usually seen by the public, so we can't promise anything, but we will do our best to fix you up.'

Mark digested this bit of information, then turned back to Kit and shocked her practically speechless by saying, 'Surely if you told them your son would like to have a look around they may let me.' Kit nearly choked but as usual was rescued by Wiggy. 'I am sure between us we will be able to fix something up, Mark.'

Mrs Thorpe told Mark that she was sure that Wiggy and Christine would do their very best for him and to let them get on with their dinner.

Kit mentally heaved a sigh of relief at this and got on with her dinner. At the end of the meal Kit told her father that Wiggy would pick him up on Sunday at 1315 and that the others would be picked up by Penny Soames at 1330 and taken to the small Chapel in the hospital. She also told them that they would meet Penny on Saturday night for dinner here. So she and Wiggy left them to it and made their way back to Faslane.

'I expect that came as a bit of a shock, Mark more or less calling you his mother.'

'It sure did. Thanks for coming to my rescue.'

'I've just had a thought. Isn't Val Kennedy's husband on a more or less conventional boat?'

'Wiggy, you are a genius and they have accepted the invitation. I may get him to invite Mark onto his boat. Yes, I'll try and have a word with him.' She heaved a sigh of relief at hopefully sorting that out.

CHAPTER 41

Sunday had come and it was a beautiful sunny day. Looking across the Gareloch Kit just hoped that the local saying wouldn't be true today.

Wiggy had dropped her off last night and taken the car back with her so that she would be able to pick her father up and bring the bouquets for Kit and herself. They were yellow roses and a single yellow rose for the ladies and white for the men. Penny would hand them out in Chapel when the people arrived and also act as usher. Penny was going to put Steven's parents and Mark on one side of the chapel and Kit's the other side and then just let the rest sit where they liked.

Kit ate a hearty breakfast, just like the 'ish she used to get on board, and sat and thought if she had done everything that needed doing.

All the invitations had been accepted in record time so Kit was able to tell Pip Jones, the Wardroom Mess Manager, the exact amount of people to cater for in the wardroom.

She couldn't think of another thing that she could have done towards the wedding. Wiggy and Penny had themselves worked their butts off to help Kit. They had been a Godsend to her. She had brought some of Steven's clothes from his flat, including the two dressing gowns that she had washed and pressed ready for tonight or even earlier! She grinned to herself at that.

Yes, she thought, she couldn't have done another thing. Kit thought she had logistically done everything right and just couldn't think what else she could have done.

She washed and stacked the dishes then went for a shower

and washed her hair. Fortunately she had the type of hair that didn't need setting and just needed towelling dry, combed and left loose. It was a bit too early to get dressed in her finery so she just wore a dressing gown over her bra and pants.

Kit wandered around the cottage, making sure that everything was okay for Steven's home coming. She just hoped he liked the cottage as much as she.

Wiggy had left her finery with Kit and Kit had laid it all out in the second bedroom and pressed it where necessary.

What would she have done without Wiggy and Penny? She just hoped that they wouldn't be embarrassed at the gifts she had bought them both, a gold Omega wrist watch each.

Her father and Wiggy arrived and Kit and Wiggy went and got ready whilst Kit's father helped himself to a large brandy.

When the girls were ready he just whistled at how beautiful they looked. 'I am the luckiest man in Scotland to have two such beautiful ladies to escort.'

* * *

They got to the Chapel dead on 1400. Penny came and said everything was all set and Kit and her father started walking slowly down the aisle with Wiggy behind them.

Everyone turned to watch, smiling at the procession as they made their way forward.

Kit had eyes only for Steven. He looked so handsome in his light grey suit and he was even standing with just the aid of a walking stick. Even the scar that had marred his cheek had nearly healed, giving him a piratical look.

When Kit and her father got down the aisle she turned to give her bouquet to Wiggy but she, Wiggy was mesmerised as she looked at the Best Man. Kit whispered to Wiggy who was blushing as she looked back at Kit. Kit just smiled as Wiggy took the bouquet from her. When she turned back to Steven he was looking at her with such love in his eyes that she could hardly wait until later.

They both turned as the Vicar said, 'We are gathered here today…' It all went over Kit's and Steven's heads, except for when they had to make a response, until the Vicar said, 'You may kiss the Bride.' Just before he kissed her she whispered to him so only he could hear, 'Don't you dare.' Then his lips were on hers and he crushed her to him. She was breathless when she pulled back from him and they both laughed then went to sign the Register, followed by Keith and Wiggy. Kit made hasty introductions then asked Steven if he was alright.

'Yes my love. I am now.' He chuckled as they walked slowly up the aisle, followed by Keith and Wiggy, arm in arm.

When they got outside the hospital church there was a Guard of Honour formed by the Naval officers with their swords. Kit was so surprised that she was laughing and crying at the same time. Then everyone was around them, congratulating them. Someone had thoughtfully brought the wheelchair for Steven, who heaved a sigh of relief as he settled himself down in it and Keith pushed him up the hill to Neptune wardroom.

Before everyone else got there Keith asked if could kiss the bride and Matron of Honour. This was a new one on Steven, who said by all means. So Keith kissed Kit on the cheek and kissed Wiggy on the lips. Wiggy was very embarrassed at this and was blushing very deeply. Kit laughed and wrinkled her nose at Wiggy and smiled at the same time.

Wiggy then squeezed and kissed Kit, whispering 'Rotter.' Kit just bellowed with laughter as Wiggy went on to kiss Steven. They had all calmed down and waited for the rest of the wedding party to arrive. Meanwhile Keith was holding Wiggy's hand and she was looking up at him and as far as Kit could see, they were both really smitten with each other.

The rest of the guests arrived and formed a queue as they congratulated the bride and groom. Even the Admiral Ambrose and his wife kissed Kit and shook hands with Steven. Soon everyone had been down the line and was now in the Wardroom.

Kit, Steven, Keith and Wiggy made their way to their table and Kit was so surprised at the way Pip had decorated the mess. And a wedding cake too, that was beautifully iced all in white. That was one thing that Kit hadn't thought of. She must find out later who had ordered it and thank them for their thoughtfulness.

Everyone was chatting to each other and had charged glasses of champagne when Keith got up to toast the Bride and Groom. All the guests stood up and said, 'The Bride and Groom, Christine and Steven.'

After that were speeches from her father and eventually one from Steven. Then the meal was served and everyone got on with the meal, interspersed with laughter. At one stage someone called over to the top table, 'Kit, I didn't know that your full handle was Christine Georgina. Are you going to be called Christine now?'

'No,' she laughed. 'Even though I was nicknamed after that legendry cowboy, Kit Carson, Kit is still the diminutive of Christine according to my husband, Steven, so I'll still be known as Kit, anyway, and it is easier to spell.'

This caused everyone to cheer and laugh at her answer.

At one stage, Keith whispered to Wiggy, asking her out tomorrow evening for a meal. Wiggy whispered back, yes please, and they made arrangements for him to pick her up at the WR entrance at 1800.

The reception went on for quite a while and Steven nudged Kit and said they had better get going. He struggled up and told everyone that it had been a long day for him in his condition and he was sure that his Doctor would agree, and Keith nodded, as Steven continued. 'Thank you all for coming and making it such a special day for Kit and myself. The drinks are on me, so don't be shy.'

Everyone went ooh and laughed and cheered. Kit was a bit embarrassed when she got up and she threw her bouquet at Wiggy who caught it. Kit winked and smiled at her and mouthed her thanks to her.

Steven and Kit made their getaway with everyone seeing them off. It was only seven fifteen. Kit turned to Steven and said, 'I won't know what to do with myself.'

'You won't have to do anything. Leave it all to me.'

'Will you be able to manage, darling?'

'I am sure I can, but may need a little assistance from you, Kit.'

'I'm sure I will be able to help if needs be.' She laughed as she turned on the ignition. 'What do you think of the new car, Steven?'

'I was just thinking that it is lovely and comfortable. How old is it?'

'Only a year and it is still under warranty. I must say that I do like BMWs.'

Steven laughed and said, 'I gathered that.'

They arrived at the cottage. Kit asked him, 'What do you think of it?'

'It looks very nice from here. I can't wait to get inside.' He grinned. 'Neither can I,' Kit agreed with him.

She parked the car beside her Z3 and got out to help Steven out. If he had had his leg still in a cast he would have struggled to get out. He hung on to Kit as he walked slowly up the drive. She unlocked the door and helped him over the step. She opened the door on the left that led to the lounge. He laughed and said that she was right, she had got a nice big settee just like his.

'Well, we did have so much fun on that, didn't we?'

'Yes we did,' he said, and grabbed hold of her and started to undress her. She said that she'd better draw the curtains or go to the bedroom for no one would be able to see them there.

* * *

Keith picked Wiggy up at the Wardroom dead on 1800. She was waiting for him in the doorway and she went down and got into his car. Keith gave her a peck on the cheek and asked her if the Commodore hotel would be alright for dinner. Wiggy said of course, and she hadn't been there before so that should make a pleasant change. She was still blushing from the peck on the cheek.

When they got there Keith rushed round to open the car door for her, and helped her out. Wiggy was rather tickled at this sign of chivalry from him.

They went in to the bar and Wiggy asked for her usual gin and tonic. He had the same as she and sat down and started chatting with Keith, and he answered her questions and she answered his except when he asked her if she had been out with anyone else from the base. It stopped the conversation dead. She didn't quite know how to answer him. He said, 'Oh, I'm sorry. That was rather clumsy of me. You don't have to answer that.'

'No, it is okay, yes I have, but it's over now and he has left the Navy.' She smiled half-heartedly.

'I'm sorry,' he said again.

She smiled at him and he could see the hurt in her eyes. It made him feel sorry for her and so he changed the subject and decided he had better take it easy with her. The talk turned around to their siblings. She laughed at the sudden change but she was very relieved and went on to tell him that she had a brother and two sisters. Her father had died about fifteen years ago after a prolonged illness but her mother was still going strong.

He said he had one sister who was very bossy and a mum

and dad. Wiggy asked if his father was a Doctor. 'Well sort of,' he said, 'but a vet'. She laughed at this and said that it was a perfectly respectable vocation to have and being a vet was a sort of doctor.

At that moment a waiter came and told him their table was ready when they were. Keith thanked him and helped Wiggy up and they followed him to their table. Once they sat down the waiter asked if they would like another drink or would they like to order some wine? Keith looked across at Wiggy who, for some reason, was trying to control a bout of laughter. 'We'll order some wine please.' The waiter went away and Keith asked her what she was laughing at. At that she just burst into laughter again. She managed to control herself and tell him. 'The waiter; the way he minced and spoke. I am sure he is a queer, or as they prefer, gay.' And she laughed again. Keith was laughing too by this time. 'I did notice but I'm surprised you did, Wiggy.'

'Oh come off it, I've been in the Navy too long not to notice.'

For some reason this conversation seemed to clear the air and break the ice. After which they both seemed to relax and be easy in each other's company. The rest of the evening went off like a dream, and then Keith looked at his watch and said that it was time to go back on board.

Wiggy was surprised when she looked at her own watch and saw the time, as it was five to twelve.

'I must say I was having so much fun that I never gave time a thought. I expect my coach with six white horses will be waiting outside,' she said. Keith laughed and said he would have to go round the back to get it. It would probably have more horses than six though.

He went round to get his car and left Wiggy at the front of the Commodore. She waited there, sighing with contentment, and taking deep breaths of fresh air that was being wafted from the Gareloch. He wasn't too long and when he got there he leapt out of the car and said, 'Your carriage awaits, Cinders.' And he held the door open for her. She laughed at him and got in the car.

He drove them back to the base and on to the wardroom. When they arrived outside he pulled her toward him and kissed her. She was a bit surprised by his fervour but gave herself up to him. He said, 'I've been wanting to do that all evening, how about the same time tomorrow night?'

'Yes please.'

'Good.' He kissed her once again, then, 'I'll see you at the same time then.' He got out of the car and came round to open the door for her. He kissed her once again, then said, 'Goodnight, Cinders.'

'Goodnight, Keith.' She went into the WR, chuckling. When she got to her cabin she just stretched with pleasure and thought how much she had enjoyed the evening.

He picked her up at the same time on Tuesday evening and did the same thing with the door. She thanked him and wondered where they were going tonight. Keith must have read her mind as he said to her, 'I hope you don't mind Chinese, Cinders.'

She laughed and said, 'Not at all. It seems ages since I've had a Chinese meal.'

'Good, because I've booked us a table in the one in Helensburgh.'

'Oh great, it's smashing in there.'

They were chatting away and were halfway through their dessert when Keith's phone went off. He frowned and said excuse me. Wiggy watched him as he answered it, not saying anything until he looked at his watch and told whoever had phoned him that he'd be there as soon as he could, and switched his phone off. He was looking quite worried, as was Wiggy. 'What is it?' she asked.

'A head on collision with two cars just north of the base. I'm sorry, we'll have to go.'

BRENDA MURRAY

'Of course.' She put her cardigan on whilst Keith paid the bill.

'I hope you don't mind, but I've booked a table here again for tomorrow evening.'

'I don't mind at all. I just hope the head on isn't too serious though.'

'So do I, anyway, I'm not on call tomorrow, Wiggy so we can relax.'

They drove the rest of the way in silence until they got to the wardroom and he leant over and kissed her. He apologised again and said, 'Same time tomorrow, Wiggy?'

'Yes, that will be fine. Goodnight, Keith.'

'Goodnight, Cinders.'

She got out of the car and watched him drive off. She was quite worried about it all. She knew it was pointless as she couldn't do anything to help, so she just prayed for him and the people involved.

True to his word he picked her up at six o'clock and she was waiting just inside the WR doorway. He got out and opened car door for her. She thanked him and as soon as she was settled she asked Keith how the occupants of the cars were. He said they were very lucky, just a few cuts, bruises, and a couple of broken legs.

'Oh, thank God for that. I'd imagined all sorts of scenarios.'

He leant over and kissed her and thanked her for the thought.

'And the prayers.' He looked at her and smiled then started the car.

They got to the restaurant at six thirty with time to spare, so they had a couple of drinks before ordering. 'We will be able to eat our way through the menu with no interruptions this evening,' said Keith.

Wiggy smiled and answered by saying, 'That sounds a good idea but I won't be able eat any more than I did last night.'

He just laughed. After a while he asked her when she was going on leave.

'Friday. Why, is there an ulterior motive in that question?'

'No, just curious.' He chuckled.

'Oh good, as I thought you were fed up with me already.'

He just roared with laughter and said, 'Of course not, Wiggy,' and reached for her hand. He squeezed it and said quietly, 'I think I'm falling in love with you.' He smiled sheepishly.

She couldn't believe what he'd said, she was so astounded. 'What a lovely thing to say. Are you serious?'

'Yes, of course I am.'

'Thank you,' she said with tears welling up in her eyes.

'Don't cry, Cinders. I mean it, honestly.'

When she looked up at him she could see the love shining in his eyes.

He called for the bill and they chatted while waiting for it. When he had paid it they went to the car.

Keith held the door for her and she got in. She did like that touch. He went to the driver's side and switched on the ignition once settled and drove off.

He drove off at a leisurely pace and Wiggy was miles away and it wasn't until Keith drove past the entrance to the base that Wiggy started to take notice of where they were going.

He looked over at her once and just smiled. He drove around to the opposite side of the loch until he was opposite the base and drove into the first layby. He switched the engine off, undid both seat belts and reached out for Wiggy. She came to him reluctantly. Fortunately it was dark so he didn't see the look on her face.

Once he started kissing her she relaxed. He started undoing the buttons on her blouse. He managed to undo her bra, very skilfully with one hand, and then he was fondling her breasts and Wiggy was really enjoying the sensation and groaning with delight. Keith then started sucking at her nipples and then he spoke, 'God I have really wanted you for days, since just after the wedding.'

'I've wanted you too but at the moment, it's the wrong time of the month. I'm sorry, Keith, I really am.'

'Not to worry. It is not your fault, it's nature's. When will you be clear, Wiggy?'

'Sunday or Monday at the soonest, Keith.'

'You'll be on leave then. How long will you be on leave?'

'Two weeks at the most. I could make it one and be back next Friday or Saturday if you would like?'

'You mean you'd give up a week's leave for me? No, I can't expect you to do that, Wiggy. Why would you do that?'

'Could be because I have fallen in love with you too.'

She had turned around and was facing him, and just then the moon came out and illuminated her bare breasts and Keith just pulled her to him again saying, 'God, you're beautiful.' He started fondling her breasts again, kissing and sucking the nipples.

Wiggy was so excited that she called out, 'Stop, stop, Keith. I can't take any more. Please stop,' she pleaded.

'Don't, Wiggy. It's alright; I can wait until you are better. Tell you what, when you are away I will look for a small furnished flat for us; how does that sound?'

She thought about it and said, 'Delightful Keith, but is that the way to go about things?'

'What do you mean?'

'Well, it is a bit much, just for a place to make love in.'

'Oh, I see what you mean. What about a hotel then?'

'That sounds a bit better, but we will have to be careful which one we stay in.'

'Think about it and we'll discuss it tomorrow night. How's that sound?'

'Absolutely fine. No, not tomorrow night, as Penny and I have been invited to Kit's and Steven's for dinner.'

'So have I. I have just remembered.'

'Great, then we can discuss it then.'

'I'll pick you both up at 1745.'

'That is a good idea, and I will have all day to think on it.'

'I'd better get you back.'

'And I'd better make myself decent.' She laughed and re-hooked her bra and adjusted it, then did the buttons up on her blouse.

He watched her and she blushed when she realised. He just laughed.

They drove back to the base and he kissed her very deeply and told her what a nice interlude it had been round the other side of the Loch. Wiggy just murmured, 'Mmh.'

He came round and opened the door for her, and when she got out he kissed her again and said, 'Remember I love you. Goodnight Cinders.'

She just chuckled and went into the Wardroom.

* * *

Kit and Steven went to the bedroom and reversed the roles. She undressed him and when she took his trousers off he was already erect and ready for her and she quickly got undressed herself. She leaned over and kissed him then she straddled him. As she sank down on him he started to fondle her breasts that she loved so much for him to do. 'Oh Steven, I have missed you so much.' She leaned down and kissed him again.

She started to gently move up and down on him and he was groaning with passion. She increased her movement until her own need was nearly satisfied. Steven had come soon after Kit started to move and he kept fondling her breasts. He looked up into her face and saw such beauty and ecstasy there it made him come again, just as Kit shouted with delight Steven's name and relaxed down onto him. They didn't speak for a while, then it was Steven who spoke. 'Apart from you, that is the one thing I have missed so much. Until I met you, I had never given sex a thought, but now it is never far from my mind.'

Kit looked up at him, smiling. 'We are rather special together.' She eased herself off him and lay on her back beside him. 'Do you know what your son, Mark, said to me when I told him that there may be difficulties in getting him on a submarine? He said, and I quote, "Surely if you told them I was your son, they'd let me on." Or words to that effect. Wasn't that sweet? I must say that I was a bit embarrassed at the time.'

'Well that is a surprise. I hope he hasn't been a nuisance or pestering you, Kit.'

'No, Wiggy came to my rescue by saying that I'll be rather busy next week,' and she chuckled and said, 'little did she know. We have a lot of loving to catch up on. But I'll be back in a minute. Excuse me please.' She put the dressing gown on that was on the bottom of the bed and went to the lounge.

When she got there she got the two crystal brandy balloons that the Officers from the *Holland* had given them for an engagement present, and poured some cognac into both glasses. She took them back to the bedroom. When Steven saw them his eyes lit up and he said, 'I am glad that Keith didn't put me on antibiotics today. He must have known that I'll be doing some boozing today.' They chinked glasses and took a sip. 'Talking of Keith, don't you think that Wiggy and he seemed to hit it off very well, Steven?'

'They certainly did.'

'I certainly hope so for Wiggy's sake.'

'Oh, and why is that?' Kit told Steven all about the chap that had let her down so very badly. 'I just hope Keith doesn't do that to her again, I don't think she would trust another man again, ever.'

'Poor Wiggy,' said Steven.

'Yes, poor Wiggy.' And she sighed. Steven hugged her to him and said that Keith wasn't that sort of chap.

'Oh, I do hope so.' And she reached up to kiss him.

He kissed her back and they just lay there quietly with the occasional caress by them both.

'I was thinking that both sets of parents are going home on Friday, so why not have them, Wiggy, Penny and Keith up for a meal on Thursday evening?'

'That sounds a good idea. Do you think you will be able to cope with that lot?'

'I don't see why not, and the dining table, when extended, will sit ten easily.'

'If you are sure, Kit?'

'It's the least we can do.'

Steven thought about it and nodded and then started caress-ing Kit. He had already undone and removed her robe earlier when they were talking and now as she was naked he leaned down and kissed her breasts, nuzzled each of them in turn and soon the nipples were very erect and then he sucked and nibbled them. He soon moved his hand down to her very core and did unbelievable things to her that had her writhing in ecstasy and she came very quickly. She then realised that Steven couldn't get on top of her so she mounted him and as she sank down on him again they both had a terrific climax that was heavenly.

CHAPTER 42

Kit and Steven were left alone for two days then Wiggy phoned them on Wednesday morning whilst they were having breakfast. Kit answered it. 'Hi Wiggy.'

Wiggy said, 'I hope I didn't interrupt anything.'

Kit laughed and said no, and then Wiggy went on to say that she had fixed for Mark with Ron Kennedy to go on his boat that afternoon.

'That is great. If you let me know what time, I'll make arrangements to pick him up at the hotel. Before you go would you and Penny like to come up to dinner tomorrow evening? It is part payment for what you have done for Steven and me?' Kit listened for a bit longer then said, 'Good. We'll look forward to seeing you at 1800 tomorrow. Both sets of parents will be here we hope.'

Kit told Steven that Wiggy had fixed up with Ron Kennedy for Mark to visit his boat at 1300 today. She said that she would go down and pick Mark up at the same time, inviting the parents up for dinner tomorrow evening.

Steven was very pleased with what Wiggy had done and said he'd be able to thank her tomorrow night. Kit said she'd go down in her Z3 to pick Mark up. Then she asked him if he would be okay on his own? He said that he'd be fine, probably do some gardening, and he'd get on and make a list for their meal tomorrow. Kit laughed.

Kit had already gotten hold of Mark at the hotel and he was very excited about going on a submarine. Kit got dressed in her best uniform with Dolphins and medal ribbons. As usual she looked very smart. She said to Steven that she hoped the boat was as clean as hers was, otherwise she wouldn't be very amused.

She arrived at the Ardencaple at 1240 as arranged and Mark was waiting outside for her. He was very impressed with the car and she said that Val's husband, Lieutenant Commander Kennedy, would be showing him round his boat. She said that perhaps Mark had met Ron at the wedding.

She swiped her card to gain access to the base and pulled over to sign young Mark in. The Mod Plod were very polite to them both. They asked how the Reverend Thorpe was and Kit said that he was a lot better now, thank you. Mark spoke up and said that Commander Carson married his father last Sunday. The Plod looked at Kit and back to Mark. 'Is that so?' they said. Kit was blushing a bit and said they were visiting HMSM *Tortoise* at 1300 so they must get going. The police saluted her and said, 'Congratulations Commander Thorpe.' Kit smiled and saluted back and got back in the car and made off to where the *Tortoise* was berthed. Ron was waiting at the top of the gangway and saluted Kit and she saluted back. 'Would you like to wait in the wardroom, Ma'am, while I show Mark around?'

'That will be nice, Ron, thank you.'

He left Kit in the wardroom with a pot of tea and then took Mark off, saying that he'd see her soon. She just smiled and nodded. She picked up a copy of *The Daily Telegraph* that was lying around there.

She was so absorbed in it that the time just flew by. It was 1400 when she heard Mark's exuberant tones coming along the passageway.

Ron and Mark came in and Mark was all smiles. 'Wow, Kit that was something else.'

'I gathered that you enjoyed the tour.' She smiled at him. Mark flung his arms around Kit and hugged her, saying, 'That was an experience of a lifetime. All my chums at school will all be very jealous when I tell them, especially that my new Mother is the first Commander of a submarine that has an all-girl crew. '

'I hope that Lieutenant Commander Kennedy told you what you can say and what you can't,' asked Kit. The boy pulled away from her, 'Yes of course, Kit.'

'Very well, thank the Commander and we must go.'

'I already did, Kit.'

'Good.' She smiled at the boy again then turned to Ron and said, 'Thank you Ron, it was very nice of you to give up a little bit of your leave for him.'

'It was no problem. It was probably more of a problem for you?'

'Yes,' she said, blushing. But smiled.

'By the way, how is Steven?'

'Getting better every day, thank you.' She ushered Mark ahead of her toward the exit. Ron came with them and saluted Kit who returned his salute and he shook hands with Mark.

Kit and Mark made their way back to Kit's car and got in. She told Mark that she had to pop into the hospital to see someone and that wouldn't take very long if he wouldn't mind waiting in the car.

She had gone in to ask Keith to dinner tomorrow evening at 1800. He said he'd be delighted and asked if he could bring anything. Kit said just hunger and a thirst. He laughed at that and said he'd see her tomorrow evening.

Kit dropped Mark off at the hotel and she said she would see them all tomorrow.

'Thank you, Kit.' He leaned over and kissed her on the cheek, saying, 'Thanks for everything.' Then got out of the car and went into the hotel.

Kit made her way home to Steven.

She was home by 1500 and Steven saw her car turn in to park next to her new BMW and went to the door to greet her.

'How did it all go?'

'Very good thanks. You didn't tell me that Mark was a very demonstrative boy, did you?'

'Is he? I didn't know that he was. What has he been up to now?'

'First he hugged me in the wardroom of the *Tortoise* then he kissed me on the cheek.'

Steven just laughed and asked her if she would like him to have a word with Mark.

Kit laughed too. 'No, not really. It's just that I'm not used to that sort of thing.'

'I quite understand, Kit, but it strikes me that you may have to get used to it.'

'Yes. Anyway, Steven, I missed you when I was gone.'

'Huh, I'll bet.' And he laughed again.

'Oh you…' She hugged him to her and gave him a resounding kiss on the lips. 'I just fancy a horse's neck.'

'One horse's neck coming up. I'll join you in a whisky and soda. Is there any ice?'

'Yes, I'll get you some.' She went to the kitchen, undoing her tie as she went. She left her jacket and tie in the kitchen but came back with a bowl of ice. She said that she'd find the ice bucket ready for tomorrow evening.

They sat down on the sofa and Steven got from his pocket the list he had made and handed it to Kit. She looked it over and said that there was one thing that wasn't on it that she hadn't got, and that was some beer and a soft drink for Mark and the mothers. Steven laughed and said that *his* mother had been known to drink practically anything. 'I don't know about yours, although she did seem to enjoy the champagne we had with our meal on Sunday.'

'I'd better add some beer and champagne to the list and a bottle of rum and some coke and some orange juice too. I think I have everything else regards the booze and the mixers. Apart from those couple of items everything seems to be on this list.' She looked up from it and found Steven watching her.

'What?'

'What to me, you will be saying Balls to the Bishop next.'

She just burst out laughing, which turned to giggles. 'Steven,' she said shocked, 'what a thing to say. I was saying "What" because you were looking at me with a strange expression on your face.'

'I can't imagine what it was, except you are very beautiful, and I do love you so.' He leaned over and kissed her. 'Why not go to bed?'

'Why not,' she agreed.

Chapter 43

When they awoke next morning they were both starving. Kit stretched and said, 'That's the best night's sleep I've had in ages.'

Steven said more or less the same thing. 'I didn't have any pain at all.'

'It must have been the cognacs we had just before we went to sleep.'

'Probably, or the loving we did.'

Kit stretched again saying, 'Yes,' through her stretch.

'Do you want some more?' Steven asked her.

'Mmh, yes please, if there is time.'

'There is always time for loving,' he said, pulling her toward him.

'Oh yes, there sure is,' she said, kissing his cheek.

'Why on the cheek?'

'Because I haven't cleaned my teeth yet.'

He said, 'Neither have I.' And he kissed her on the lips. They had a very nice session of love making and eventually Kit said she would get up and cook some breakfast. Steven said he'd have a shower.

'Will you be able to manage okay?' asked Kit, sounding a bit worried.

'If I'm careful. Anyway, I'll call out if I'm in trouble.'

'Okay. You do that,' she said as she went to the bathroom and then on to the kitchen. She made some tea before she did anything else then got on with the breakfast. She laid the table in the kitchen with some clean napkins, glasses and knives and forks. She could hear Steven singing in the shower and she joined in with him. 'All things bright and beautiful,' he sang, 'All creatures great and small.' She added her voice to his. All of a sudden she couldn't hear him singing. She turned the cooker off and went running to the bathroom.

When she got there she found Steven shaving and humming to himself. He looked at her in the mirror and said, 'Good Lord. Whatever is it?' He was wiping the shaving foam from his cheeks. She looked like death warmed up.

She held her hands over her heart. 'You stopped singing and I thought the worst. You frightened the life out of me when you stopped singing.'

'I'm so sorry, but I was listening to you when you joined in. I thought that you were better than me and it was time for me to shut up.' He shrugged his shoulders and held his arms out for her. She went to him and squeezed him tightly.

'I'm so glad you are alright, darling. I can get on with the breakfast now.' She smiled at him and went back to the kitchen and turned the heat back on.

Eventually Steven joined her in the kitchen and he asked if there was anything he could do. She shook her head and carried on.

He watched her and noticed that she was very adept at what she was doing. She looked over and smiled at him.

When they were eating she asked him if he would like to come with her when she went shopping. To her surprise he said yes. She said, 'Good,' and got on with her breakfast.

At one point Steven asked if there was anything she needed from his flat. She said no unless there was something he wanted.

When they had finished breakfast Kit went and had a shower and Steven cleared the dishes.

* * *

They managed to get all they needed in one supermarket. Steven had told Kit about a very good place to buy the vegetables but fortunately the ones in the supermarket were very good.

Then they went home and had a cup of coffee and relaxed for a while.

Steven said he'd prepare the vegetables and Kit said she would do the dining room table for the ten of them.

When she had finished, the table looked really beautiful. Kit had pulled the table out, using all the extra leaves so everyone had plenty of room. On a table beside the sideboard, she had made a temporary bar, putting out all the crystal glasses and decanters onto it. She'd topped up the various decanters with the appropriate spirit or liqueur in them and around the neck of the decanters she put the various silver labels with the names of the contents inside on them.

She stood back and admired her handiwork. All that was needed were candles or small vases of flowers. As she had no small vases she opted for candles. Kit went back to the kitchen to see how Steven was getting on. He had nearly finished and all that was to be done were a handful of peas, and while he was finishing up she turned on the oven, and put on the kettle for some tea and prepared the meat.

The meat in the oven, she took their tea into the lounge and sat on the rather large settee and chatted. Kit asked Steven how he felt and he said surprisingly well but it was still very frustrating that his leg was so stiff still and that his left wrist was still in a cast.

'Perhaps Keith could have a quick look at you, tonight,' Kit said.

'No, I've got to see him tomorrow for a check-up, so I mustn't bother him tonight. Okay?'

'Okay. It's your call.'

They drank their tea and both fell asleep. Fortunately Kit

woke up in time, and the meat was doing beautifully. Then she put the rest of the veggies on a low heat and went to wake Steven. She kissed the top of his head and said, 'Come on sleepyhead, time to get ready for the visitors.'

They both went to the bedroom to get ready, he in a nice pair of slacks and pale blue shirt with a navy cravat and Kit in a simple summer dress that had a hint of blue in it. Steven had tried to make a grab for Kit but she had managed to sidestep him with a laugh and went back to the kitchen to check on the dinner's progress.

It was going fine and when she got back in the lounge Steven had poured them both a drink. 'Thanks darling.' And she took a welcoming sip of hers. 'Mmh,' she murmured in appreciation.

Just then the guests started to arrive. Keith with Wiggy and Penny, followed shortly afterward by the parents with Mark. All the women kissed and the men shook hands. Mark kissed Kit and Steven worked the bar. All the men had a cold lager and the women what they asked for. Kit couldn't remember whether Penny had tonic with her vodka or lemonade, or was she drinking rum and coke? They had bought both so they were alright.

As Kit was busy greeting the guests, Keith whispered to Wiggy, asking if she'd made her mind up. She whispered back that a flat would be a good idea. Keith beamed at her.

Neither of the mothers had seen the cottage and Kit told them to wander around at their leisure. Wiggy and Penny went with Kit to the kitchen and Penny said, 'Something smells good, Kit.'

'Thanks, Penny. It is surprising what you can do with a tin of Baked Beans these days.' All three women laughed and Kit said, 'I'm glad that I had a minute alone with you both.' She went to one of the drawers and took out two identical sized packages. 'I hope you won't be embarrassed by this thank you gift. But your help was much appreciated by Steven and me. Enjoy.'

Both women were over the moon with their gift. To such an extent that they couldn't say anything at first then both started at the same time.

Kit held up both hands, saying you both deserve them and I don't want to hear any more about it. She was rather embarrassed at their reactions.

'Anyway, it's time to eat these beautiful Baked Beans.' And they all laughed again as Kit carried in the roast beef, Penny the roast potatoes with Yorkshire puddings, and Wiggy two dishes of vegetables and went back for a third.

'Please sit down everyone where you like but leave the end chairs free for Steven and me.'

Steven said grace and then carved the meat as Kit poured the wine. 'Help yourselves to veggies and anything else you want.' She turned to Mark and asked him what he would like to drink and he said orange juice please, at which Kit went to the fridge and got him a glass full.

Keith tapped his fork on a glass for attention and when he had it he raised his glass and said, 'It has been my singular pleasure getting to know you all, especially Kit and Steven, and I would like to propose a toast to them. I give you, Kit and Steven, hoping they have a long happy and successful marriage.' They all raised their glasses to the happy pair. 'Kit and Steven.'

THE END

ABOUT THE AUTHOR

I was born during WW11 in Kingston, Surrey and have fond memories of spending time in air raid shelters with my mother and two older brothers. My Father had been captured in Crete and spent the rest of the War in prisoner of war camps so we didn't meet until he returned home at the end of the War. In 1946 the family moved to Westminster where we stayed until 1954, by which time I had a further brother and a sister and we moved to Enfield, Middlesex.

In October 1959 when I was 18, I joined the WRNS and, after training, I was posted to HMS *Seahawk,* a Royal Naval Air Station at Culdrose in Cornwall. After only two months I was drafted again to HMS *Heron,* another air station in Somerset. Soon after joining there, I met my husband to be, John, and eventually we married in1967. He was also in the Navy and the week after our wedding he was posted to submarines. He served in nuclear powered and nuclear armed submarines for the next seven years. It was a secret world and he never told me anything about it so, when I wrote *Holland II,* I was not constrained by knowledge. I had left the WRNS in April 1967 and spent the next forty odd years following my husband around the world. I worked in various jobs, mainly in Naval Bases and mainly for NAAFI. I stopped working for them when John was posted to HMS *Rooke* in Gibraltar in 1976. There I was a lady of leisure, we had a great time and made great friends, some of whom we are still in touch with.

In September 1991, when John finished his service in the RN, he joined the Royal New Zealand Navy on a short-term contract. This lasted for over 18 years until he finally retired as a lieutenant commander in 2009 after 51 years in uniform.